Oathsword

Book 2 in the Danelaw Saga

by

Griff Hosker

Published by Sword Books Ltd 2021

Copyright ©Griff Hosker First Edition 2021

The author has asserted their moral right under the Copyright, Designs and Patents Act, 1988, to be identified as the author of this work.
All Rights reserved. No part of this publication may be reproduced, copied, stored in a retrieval system, or transmitted, in any form or by any means, without the prior written consent of the copyright holder, nor be otherwise circulated in any form of binding or cover other than that in which it is published and without a similar condition being imposed on the subsequent purchaser.
A CIP catalogue record for this title is available from the British Library.

Contents

Oathsword i
Prologue 1
Chapter 1 9
Chapter 2 27
Chapter 3 41
Chapter 4 52
Chapter 5 65
Chapter 6 77
Chapter 7 90
Chapter 8 98
Chapter 9 111
Chapter 10 123
Chapter 11 138
Chapter 12 150
Chapter 13 161
Chapter 14 174
Epilogue 188
Norse Calendar 189
Glossary 190
Historical Notes 193
Other books by Griff Hosker 195

Dedication

To Rex, Geoff, Steve, Rich: my Beta reading team! Thanks, guys!

Prologue

I am Sven Saxon Sword and I own one of the mystical and magical dragon swords. Ordered to be made by King Alfred, it was given to the Danish warrior Guthrum when he became a Christian. I am still unsure why it came into my possession except that my father, Bersi, was obsessed with the idea of owning a dragon sword. That I took it in a battle in a small Saxon village makes me think that I was meant to own it and, certainly, it changed my life and that of our clan, the clan of Agerhøne. It made me a warrior of renown but, at the same time, it attracted enemies to me like flies around a dunghill. Whenever I fought and no matter who the enemy was, they always sought me out. Christians sought to kill me for I owned a sword which was touched by the king they called '*The Great*' and Danes and Norse could not believe that such a callow youth should wield the weapon.

It was after I had returned from the last raid on Wessex that I discovered the true story of the sword. The priest who told me did not survive the voyage and that left nagging doubts in my mind that perhaps his story was untrue. I had wanted Mary, the Saxon whom I had taken back to help my mother, Gunhild, to question the priest. Perhaps the Norns, Urðr, Verðandi and Skuld had been spinning for my mother lasted barely a week after my return. She had pined for my dead father for years and despite the care and love lavished upon her by the Christian slave, she slowly went into herself. Her smile, when I returned, was joyful but the eyes were sad and I think she chose to die. The day she died Egbert, our Saxon thrall, fetched me to the longhouse. "Your mother is close to the end, Sven."

I could not believe that my mother would leave me, "She is not! It is just another chill. Mary will tend to her and she will be well!"

The Saxon shook his head, "You will see."

When I entered the chamber in the hall used by my mother, I saw a thin, grey and gaunt figure. Holding her hand was Mary, the Christian maid I had brought as a slave. Gunhild, wife of Bersi and sister to Sweyn Skull Taker beamed when I entered and held out a thin and bony hand for me to take. She put my hand in Mary's and smiled at us both. "Soon I shall see the Allfather and I am happy knowing that you two are together."

"What do you mean, mother? You are not dying!"

"I am and Mary knows it."

I looked into Mary's eyes and saw the truth of her words. It was as though the woman who had borne me had developed second sight and could see into the future.

"You will marry." She placed our hands together and said, "It is my wish." She smiled and then her eyes rolled and, after saying, "Bersi," softly she died. It was as though she had hung on to the thread of life until she had given me a command which I could not refuse to obey.

Mary made the sign of the cross and folded my mother's hands together. She gave me a sad smile and I saw a tear trickle from her eye, "I knew this day would come. When you were at sea, I saw her weaken each day and knew that she was staying alive just to see you return. This week we enjoyed with her gave me hope that she might have a release from the pain but she had endured enough of life."

Egbert smiled, "She has a release now, for she is with your father, Sven."

"My father is in Valhalla."

He shrugged. He was a Christian and he could know nothing of the ways of the old gods. "When she passed, she spoke your father's name. She is with him for no matter what you believe I believe that the one God is merciful, and he would wish them to be together."

"Amen." I looked at Mary who nodded as she said the word.

I should have said something then about the marriage, but I did not. I was too upset and confused by the death and the words of the Christians. That I did not was a mistake. I was also afraid. I know that my shield brothers would have been surprised that I should be afraid of anything, but Mary always seemed to hold a power over me and I was afraid that if I asked her and she rejected me then I would not be able to face her. My father had been plagued with flaws. I suppose all men are but my flaw was a fear of rejection and I said nothing. It was foolish and, looking back a mistake but all men have a weakness and that was mine.

The other reason I said nothing was that the day after my mother was buried, the hersir, her brother Sweyn Skull Taker, was summoned to King Sweyn and all the warriors were too distracted to think of anything except the summons. We knew that King Sweyn did not hold our clan in high regard and that, while we had served the King of Denmark each time he had asked. he was a wilful king and he could take it upon himself to punish us in some shape or form. We prepared weapons and took to attending to the needs of the drekar. Mary, for her part, had my mother's clothes to distribute to the poor. We did not see much of each other for a few days.

The Danish warriors who raided Wessex and Frankia were not concerned with gaining land or power but our kings were. King Olaf Tryggvason was angered by an alliance of Svein Forkbeard, King of Denmark and Olof Skötkonung, the King of Sweden. At the time we knew nothing of this but when Sweyn Skull Taker was summoned to the court then we knew that something was afoot. Lodvir had ordered us to make our ships ready for war. He had an idea why the hersir had been summoned. We were busy repairing our two drekar. We had raided successfully, and our men were keen to sail across the seas once more and ravage the weakly defended lands of England. Our drekar were hauled from the water and their hulls scraped. It was not a pleasant duty, but we knew that it was necessary. Lodvir's ship. *'Hyrrokkin'*, was relatively new and did not need much attention but ours did for she was old. We had just finished *'Sea Serpent'* when my uncle returned from King Sweyn. That he was not happy was clear and his face was as black as thunder.

He forced a weak smile when he saw that we had cleaned the hulls of the two ships, "You are becoming fortune-tellers for we go to war!"

Lodvir nodded and asked, "When?"

My uncle paused and, shaking his head, said, "We are to muster in the Østersøen. There is an island in the channel there, we call it Anholt but the Norse call it Svolder. The Swedes are bringing their ships and King Olaf Tryggvason comes to do battle with us."

Griotard used a splinter of wood to remove a tough piece of gristle from his teeth, "King Olaf has the largest ship afloat. **'Long Serpent'** will not be easy to defeat."

"You are right, my friend, but there is treachery for King Sweyn had suborned some of the Norse jarls and when the Norwegians sail, it will be with just a handful of ships. Our brave king leaves nothing to chance!" Sweyn shrugged, "We follow the other ships, and we will do our duty but my heart is not in this." My foster father was an honourable man.

I had yet to fight in a sea battle, certainly one of this size. I spoke quietly thinking that only Lodvir heard me, but the sudden silence meant that all heard my words, "But if we outnumber them by so many then where is the danger? We fought the Saxons at sea and did not lose a single ship!"

Griotard laughed, "The Saxons? They are not seamen. They are poor warriors whom we can defeat easily on land. At sea, they are even worse. No, Sven, we face the Norse, and you would be a fool to underestimate them. In a battle such as this then you either win and sail your ship home or sink beneath the waves. Even if we outnumber them by ten to one, and that I doubt, they will fight hard and we could win our own battle and still die!"

That evening, as I returned to the home I now shared with Mary and Egbert I was, I confess, fearful. I had every confidence in my ability with Oathsword and I knew that I could fight well but a drekar tossing on the sea was a different matter. After Griotard had given me his stark assessment of a sea battle I had spoken with him as we hauled the drekar back to the sea. "Then it might be better to fight without mail."

"There would be less chance of drowning, that is true, but it means you would be more likely to die from a wound. When a sea battle is over then the survivors of the losing side flee. They have no time to look for survivors and the winning side only rescue their own."

"You make it sound hopeless!"

He gave me a sad smile, "Sven, you are a good warrior and I have seen you fight. Your Saxon sword and your dancing feet make you an opponent to be feared but the tossing deck of a drekar is not the place for dancing feet. A lumbering Norse who spreads his legs and swings his sword in an arc is just as likely to kill you by accident when you slip as he is to make a skilled scythe with a well-timed blow. A battle on a drekar is always about luck."

When I reached the hall I was preoccupied and after Egbert had fetched me a horn of ale I sat before the fire. We kept a fire going even on a summer's day. I heard movements in the room which was hidden behind the wall hangings. It had been my mother's room and she had been given privacy on the orders of Mary. She had been quite clear about what my mother had needed. "What is that noise, Egbert?"

He looked embarrassed and shifted his weight onto his good leg, "Lord, it is Mary. She is sorting out your mother's chamber."

"Sorting it out?"

He shook his head, "Better that you ask her for she does not take kindly to my questions!"

I sighed and emptied the horn. I needed the drink, but I would not be able to enjoy it. What was she doing? The room needed no sorting out. I moved along the wall hanging. She had been making so much noise that I doubted she had heard our words. I saw that she was trying to move the bed.

"What are you doing?"

She had an angry look on her face but I think that was because I had found her out, "I wished to move the bed is all!"

Perhaps my mind was still filled with the prospect of a sea battle for I said, "Why? Mother is dead."

"And you are going to let the best bed in the house remain unoccupied." The anger left her face and her voice, "I thought to move in, but the bed must face east to west."

Her actions now became clear, but I wondered why she had not asked me to help and then I realised; she had thought I might say no. Nodding I said, "It will be easier if we all help. Egbert!" The thrall appeared, "We need to move the bed to face east to west."

"You are not angry?"

I smiled, "No, Mary, for you are right in one respect; the bed needs to be used. Come, with three of us we can move the bed and then I can enjoy my second horn of ale in peace!" I was right and it did not take long.

When we ate our evening meal which the kitchen thralls had prepared, I told Egbert and Mary of the prospect of war. Surprisingly, Mary did not seem that upset. "The Norse are an evil people! They took the precious books from Lindisfarne and destroyed them. Why? Because they did not understand them!"

"We take holy books too, Mary!" I saw Egbert shake his head.

Mary gave a smile, "You are practical men and sell them. They end up with Christians and while I cannot condone the attacks the result is not as bad as an attack by the Norse!"

The woman with whom I shared my house was complicated and I did not understand her at all. She always gave me the impression that she knew more than I did and men do not like that. The truth was she was the cleverest woman I had ever met and that made me a little afraid.

We were to leave three days later for the sail to join the other ships close to the isle of Svolder. I was kept busy with the drekar but it did not bother Mary for she was busy making the room her own. She had Egbert move a chair into the room for her. She had sat on a stool when she had tended to my mother, but she now wished a chair. She also had a small altar with a cross made by one of the thralls. She had a cross but I knew, from comments she made that she wished for a better one, and I also knew that it had to be paid for and not stolen.

I still sailed on my foster father's drekar but now it felt familiar, almost like home. Lodvir's was a newer ship but *'Sea Serpent'* was comforting, like an old pair of boots which were well worn in. We did not know how long we would be at sea and we loaded supplies for we did not know exactly when the King of Norway would come to do battle. King Sweyn would be most unhappy if any of his ships had to return to port because they had no food left. We were able to load our chests earlier than we might for we knew what was expected of us. I had my byrnie, sealskin cape, fur and dried food prepared by Egbert. I left the fine new Saxon sword in the hall. Oathsword would be sufficient. I fastened Saxon Slayer, my spear, to the thwarts.

The night before we left, Sweyn Skull Taker held a feast in the mead hall we had built after we came back from our last victory. We wanted somewhere we could celebrate. It was a measure of the ambition Sweyn Skull Taker had. My father had been more of a dreamer and such a hall would have remained in his head. This would be the first time we would sit and feast. Sweyn One Eye, now more comfortable with his one eye, gave us a song. The birth of his son and the love of his wife, Bergljót had helped him to recover his confidence.

Sweyn Skull Taker was a great lord
Sailing from Agerhøne with his sons aboard
Sea Serpent sailed and ruled the waves
Taking Franks and Saxons slaves
When King Sweyn took him west
He had with him the men that were best
Griotard the Grim Lodvir the Long
Made the crew whole and strong
From Frankia where the clan took gold
To Wessex where they were strong and bold
The clan obeyed the wishes of the king
But it was of Skull Taker that they sing
With the dragon sword to fight for the clan
All sailed to war, every man
The cunning king who faced our blades
Showed us he was not afraid
Trapped by the sea and by walls of stone
Sweyn Skull Taker fought as if alone
The clan prevailed Skull Taker hit
Saved by the sword which slashed and slit
From Frankia where the clan took gold
To Wessex where they were strong and bold
The clan obeyed the wishes of the king
But it was of Skull Taker that they sing
And when they returned to Agerhøne
The clan was stronger through the wounds they had borne
With higher walls and home much stronger
They are ready to fight for Sweyn Skull Taker
From Frankia where the clan took gold
To Wessex where they were strong and bold
The clan obeyed the wishes of the king

But it was of Skull Taker that they sing

When Sweyn One Eye had finished the song then the table was banged with the hilts of daggers as men chanted the name of the hersir. Of course, I had heard fragments when Sweyn had told them to Alf, my other cousin, and me. We had spent a long time trying to find a rhyme for stake filled ditch but we could not. I had persuaded my cousin to make my part smaller. I had not wished to be named for I did not think I was important enough. It was well-received. We all knew that it was not exactly the way it happened but as with all battles it was the way men would remember it when it was retold in the future.

The hersir stood and thanked his son, "I am honoured that my son, a great warrior and a skald should compose such words. I am humbled. Know this, Sweyn One Eye, the next battle may be even more bloody. I just hope that there will be warriors left to compose it."

The euphoria of the moment evaporated and I wondered at the wisdom of the hersir. My father would have revelled at the moment. They were different leaders that was for sure.

Griotard the Grim had, despite his name, a wicked sense of humour and a total disregard for kings and princes. He lightened the moment and made men smile, "Now, think on this Sweyn One Eye, do not make the mistake of singing that song when King Sweyn is near for he would want all of the glory and be most unhappy that he barely has a mention." He paused and swallowed a large mouthful of beer, "Of course, no matter how far he shall be from King Olaf's ship in this coming battle, I can guarantee that he will be the one accorded the glory of the victory!"

Lodvir grinned and rolled his eyes while Sweyn Skull Taker just looked to the table.

That night when I returned to the hall, a little drunk I confess, Egbert was waiting for me, "I heard the singing, lord, it was a good night?" Since I had returned from our last victory the thrall had called me lord rather than master. I think it was because he now knew the true story of the sword. The term flattered me for I was not a lord. I was bondi as were the others. The only title I had earned was hearth weru. I guarded Sweyn Skull Taker.

Nodding, I laughed unsteadily towards my bed. I was never a great drinker and usually stopped earlier than most men but the praise my cousin had received had made me foolish. "Aye, Egbert and tomorrow I leave. Has Mary retired?"

"She is on her knees saying her prayers."

I laughed, "Her God seems to like his subjects in that position. He seems to be like Sweyn Forkbeard."

Egbert just made the sign of the cross with his free hand. He said nothing as he led me to the bed to undress me. He had little to take off, my boots, breeks, and kyrtle. He laid me on the bed and went to fetch the bearskin but I waved him away. "It is hot!"

"Aye, lord. Good night."

I almost passed out immediately, but I had enough wit to turn on my side. I dreamt a strange dream but it was about Mary and not the coming battle. I dreamed that I held her and kissed her but the moment my lips almost touched her she became a dragon and devoured me. Then I felt the ale rising in my gut and it brought me awake. I put my head to the side and vomited. I retched until my stomach hurt. I had eaten well and it took some time for my stomach to empty. The action partially sobered me up and I thought to rise, rinse my mouth and then clean the floor for I was embarrassed by my action.

When I opened my mouth and looked down I saw that there was no mess but Mary's hands held a pail and she had stopped the vomit from reaching the floor. I was mortified for I was naked! I grabbed for the bearskin. She laughed, "Sven, it is a little late for that!"

"How…?"

"I heard your words when you came in and your mother had told me how your father when he drank too much, would oft be sick. She said she always had a pail to hand. I was just prepared." She shrugged, "You were lucky that I was still here when you began." She poured a horn of water and handed it to me. "Here, drink this. All of it mind." My unsteady hand touched hers and it had an effect. My nakedness became even more embarrassing. She glanced down and laughed, "Now, I think, is not the moment." She stood and I drank.

It took the sour taste from my mouth and I swore I would never drink so much ale again. When I had finished, I handed the horn back to her and this time she ensured that our hands did not touch. "I am sorry for this, but I thank you."

She smiled, "Sven, I have seen the best of you, and I have seen the worst of you. I can live with both. If you are sick again make sure you strike the pail. You can empty it in the morning. I have done my part!"

She left me and I found myself smiling. She did not hate me! My mother's command came back to me. I had thought Mary had forgotten it but she had not.

Chapter 1

The Battle of Svolder

Østersøen 1000

We had a long way to sail for we had a home on the west coastline of Denmark, and we had to sail to the sea close to the east coast, the Østersøen. It would take many days. We would first sail to the port belonging to the Jarl of Ribe where Jarl Harald would join us with his ships, and slowly we would progress around the coast picking up more ships as we went. We would not be the largest contingent in the fleet but we would be a sizeable one. There would be eighteen ships under the command of the jarl. Ribe was the place that stretched along the coast. There were four or five places where ships could land. The largest was called Ribe in honour of the jarl while ours was simply named after the clan. As some of the clan lived on the islands that protected us from the worst the sea had to throw at us, they too were referred to as Agerhøne but for us, Agerhøne was the hersir's hall and the wooden quay and jetty jutting into the sea.

That first day of rowing almost killed me. I had not eaten breakfast as I could not face food and I felt nauseous all the way north. Sweyn and Alf were also suffering and so the mocking came from the older warriors. They had endured a similar rite of passage but that did not stop them from mocking us. None of us was in any shape to argue. Perhaps the rowing helped to cleanse my body. I sweated as though it was high summer in Africa and it seemed to tell me that it was the sweat that had purged me. We rowed in silence and that helped me to reflect upon Mary and our situation. I knew that I had put off for too long that which I should have done when my mother was alive. I regretted my indecision. No matter what happened during the next weeks and the coming battle I would ask Mary to be my wife. I could even take the rejection and, if she did, then I would give her freedom and have her taken back to her home. A drunken night, vomit and a hard row will do that to a man. The combination strips away all that is unnecessary and leaves him with answers, however unpalatable.

There were too many other crews in the harbour for us to be accommodated and so we slept on the drekar. We did at least eat. The jarl sent cauldrons of food and bread for us. I ate, but sparingly. The tiredness and the previous night combined to make me fall asleep on my bearskin. I was awoken before dawn with a sea fret that felt as wet as rain. I cursed my lack of foresight. The wiser, older warriors, had all covered themselves with their seal skin capes and their furs would be dry. We younger warriors would have to try to dry them on a drekar with spray flying over the bows. We resigned ourselves to the prospect of a cold and damp bed. When we reached the northern tip of Denmark our voyage changed. We were entering the Østersøen. We had been told that King Olaf had not set sail yet but who knew if that was some sort of trick? It was with some relief that we turned the northeast tip of Denmark and Jutland to head south to the muster.

Jarl Harald used the voyage south to practice the tactics and formations we would use. His ship would be the tip of the arrow, but we were honoured by being chosen as the second ship from his steerboard side with Lodvir to our steerboard. It was a measure of the success we had enjoyed. King Sweyn might not give us the credit we felt we were due but the other men of the Ribe fleet did and I felt proud of the men of Agerhøne. The exercises and the manoeuvres meant that we arrived at the island of Svolder half a day late. That was not bad after our journey, but it meant we had less of a choice over our moorings. The island had been chosen because it was large enough to accommodate all the ships which would arrive. Triangular in shape the best berths were those where there was shelter from the prevailing winds.

Thorstein the Lucky was careful as he had edged us, stern first into the beach. He had two of his ship's boys swim ashore and they guided us backwards. When they held up their hands then Thorstein had us back water and ropes were thrown to secure us to the land. Our blacksmith had made two huge, sharpened spikes from weapons that had been killed or damaged so much as to render them useless. They were driven into the sand. Each was as long as a ship's boy. I knew that they would take some shifting. At the same time, as we stacked our oars on the mast fish, other boys dropped heavy anchors from the bows. We would be as secure as it was possible on such a sandy island. We were on the long side of the island. The side which faced the Norwegian Sea only held twenty ships. When we passed there had only been ten and they were King Sweyn's. We were told that the other ten were for the King of Sweden.

While the jarl, Sweyn Skull Taker, Lodvir and the other captains went to speak with Karl Three Fingers, we set about building a camp. That the Swedes were not yet here meant that battle was not imminent and both Griotard and Thorstein wanted us to be as comfortable as it was possible. As the hearth weru of the hersir, we had to make his bed first and when we had done so we collected as much deadwood and undergrowth as there was to be found. There was little to be had but we used what there was for the hersir. The ones who came later would find nothing. We then fashioned our capes on the wood so that there was a roof over our four beds. By using piled up sand where the beds faced the sea and around the sides we ensured that we would be as comfortable as it was possible to be for however long we had to wait for the Norwegian king.

The captains had not returned by the time we had foraged the shoreline and hauled in the catch from the lines hanging from the drekars' sides. We knew that this bounty would diminish for we would soon exhaust what there was but we enjoyed it all the more for that. We also searched for seafood and that too was, when we searched, plentiful. In my case, it was the first real meal I had enjoyed since I had emptied the contents of my stomach in my hall.

The fires we had lit kept away the flies and it was a pleasant evening. There was no sunset over the sea on this coast but we all anticipated a spectacular sunrise. I had taken out my whetstone when we had finished eating and I was sharpening my seax, long dagger, Saxon Slayer and, of course, Oathsword. The long dagger was new. I had used some of my treasure to have the weaponsmith make me a knife to my own specifications. It had a strong hilt and a blade that tapered. I had a seax for close-in work, but I had wanted a weapon that was like a short sword but lighter. I had yet to use it and therefore to name it; I was happy with the work of the weaponsmith. Knowing of Oathsword he had incorporated a dragon on the handle. My weapons had all been kept from the worst that the sea could throw at us with sheepskin, but it did no harm to clean, sharpen and then oil them with seal oil. There was something soothing about sharpening a blade. The slow, regular motion made for a sharp edge while the action emptied the mind and let it drift. I had just finished and put away the stone and weapons when the captains returned. Lodvir had been summoned too. He might command a small ship, but he was still a captain.

Alf ladled out Sweyn's food while Aksel Moltisson served Lodvir and we let them eat before we pestered them with questions.

Sweyn spoke, "It seems there is a treacherous conspiracy going on. The two kings have already promised many of the Norse jarls, lands and position when they partition Norway. It means that the Norwegian King will have fewer ships than we might have expected."

Lars Larsson asked, "How many would define as *'fewer'*?"

"Some think he might have as few as twenty while others say we should expect forty."

His brother Leif said, "Then with as few as that we need no more ships. We could take them with just our ships."

"And that is the plan. We wait here, almost hidden until they pass us and then we launch our ships to attack them when they try to return through this sea. We will be as a net catching a shoal of fish."

It seemed a good plan. Alf, the youngest of us, was left to ask an obvious question, "If he has so few ships then will he fight? Might he not simply stay at home?"

"That is a possibility but if he did so he would lose his kingdom for those jarls who have switched allegiance would also fight him. No, he will come, for, with the largest drekar ever built, some say it is unsinkable, he believes that he and his mighty warriors can defeat us."

"Great warriors?" I was intrigued for I only knew the name of the king.

"Einarr Þambarskelfir is supposedly the greatest Norse archer and there are others, Thorstein Ox Foot, Ketil the Tall and Bersi the Strong to name but a few."

"How do we know all of this when we are here, and the Norse are many leagues to the north?" Lars asked a good question and it showed the sharpness of his mind.

Lodvir had finished his ale and he spoke, "We have a Norse traitor with us. Jarl Svein Hákonarson, the Earl of Lade, has deserted the Norse king's court. He knows all and he has been promised much by King Sweyn. It was he who estimated the lower number of ships. I do not like the fact that he is a traitor but he seems to know his business."

And so we waited. The King of Sweden arrived, and we saw that when the whole fleet was gathered, we had one hundred and ten ships. The Norse would be defeated. Even the upper number of forty would not help them. That was not as comforting a thought as I had expected. Any warriors killed in such a battle would have wasted lives. I found myself looking at my oar brothers and wondering which of us might not survive. As we had predicted the catches grew less and the stews we ate became more salted meat and fish than fresh fish but we did not mind. We had even built a bread oven and we ate bread. It was not as good as that which we might enjoy at home but the smell of it cooking acted as food before we had even eaten it. Then those on the far side of the island saw the ships of the Norse. They passed early in the morning when we were hidden by fog, but their masts could be seen. A drekar has a higher mast than a knarr or a trading vessel. The kings were caught napping for our ships were not manned and ready. By the time the sun had risen the Norwegian fleet were just dots on the horizon. We were ordered to launch our ships while the captains were summoned to the two kings and the Norwegian earl.

Sweyn Skull Taker shook his head as he returned and boarded the drekar, "Eleven ships we fight! Eleven! This will not be a fight but a massacre."

"Where has the Norse king gone?"

"To the Wends in Pomerania, Griotard. He seeks allies from the Wends and he hopes to have ships and men from them."

"Then there will be more than eleven ships."

"Not many more for Jarl Sigvaldi, the leader of the Jomsvikings and his men have been paid to keep the Wends at home. Our king does not battle for a crown he buys one. Now I see that all the raids to England were for one purpose, not to conquer that country but to buy another."

I turned to Sweyn One Eye, "Who are the Jomsvikings?"

The hersir answered, grimly, "A band of fanatical warriors who refuse to follow any king. They have a stronghold at Jomsborg which is so hard to take that the kings tolerate them. They raid where they will and serve any master so long as they are paid well."

And so we waited at sea. The kings chose the straits at Øresund. The sea is but a couple of miles from coast to coast there. We could almost make a longphort with the ships we had. I knew from Lodvir that a longphort was a sort of floating port. Ships would be tied together and, unless the weather was stormy would give a stable platform. It was used, Lodvir said, when there were too many ships to anchor in a port. I realised then that it could be used as a quickly erected bridge. The battle plan was a simple one and had been devised by Karl Three Fingers. As such it was clever and effective. However, King Sweyn had modified it and it was to ensure glory for him. Whilst taking away none of its simplicity, he had given himself the best opportunity of both glory and victory, it also kept him relatively safe. In the original plan, the two kings would have sailed to flank *'Long Serpent'*. Jarl Svein Hákonarson, with the ships defected from Norway would be our reserve line and our contingent, the men of Ribe, would sail around the end of the enemy line to cut off a retreat and attack the steerboard of *'Long Serpent'*. We had been honoured to have been chosen for such a role but within an hour of the decision being passed to us, an embarrassed Karl Three Fingers told us that King Sweyn would attack the rear and we would join the line attacking the centre. Our silence made it even worse for Karl when he told us. He almost shuffled back to his king. We would have the harder task and none of us was bothered about the glory!

We had all rowed in mail and that had been hard enough but now we had to wait in our mail and it was a sunny day. We took down our mast as did all the other ships. Only Jarl Svein Hákonarson, on his ship *'Iron Ram'* and the reserves as well as King Sweyn's handful of drekar, kept their masts for they had to be manoeuvrable. We could not see King Sweyn who waited to the south ready to take the prevailing wind and fall upon the rear of the enemy. We would rely, instead, upon the power and speed of the oars and the skill of Thorstein the Lucky.

It was one of the ship's boys, Guthrum, who spotted the enemy before any other of the ships. It was a remarkable achievement for we were not the closest and he had no mast upon which to squat. Instead, he was precariously perched upon the prow of our ship.

"Enemy fleet in sight!" He pointed to the south and we were facing in that direction.

The word was passed to the drekar closest to us and the words rippled out to the rest of the fleet. The southernmost ship would signal King Sweyn and the rearmost ships then signal Jarl Svein Hákonarson. The order was then given to row. Speed was not essential at first for the enemy would not yet see us; we had no masts. It was when they came to within half a mile that we would speed up to allow us to smash into them. Then there would be a terrible collision of shattered wood and oars. Some ships would sink and those men with mail would sink beneath the waves. We did have some snekke, just eight, and their task was to pick up survivors. The odds, however, were against survival if we were holed.

The hersir shouted, "How many do we face, Guthrum?"

Balanced on the prow and with a hand shading his eyes from the morning sun he paused and said, incredulously, "Eleven!" There was another pause and then he said, "They are stopped and taking down the sails!"

Griotard said, "The old fool intends to fight! Allfather but he is a true Viking. He makes a longphort."

Sweyn Skull Taker cupped his hands and shouted across to Jarl Harald Longstride on *'Stormbird'*, "Longphort!"

The words drifted back, "Aye, the Swedish king wishes ramming speed! May the Allfather be with you!"

It made a sort of sense. It would take time for the Norse to unstep their masts and then bind all their ships together. If we could hit them while they were doing so then there would be confusion and, possibly, victory. It was, however, a risk and one I knew that the jarl, Sweyn and Lodvir would not have taken. Now we chanted and it was Sweyn One Eye who was given the order to do so by his father. We used, Bluetooth!

Bluetooth was a warrior strong
He used a spear stout and strong
Fighting Franks and slaying Norse
He steered the ship on a deadly course
Njörðr, Njörðr, push the dragon
Njörðr, Njörðr, push the dragon
The spear was sharp and the Norse did die
Through the air did Valkyries fly

A day of death and a day of blood
The warriors died as warriors should
Njörðr, Njörðr, push the dragon
Njörðr, Njörðr, push the dragon
When home they came with byrnies red
They toasted well our Danish dead
They sang their songs of warriors slain
And in that song, they lived again
Njörðr, Njörðr, push the dragon
Njörðr, Njörðr, push the dragon

We flew. Lodvir, next to us used the same chant and they kept pace with us. We were making no attempt to overtake our jarl but the crew of the threttanessa, *'Fire Dragon'*, captained by one of the jarl's sons must have had a rush of blood for it began to edge ahead, not only of the jarl but also King Olaf of Sweden. We could see nothing of this but Guthrum gave us commentary as he kept us informed about the Norse fleet.

It was when he shouted, "They are all secured!" that we knew that Olaf Tryggvasson had well-trained men. That was followed by, "*'Fire Dragon'* is going to strike!"

We had to forget our comrades for Thorstein's voice took over, "Prepare to withdraw oars!" The last thing we needed was shattered oars which could splinter and blind or maim a man.

We knew that we would be close to striking. There was a mighty crash ahead of us and the sound of screams and cries. Even as Thorstein gave the command to withdraw oars we heard the voice of Guthrum telling us that *'Fire Dragon'* had sunk. The jarl had lost a son! A moment of madness, an almost berserk act, had taken the men of a whole village beneath the sea. It was a waste!

We heard all this as we calmly stacked our oars. As soon as we had done so we each took our shield from the gunwale, donned our helmets, and took our weapon of choice. Mine was obvious, Oathsword. Saxon Slayer would be too unwieldy to use aboard a drekar as there would be too many men packed closely together. I joined Sweyn One Eye and Alf and followed Sweyn Skull Taker down the centre of the drekar to the prow. It was then I saw the wall of wood we faced and, to our left I saw the enormous behemoth that was *'Long Serpent'*. Its prow stuck out half the length of a threttanessa from the rest of the Norse fleet. Even as men made our way forward I saw Jarl Harald and his men attempting to board her but before them stood the mightiest mailed warriors I had ever seen. Then I had to concentrate on our job for arrows were sent towards us and our job was to protect the hersir.

Sweyn and I lifted our shields to cover his father's head. The ship's boys, with no protection whatsoever, were trying to put in place the planks to help us cross to the Norse longphort. Our archers were duelling with the Norse. I saw Lars Siggison plunge over the side pierced by an arrow. It made Sweyn Skull Taker move even more quickly and we hurried after him, careful not to slip. I felt Griotard's shield in my back and was comforted for I knew he would urge the rest of the crew to follow closely. This was a mighty battle, already I could hear the crack and creak as ships struck and the cries of the dying but our own battle was a small one. It was the hersir and his hearth weru. We would fight our own small battle and hope we won.

It was when Sweyn Skull Taker stepped up to the plank that he was most vulnerable. He was a skilled warrior and the Norse warrior who ran at him swinging a boarding pike was not; he was just reckless. Showing great balance for a man of his age the hersir simply swung to his right and the boarding pike slid along his mail. Sweyn One Eye smacked the edge of his sword against the head of the pike and that simple action caused the man to overbalance and plunge, fully mailed into the sea.

The hersir did not wait but shouting. "Agerhøne!" ran along the plank to board the Norse drekar. The cry of the clan was inspiring.

Their warriors were waiting for us. These were not reckless like the one whose body was now tumbling towards the bottom of the shallow sea, but they were determined and a wall of shields and mail bristling with spears and swords awaited us. Sweyn Skull Taker halted and shouted, "Wedge!"

Sweyn One Eye and I were already in place and Alf slipped behind us with Griotard behind me. Dreng was the other to flank Alf and the six of us were enough to move forward. Griotard began the chant to help us keep step and to give heart to the clan. For some of the younger warriors, this was their first battle and I still remembered the first time I had chanted my way to battle. The chants helped.

We are the bird you cannot find
With feathers grey and black behind
Seek us if you can my friend
Our clan will beat you in the end.
Where is the bird? In the snake.
The serpent comes your gold to take.
We are the bird you cannot find

With feathers grey and black behind
Seek us if you can my friend
Our clan will beat you in the end.
Where is the bird? In the snake.
The serpent comes your gold to take.

Sweyn Skull Taker headed for the tall warrior with the long spear who stood in the centre of their line. He had filed teeth and a tattooed face. His shield bore a red skull on a white background and at his waist hung a good sword. Sweyn Skull Taker knew his business and, with my shield pressing in his back and his son's protecting his left side he stepped forward with his sword held high. I knew my business too for we were not fighting a wedge, but a line and that line was backed by ever-widening lines of warriors. There was a warrior to Sweyn Skull Taker's right, and I would need to deal with him. He was a squat warrior, and he held a sword which was held to strike a backhanded slash down my foster father's right side as he sought to kill the mighty spearman. I had no shield to use for that was in Sweyn Skull Taker's back and as soon as I stepped forward to strike then there was another Norse who would have a free blow to my right. I was hearth weru and this was my job. I had to risk my life to save the hersir. It was as the swordsman slashed and I lunged that I felt, rather than saw, the coiled rope thrown by Griotard. I had been aware of it as I had passed it, close to the prow of the Norse vessel, but I was young and did not see it as a weapon. Griotard was a veteran and he used anything to hand. The rope hit the swordsman and his strike missed.

I was young and had quick hands and Oathsword was longer than the Norse blade and I caught the warrior beneath the chin. The sword entered his head, ripping through his throat and skull and his blow was not struck. Griotard's shield and sword appeared next to me followed by his body. He roared, "Agerhøne!" and he swung his sword at the Norseman who filled the gap vacated by the man I had slain.

To my left, the hersir was winning his battle with the mighty warrior who was now hampered by his weapon. Sweyn Skull Taker had whittled chunks from the shaft of the spear, and it would not be long before it broke. From a few rows back I heard Lars as he shouted, "Push!"

I felt the weight of the clan as those who had boarded the Norse drekar now leaned against their shields. If we were to get more men aboard we needed to shift the ones from before us. The deaths we had caused meant we had gained the length of a spear but now we were shield to shield. Another Norseman with filed and blackened teeth pulled back his head to butt me. It was not a new experience for me but I was helped by the pressure from behind. As I stepped forward and he butted I lowered my head so that the nasal of the Norseman would strike the crown of my helmet. There was a ridge of strengthening metal there and would be able to resist the blow. The man had concentrated so much on the butt that he failed to move his feet and as his head came down, he found himself moving backwards for we were pushing hard. His head still connected but it was a weak blow, and I pushed hard with my head. His feet left the ground and his weight of mail made him start to fall. He naturally spread his arms for balance I had enough space to stab with Oathsword. I even had the luxury of aiming for a broken link and I thrust hard to enlarge the break and tear into his flesh. His falling had already forced the ones behind to move backwards and Sweyn Skull Taker slew his man as did Griotard. We gained another spear's length and more men from our clan stepped aboard. We were almost at the mastfish.

It was then I heard Alf's voice. We had practised many moves at Agerhøne and when he shouted, "Leif, Lars, shield I knew what he intended. It was a most dangerous thing to do and I knew that his father would not be happy, but I also knew why he did it. He was the only one not using his weapon for he was behind Sweyn and me. With the space we had created, Lief and Lars held a shield between them. Alf ran at the shield and as he stepped on it, they threw him in the air. He cleared his father and the first rank of the Norse. He managed to aim his feet so that his weight struck two men while his sword drove into the neck of a third. The sword which was thrust almost blindly at him merely scraped along his mail. The effect was devastating. Not only were many of the Norse so shocked and surprised by the act that they stopped fighting but also it cleared a space in the second and third ranks. Sweyn One Eye and his father both slew two surprised Norsemen and I brought my sword down to smash into the helmet of another. He fell to the ground and Griotard swung his sword in a wide scythe slicing through the noses and faces of two men. Suddenly the Norse before us were shattered and having reached the widest part of the drekar the clan who had just boarded with freshly sharpened weapons flooded around the flanks of the demoralised Norwegians. I could not believe the speed with which we dispatched the rest. Although most we now faced had no mail they had not yet been in combat but each blow struck by one of the clan brought a wound or death. It was as we neared the steering board that I realised that Jarl Svein Hákonarson had attacked the left flank of the longphort and had already taken one ship. He had disobeyed his orders but, in doing so had given us an advantage. We were winning!

As we slew the last of the Norse crew Sweyn Skull Taker turned, "Agerhøne, we make for *'Long Serpent'*. Alf the Swooping Hawk has shown us that we are the hunters! Let our swords feast on Norse flesh!" I knew that Alf would be happy for he now had a name!

We had the advantage now of attacking the next drekar, two down from *'Long Serpent'* from the side and as the crew of *'Stormbird'* were fighting on one front we had the chance to outnumber them. When they saw us haul ourselves onto the gunwales a voice cried. "Face larboard! The Danes have come!"

Even as I stood and prepared to follow our hersir into the heart of the ship I saw Jarl Harald Longstride fall. His hearth weru had fallen already and three men fell on him. They hacked and chopped long after he was dead. With the best men of Ribe dead, the rest began to fall back and the Norse surged to throw them back aboard *'Stormbird'*. We owed more to our jarl and the men of Ribe than a self-serving king and Sweyn saw the danger. He leapt down and began a furious attack on the back and sides of the Norse. His sons and I were with him instantly and the four of us locked shields to hack, chop and slash into the backs of the Norse crew.

Behind us, I heard Griotard shout, "Protect the hersir!" It gave the four of us the confidence to push on as we had support.

We could now see that ships had been sunk. The longphort meant that the Norse could drop huge rocks from the higher sides of *'Long Serpent'* and ships had been holed. Others had been damaged by the ramming speed they had employed. The result was that despite our successes the Norse were still a force to be reckoned with as they had yet to lose a ship. I had not seen King Sweyn and his men appear in their surprise attack on the rear.

When we reached the butchered, mutilated bodies of Jarl Harald and his hearth weru Sweyn Skull Taker roared, "Men of Ribe! We guard the body of our jarl; come and take revenge on these barbarians!"

With a roar, the deflated warriors, who had returned to their sinking ship, renewed their attack with such vigour and ferocity that the Norwegians, overextended as they were, began to fall back. The ones at the rear turned and faced the four of us. The ones we would fight had no mail and we did. More than that our weapons were the best and when I blocked the blow from one warrior, well-struck though it was, it simply bent on mine. I punched him in the face with the boss of my shield and as he reeled, skewered him. The ones whom we fought lasted just enough time for Griotard to corner the captain and his oathsworn at the steering board.

As we made our way back, I slipped my shield over my back. The arrows had long ceased to be used and, in any case, their best arrows had already been sent. The ones they had left would not penetrate my byrnie. Instead, I drew my long dagger which was almost like a short sword. The fighting would be even closer from now on and I wanted more offensive options. When we reached the steering board, I saw that we had lost men. That was no surprise for these men were the best that this crew had to offer. There were eight Norsemen left and all were bloodied. Some bore wounds and one had a left arm which he would never be able to use.

Griotard, Leif and Lars moved aside when we reached them. Sweyn Skull Taker said, "The rest of you finish off any wounded, tend to our men and then prepare to take the next ship. The eight of us are enough to send these eight men to Valhalla."

The captain, I could see that he too was a hersir, laughed, "You are that confident, Dane?"

My foster father nodded, "One man is so badly wounded that he will last but a moment and then we will outnumber you. Your men butchered our jarl and so we are honour bound for vengeance. I am Sweyn Skull Taker of Agerhøne and if you have not heard of me, your widow will, and finally." He nodded to me, "My hearth weru has a dragon sword once wielded by King Guthrum." He smiled, "Yes, I am confident! At them!"

It was a brilliant strategy for his voice was even throughout and it was as though he had lulled them with a spell. The reference to the dragon sword made every eye go to me so that when our eight swords struck, the one-armed man and a young hearth weru, died without even raising their swords. We now outnumbered them by two warriors and when the man facing me put all his energy into a blow to smash the dragon sword from my hand, he did not notice the dagger stabbing up from beneath his byrnie to gut him. Griotard attacked his man so ferociously that the warrior tripped over a rope and tumbled over the gunwale into the sea. Griotard was so angry that he had not slain his opponent, that he slashed his sword into the spine of the captain of the drekar, the hersir. It showed the anger in our oldest warrior, but he knew he had done wrong.

"I am sorry, Sweyn Skull Taker but the blood was in my head and I could not see straight." The rest of the Norse hearth weru lay dead.

Sweyn nodded, "This will be a day like no other, old friend. The Norns have spun. It was *wyrd*."

The ship was ours and we saw Lodvir lead his men from the first ship we had taken. Like Griotard the blood lust was upon him. He shouted, his face covered in blood, "It is our turn to be the first, hersir, for I do not wish Griotard to gain all the glory. With me!" Some of the men we had led followed him.

Sweyn said, "This fight is not over. It is not a land battle where men can flee. They fight and win or fail and die." He pointed, with his sword to the southwest, "See, our brave king brings reinforcements." The sarcasm in his voice was clear. "Alf, that was a brave thing you did, but no more. Be as cold as a firedrake. We fight to win and win we shall, but I want no more dead!" We nodded for he was right. As soon as King Sweyn and his ships arrived at the rear of *'Long Serpent'* then the battle would end.

The others now did as I had already done and slipped their shields around their backs. It made it easier to clamber over gunwales. Griotard picked up a small hand axe while the others all drew seaxes or short swords.

Lodvir and our men had carved out an enclave on the ship which lay next to *'Long Serpent'* and despite his apparent recklessness, he had organised the men to make a wall so that when we boarded, we had no fighting to do. It gave us the chance to assess the situation on the last drekar. King Olaf of Sweden held the bows of the great warship but as the ship was forty-five paces long his success had not brought him any closer to King Olaf Tryggvasson.

We had another ship to cross before we could reach our king's enemy but survivors, few though they were, from the other ships had made their way to the surviving Norwegian ships. It would become harder for us all. Sweyn Skull Taker used the time to make another line of our strongest warriors. We gathered those with the best mail as Lodvir and the others wearied the men they were fighting. I think that the Norwegians had long ago given up any hope of victory. They were just fighting now to take as many of us with them as possible. I knew, as my foster father did, that there would be no glory in this and certainly no honour. We had become Forkbeard's human butchers. With a block of twelve of us, Sweyn One Eye and I flanked his father, the hersir shouted, "Agerhøne, charge!"

Lodvir shouted, "Break!" It was a tactic we had practised and the men alongside whom he fought, all lunged and then turned to the side. Their opponents, who were weary already, were too stunned to move and our wall of steel simply broke them. Oathsword and my long dagger both drew blood. The men who died had resignation in their eyes. They knew they were dying, and they all held tightly to their swords to be guaranteed entry to Valhalla. Their king might be a Christian and some wore a cross but at the end, when things really mattered, it was the old ways that gave a man hope. We were suddenly at the side of *'Long Serpent'* and we were faced with a wall to climb. Before we could consider how to do it warriors appeared behind us. It was Jarl Svein Hákonarson and his men. They had fought their way across the other ships to join us.

He greeted our hersir who gave a half bow, after all the man was a Norse and they were the ones we were fighting, "You and your men have done a magnificent job, hersir. King Olaf is my enemy. We will lead this attack!"

It was a command and as such, had to be obeyed. I did not mind but I saw, from his fiery eyes that Griotard did. Sweyn Skull Taker took the sting out of the order, "And we, of course, will follow you, Jarl Svein Hákonarson, so that we can bring this battle to a speedy end."

"I would expect nothing less from the men of Agerhøne and the warrior with the dragon sword. You have lived up to your reputation Sweyn Skull Taker and that is rare."

While we waited to climb, I saw that the Norns had been spinning once more for the first ten of Jarl Svein Hákonarson's men who tried to board the huge drekar were slain and their bodies hurled back to the deck where we stood. That would have been the hersir and the hearth weru had the jarl not arrived. I kissed the hilt of Oathsword in thanks. It took longer for the jarl to reach the deck of the great ship than he had expected, and he turned when he reached it, "I think, Dane, that I shall need your help now for my best warriors are fallen."

When we ascended the side of *'Long Serpent'* we were greeted with a sight that looked nothing like any deck I had ever seen before. The height of the gunwale had allowed us to see the King of Sweden at the prow, but it had not prepared us for the sea of bloody bodies which covered the deck. Two of the jarl's hearth weru lay there and I saw that he and the survivors of his attack had a tiny enclave. They were fighting for their lives. This was the king's ship and still aboard it were the finest of his warriors. All wore the best mail and had fine helmets and weapons. They still retained their shields and I estimated that there were more than twenty-five of his best warriors gathered before him. His lesser warriors were closer to the prow and were fighting the King of Sweden.

Once more it was Sweyn Skull Taker who took command, "Lodvir, take half of the men and make a wedge of warriors to our left. We will support Jarl Svein Hákonarson."

"Aye, hersir."

He turned to the ones he had selected aboard the last drekar. "When I give the command, we drive along the gunwale to support the jarl!"

I saw his cleverness in those simple orders. Jarl Svein Hákonarson was surrounded and Lodvir's men would give him protection from the left. By attacking the men on the jarl's right and using the gunwale to protect our right we would be able to stretch the Norse defences. The warriors we faced would fight until night fell if necessary.

"Agerhøne!"

The jarl's men heard us coming and the ones on the right, still fighting, shifted back, echeloning their line. It meant that we hit the right side of the mighty hearth weru and oathsworn of King Olaf Tryggvasson. They were truly great warriors but as Sweyn One Eye, his father and Oathsword all struck the two huge warriors even their mail and strength could not stop our swords causing such wounds that the two Norse shields were dropped and, when Oathsword drove up under the arm of one to appear at the other side of his neck, Bersi the Strong finally went to Valhalla. Sweyn Skull Taker's sword hacked through the throat of the other and suddenly we had a more solid line of warriors. Lodvir's movement meant that Jarl Svein Hákonarson and his men now filled the drekar to the steerboard gunwale. There were two battles: behind us were the Swedes, battling the bulk of the Norse and there were two small groups of warriors facing each other. King Sweyn Forkbeard had managed to bring his ships to board the Norse, but it was not **'Long Serpent'**. He was four drekars away.

It was Jarl Svein Hákonarson who spoke as both sides stepped apart to recover a little. Such events often happened in battle. It was as though the two sides mutually agreed to rest to make a final battle worthy of remembrance. "King Olaf Tryggvasson, you have lost. The battle is over. You cannot win."

The king laughed, "And you expect me to surrender to a backstabbing traitor? Do not think that I do not know why my ships did not follow me. Had I brought the full force of my ships to bear, then the sea would be filled with the wreckage of Danish and Swedish drekars. Try to take me, Jarl Svein Hákonarson, and you will see that my oathsworn have even more reason to hate you!"

It was as he spoke that I saw that he too held a dragon sword. That was strange for he was a Christian. Perhaps, like his men, he still had a pagan heart.

We stood facing each other in silence. Around the king, the deck was bloody but clear of bodies. The king was protected by four of his crew with shields, but the rest, the real warriors, were in one line. Then one warrior nodded, and the Norse ran at us. Some of them had shields but others were like me and had two weapons. I was still next to the hersir and I would be fighting. It never occurred to me that I might die even though the men who came to kill us were the best that the Norse had left. Sweyn One Eye and I were there to protect the hersir and nothing else mattered.

The warrior who came at me was the same height as I was, but he was broader. He had a hand axe and a sword. The worst thing I could have done would have been to stand and await the blows and so I stepped forward to close the gap. The Norwegian brought the axe down in a swing to strike my head while his sword, held in his right hand, came up to stab me in the neck. That suited me for while such a blow might buckle a lesser sword, Oathsword would take the blow easily. When my sword stopped the axe, I saw the look of surprise on the face of the Norseman. Slivers of wood were peeled from the haft. He had seen a youth and expected fear. My left hand acted instinctively, and I deflected the sword which scraped along the hersir's mail. While the man was still surprised, I turned the long dagger and drove it towards the Norse's thigh. He had a split byrnie and my blade drove into his thigh. I twisted and pulled. As his leg buckled a little, I punched him in the face with the hilt of Oathsword. At the same time, I rammed my knee between his legs. It increased the flow of blood as well as making the Norseman double in pain. I have quick hands and inverting the sword I drove it into his neck, "Go to the Allfather! You have done your duty."

I looked to my left and saw the hersir fighting another mighty warrior while Alf and Griotard fought the tallest Viking I had ever seen. My duty was clear. The warrior fighting Sweyn Skull Taker had a shield, but the folds of his byrnie allowed me to slice into muscle, slide along the bone and then drive through his body to the other side. As his arm fell and I withdrew Oathsword, Sweyn Skull Taker ended his life. There was now a gap between us and the king and it was tempting to rush forward, full of the joy of battle and fight with the king. I had no wish to die and I knew that I would die if I attempted such a thing. Others were still fighting and until his oathsworn were killed then the king was safe.

I saw Griotard slump to his knees and knew that it must be a serious wound for he was a hard and tough warrior. The Norseman turned his attention to Alf who was struggling to defend against the mighty warrior. His sword had bent a little. I dropped my dagger and taking Oathsword in two hands swung it into the back of the Norseman who was about to take Griotard's life. He had the best of mail and I only broke a dozen or so links but the force was enough to hurt his spine and as his head came up Alf drove his sword through the Norseman's neck, "Take Griotard to safety!"

"I will stay!"

"You are hurt. Do as I say, Alf. There are others to take your place." Even as I spoke Dreng and Eystein stepped forward with Folki close behind. Alf obeyed.

I heard King Forkbeard shout, "Tryggvasson is mine!" He was clambering over the gunwale of *'Long Serpent'* to join us.

As the last of the oathsworn was slain King Olaf Tryggvasson using a stay for support, stepped onto the gunwale. He was defiant to the end, "I am King Olaf Tryggvasson and I die not through an honourable defeat in battle but by the hand of treachery. I will not give a treacherous Dane the glory of my death and I curse you, Sweyn Forkbeard. You shall never know peace." Many men say that the king died a Christian, but I saw that he clutched the sword in two hands as he threw himself over the side, his mail, boots and weapons guaranteeing that he would die, and I knew that he hoped the Christian heaven would be Valhalla.

That was not the end of the battle. The men who had followed King Olaf Tryggvasson on this voyage to the next world fought to the end and were butchered where they stood. There was great slaughter on both sides. It was, however, the end of our battle and as *'Long Serpent'*, damaged from all sides and below the waterline, began to sink, we headed back to our own ships. As we boarded *'Sea Serpent'* we saw the sea take the greatest warship ever built. There would never be another like it. As the sun set, we saw that all eleven Norse ships had been sunk but there were twenty-five of our drekar to keep them company. Many of the Danish and Swedish drekar which headed home had barely enough men to man the oars. We had lost five men killed as well as Griotard and two others with wounds serious enough to keep them from the oars. We rowed west in silence for the sea seemed filled with the dead of a bygone era. I did not think there would ever be a sea battle like this one and when the island of Svolder hove into view and we sought a berth, I for one was glad that it was so.

Chapter 2

Griotard's wound needed attention and we lit a good fire to help us to see the problem. His left thigh bone had been cracked by an axe head. It was a wound that would change Griotard's life. He would be able, when it healed properly, to row and he would be able to stand in a shield wall, but he would be a liability in a battle for he would not be able to move quickly and his movements would be impaired. As his friend Lodvir the Long tended his wound the two of them spoke of this.

"My life as a warrior is over, Lodvir."

"This life as a warrior is over but there are other things you can do."

He laughed, sardonically, "Oh you mean watching Agerhøne with the other old men and cripples? No thank you!"

"If you think you are crippled then that is sad, but it is not what I meant. I need a captain for my drekar. I need someone who can navigate but also fight. Is that you or are you too crippled for that?" That is the way old friends can talk to each other.

"Is this because you feel sorry for me?"

Lodvir laughed, "Feel sorry for you? You are alive! There are many at the bottom of the sea who would change places with you."

"Then I accept." He looked up at Alf, "Sorry that I almost caused you to be skewered, lad. It was fortunate that Saxon Sword here has a quick arm and a strong one!"

Alf shook his head and smiled, "It was my own fault for I was still thinking of the moment I won my name. My father was right when he said to concentrate on fighting the man before me."

Griotard laughed and then grimaced as the laugh made his leg hurt, "Aye, I forgot to give you your full title, Alf the Swooping Hawk!"

Generally, we referred to Alf from then on as either Swooping Hawk or simply Hawk. It was his mother and father who still used the name Alf, although when we went to war his father called him Hawk.

Sweyn One Eye said, "And did you name your new weapon, Sven?"

I nodded, "Norse Gutter for it did its job well. They were hard men."

Lodvir nodded as he finished bandaging Griotard's injury, "Aye, and I did not enjoy slaughtering them. They did their duty as did almost every other warrior, but it still did not feel honourable."

Every eye was drawn to the fire of the king and Jarl Svein Hákonarson. The captains who had survived were there now, reporting to him. His name was not spoken but every warrior knew that King

Sweyn Forkbeard had a bloodless sword. He was a hard man for a warrior to be loyal to. Karl Three Fingers arrived and said, "The king wonders why you are not in his presence, Lodvir the Long?"

Lodvir stood and looked his old comrade in the eye, "I was tending to a warrior who fought Olaf Tryggvasson's oathsworn and thought that a more immediate priority." He sheathed the dagger he had used to improvise a splint, "Had the king been closer to the battle he would have known that."

Karl sucked in air through his teeth, "I am an old friend, Lodvir the Long, and I know you meant no ill but there are others who would have taken offence at your words. Tread carefully."

Lodvir smiled, "Am I not among friends now?"

Shaking his head the old warrior said, "Come; you have tried his patience." The two left for the king's fire.

Griotard looked to be asleep and Alf the Swooping Hawk asked, "Do we need a king?"

Griotard's voice made us jump when he spoke, "There were many who thought we did not need one in the same way that there were many who did not agree with Harald Finehair making a throne in Norway. The ones who fought both kings went to the west and the isle of ice and fire and beyond. We chose to stay and that means that we bend our backs and necks a little. Let us see what the two kings make of Norway. For myself, I know not why they wish it. There is little farmland and half of the country is under snow and ice for half of the year." He sighed, "Keep your voices down. Not only does it keep me awake but there are ears close by who would love to tell King Sweyn of disloyalty. If you think you live in a land where a man may voice his opinion, then you are wrong."

I said, in a quiet voice, "Cousin, we are hearth weru. We have no opinion save that of our hersir. What does Sweyn Skull Taker think about this matter?"

Hawk looked confused, "I know not for I have not asked him."

Sweyn One Eye ruffled his brother's hair, "Brother, today you showed you are brave but sometimes I wonder if you are from our family at all! Listen to our cousin who is wise beyond his years. Do as Griotard said and keep your mouth shut else The Swooping Hawk might be better named, the cackling cockerel!"

It was such a funny image that all of us laughed and it eased the tension.

We had fought all day and we were all weary, but none could sleep. In the case of the hearth weru part of that was the absence of the hersir. We had to wait until he returned before we could position our bodies around his when he slept. However, even had I been an ordinary warrior I would have found it hard to sleep. My dreams would have been filled with the butchered, bloody bodies I had seen aboard the Norse ships. It was a waste. Had the three kings put aside their differences then we could have sailed to England and after we had destroyed their army, been the richest warriors the world had ever known, for England was richer than all save the eastern empire! King Sweyn's wife's hatred of Olaf Tryggvasson had made our king blind to the possibilities we had. Sigfrid the Haughty was a vengeful woman and the slight done to her by King Olaf had been paid for with the deaths of hundreds of Norsemen. Men were still talking of the battle and the famous warriors they had seen die when Lodvir and my foster father returned. They had been away so long that some had feared King Sweyn meant to do them harm. Karl Three Fingers' words had been ominous. However, the two were smiling as they entered the firelit camp.

They both went to see Griotard. He was the only one who had succumbed to sleep but we had plied him with strong ale and he had almost collapsed. The two stood over him, "He fought well today, Lodvir."

"Too well. I fear that if we use him in a shield wall, he will be the one who slows us."

"Then we use that and Griotard becomes an anchor." Sweyn Skull Taker stretched, "Alf, ale!"

My cousin had a filled horn ready almost before the words had died and I poured one for Lodvir who smiled his thanks. He raised his horn, "Men of Ribe and Agerhøne, let us drink to the dead."

"The dead!"

Lodvir grinned as he added, "And to the new Jarl of Ribe and Agerhøne, Sweyn Skull Taker!"

My foster father was ever a modest man and to deflect some of the cheers and praise with which he was showered he said, "And to the new hersir of Agerhøne, Lodvir the Long."

The news guaranteed that it would be some hours before we slept. It was Lodvir who told us what had happened at the king's camp. It became clear that the king had been anxious for what amounted to a court to be ready before he spoke hence Karl's urgency. The two kings must have already divided Norway in anticipation of victory. Men will say that the odds we had in our favour guaranteed that we would win but they were not there! Jarl Svein Hákonarson would rule the parts of Norway given to Denmark and confirmed that the motives for the battle were personal and had nothing to do with the land. Jarl Svein Hákonarson would supply men when we went to war. It had been the jarl, as well as Karl and many of the other drekar captains who had first asked and then demanded that Sweyn Skull Taker be given the title of jarl. Jarl Harald's sons had died fighting with their father and there was no other who could have been given the title. That the king had been reluctant was curious but Lodvir explained it away.

"Sweyn here is a modest man but others can see what he cannot, that he is the most popular Dane and men would happily follow him to battle. He has shown in every war we have fought that he is resolute and brave and does not let his comrades down. The king fears him. He sees a potential rival for the crown. Sweyn Skull Taker has no desire to be king but those who take a crown fear that others will have the same view. We will be given the hardest tasks in any war."

It was then that Sweyn finally spoke, "I am not saying I agree with all that Lodvir said. He talks far more than I would have done and speculates without knowing all! I will say that I was reluctant to accept the title. I told the king that I will not live in Ribe. The home of the Agerhøne clan is where I shall continue to live and now that we have made it stronger, I would be a fool not to do so. Lodvir will live there for I know it will be in good hands."

I was a little sad for I would not see as much of the man who had made me the warrior I was.

He then shook his head as he continued, "This battle cost us men and ships. *'Stormbird'* was just one of many which sank. If there was any profit to be had then it sank beneath the waves."

That was not quite true for while the King of Sweden had destroyed the last of King Olaf's men, we had taken coins, swords, helmets, and other weapons from the oathsworn. Better that we have them than the fishes.

While we were all awake Jarl Sweyn gave us more information about what we would do in the future, "We have a winter to prepare for King Sweyn intends to spend the next raiding season in Wessex. There we will make the profits that will see us enriched. We have the next months to train warriors and to repair the damage to our drekar. Ramming such a fine vessel into another one can do it no good. Enjoy this night for tomorrow we begin to become not just the warriors of Agerhøne but Ribe and Agerhøne. The next time we go to war there will be more than one hundred and fifty spears following my banner. We need those men to be of the quality I see before me, the warriors who won the Battle of Svolder."

It was a stirring speech and we sat up until the dawn was almost upon us talking of the future. When I went to sleep my mind was filled not only with future battles and Wessex but also Mary. If I was going to England again then our future must be decided.

Thorstein the Lucky kicked us awake and when I opened my eyes, I saw that Sweyn Skull Taker was no longer there. I rose with a start. Thorstein grinned, "A poor start for the hearth weru of a jarl, Sven Saxon Sword. He is aboard the ship already. Still, my ship's boys are handy should any make an attempt on his life."

I shook One Eye and Hawk, "Come, the jarl has gone!"

My foster father was smiling as we boarded the drekar. The king and many of the other drekar had sailed already and the ship's boys were preparing the ship for sea. We would raise the mast once the rest of the crew were aboard. There were just five warriors aboard, Griotard and four of the Ribe men who had survived. "Sleepyheads, eh?"

I spoke for the others, "Sorry Jarl Sweyn Skull Taker. It will not happen again!"

He laughed, "The title has not changed me, and I care not if our king takes it away. If I am not safe aboard my own ship, then I am safe nowhere. You three showed yesterday that you were a wise choice for hearth weru. I was able to do what I did because I knew that the three of you guarded me and that helps the rest of the clan. You three must stay alive for while you live then we shall win." He looked at his youngest son, "And you, no more heroics! You have a name and be satisfied with that. A spear held aloft could have ended your life and no father should bury his son. Sweyn and Sven show you how to fight, with courage and fortitude but not recklessness."

I had spoken to Hawk and knew that even as he had leapt, he had regretted his action but by then it was too late to undo it. On a more positive note, the three of us had sat and begun to compose the saga of the swooping hawk and we hoped by the winter solstice to have it ready. We had other chants and songs but they were of the past. The Battle of Svolder had been too dark a chapter to be commemorated in a song but Alf's action merited one.

Our two ships finally left the island at noon. Our departure was marred as we found ourselves sailing through not only broken pieces of wreckage but bodies and body parts. The battle would throw up its reminders through the next months and I, for one, was glad that living on the other coast of Denmark, we would not see them. In fact, the journey back was one of constant reminders for we had sailed to the battle in a fleet led by Jarl Harald and the sea had seemed crowded. Now we led *'Hyrrokkin'* and it seemed empty and lonely. There were ships ahead of us, but we could not see them and others who would be following. so for two days and nights, it was as though our two ships were alone. We called in at Ribe to let ashore those survivors who had crewed with us and to tell the jarl's wife and daughters of the deaths in battle of their men. They would continue to live on the jarl's lands for he had many thralls. They would not be poor, but they would have changed it all for the return of their menfolk. I knew this for my mother had said so when my father and brothers had died. He also took the opportunity to tell the burghers that he was the new jarl and that Lodvir the Long would rule in his stead. We left for the short voyage home after a brief visit. I do not think that Jarl Harald's family needed us there. It was their time to grieve and to remember. The time for conversation would come but not yet.

We were our own harbingers and when the folk of Agerhøne saw the sail they would rejoice but, as I knew from when I had stayed at home, they would fear that while the crews returned, their loved ones might not. The mighty horn would sound and families would leave the stronghold and make their way down to the jetty and quay. I felt especial sadness as my mother would not be there to greet me. Sometimes she had been too ill to make the jetty but, until this return, I had always known that I would see her and now I knew I would not. The whole crew seemed to have similar sombre thoughts and we tied up in silence. Those waiting for us were silent too as they waited to see a face they sought. When the families of our dead saw that their father or husband was not returned there would be a wail. The others would not cheer but the hugs and embraces would be all the more powerful for that.

We each took our shields from the side of the drekar; our chests could wait but it was bad luck to leave shields on a drekar in your own port. The figurehead was also removed by Thorstein the Lucky. The jarl was the first off. None knew of his title and he would not speak to the clan until he had told his wife. As he stepped off every warrior banged their shield with the hilt of their dagger. It was like Thor's thunder. Still banging our shields the hearth weru followed him, I was the last of the three. The jarl and his family quickly moved off to allow others to disembark and I slipped my shield over my shoulder so that I could hurry home. I saw Mary and, behind her, Egbert. For no reason that I could tell she suddenly burst into tears and ran at me. Throwing her arms around my neck she planted a kiss and lifted her feet from the ground. I kissed her back and Lars and Leif whooped with joy behind me.

Her tears had wetted my face and when she descended to the ground, she looked up at me and said, "See how you have made me a wanton? My father will be an unhappy man!"

I nodded, "Then let us remedy that. We shall be married as soon as we can."

She beamed and then frowned, "A handfast marriage? In the Danish style?"

I laughed, "I care not. In any way you wish. If you can find a priest, then in the Christian manner. I do not worry how we marry just so long as we are wed and can be one!"

"We will find a priest!"

The hall seemed empty without my mother, but I knew, as I entered, that this was my hall now and mine to do with as I chose. I had a winter to make it my own. Then I realised it would belong to Mary and me, it would be ours to change. After Egbert and the other thralls had fetched my weapons and chest, I bathed for I stank of blood, seawater and sweat. Mary and her women prepared the evening meal. I invited Egbert to eat with us for I needed his advice and knowledge. He was a little embarrassed to be dining with us, but Mary made it easy and often deferred to him.

"Egbert, I shall be home until the spring." I saw Mary frown. That was a bridge I had yet to cross. "Before I go, I wish to ensure that my lands and my hall be left in a healthy state. Until this moment I have spent my whole time worrying about a sword. I can see now that Oathsword is part of my life and not the whole thing." Both nodded and smiled. "Mary and I are to be wed and that means we will have children. I wish my hall to reflect that. Have the thralls work with Mary to make it easier for all when there are young Svens and Marys in it."

"Aye, lord. It will mean cleaning out parts which have remained unused and we can make better, more solid partitions." He hesitated and said, "In the Saxon style."

"You will not offend me by doing so. How are we for livestock?"

"We could do with more pigs and a man can never have enough sheep."

"Then we will go to Ribe and buy more when the livestock markets reopen." He nodded, "And crops?"

"More land could be cultivated but we do not have enough hands to work it."

"I will fetch more thralls." A thought had occurred to me as I had sailed home. "There is one thing more, Egbert. I would give you your freedom. You shall be paid for running my lands." I paused and realised I had made assumptions. "Of course, as a freeman, you could return across the seas to your home."

He shook his head, "I thank you for the gift of freedom lord, it has oft been a dream and your mother promised it towards the end of her life. I have no family there now and my only family are yourself and your good lady."

Mary put her hand on mine, "That was well done, Sven."

"It was not, Mary, for it had been well done if I had done it when my father died for Egbert was his thrall."

"There is a priest in Ribe, lord. He can wed you."

"How do you know?"

"When your father would visit with his friend Jarl Harald and took me to watch his horse, I would sneak off so that Father Oleg could hear my confession."

I nodded, "Before we can arrange a marriage then I need to seek the permission of Sweyn Skull Taker."

"Of course."

The next morning seemed an appropriate time to do so but as word had got out that he had become jarl then his hall was crowded with those wishing to congratulate him while there were others, the ones who were not warriors but merchants and farmers who sought to profit from the news. I waited a while and tried to catch his eye but it was impossible and I joined Hawk and One Eye outside the hall. I gave them my news and they were delighted. My cousin Sweyn said, "Go and speak with my father for he will like this news. I know that he approves of Mary, we all do for she has been good for you."

"Good for me?"

They both laughed and he continued, "Aye, you were withdrawn and quiet when your father died. It was why my father put you with Siggi for he too was a quiet and reflective youth. We all knew that he would not last many voyages, but it mattered not. Mary took his place and once she came into your life you smiled more."

"Aye," said Hawk, "and became a better warrior."

Shaking my head I said, "You give me more credit than I deserve."

Sweyn said, "When Griotard was wounded who took command? You did. You are a different warrior now and that is down to two things, Oathsword and Mary. When you marry her and have children you will change again. I know that the birth of my son had a profound effect upon me."

Before we could continue our conversation Lodvir came out of the hall and made for us. We all stood; were we to have a duty?

"Sven, the jarl knows that you wish to speak with him, and he has dismissed the throng."

As we passed the disappointed farmers and merchants who emerged I asked, "But how…"

"You are hearth weru, Sven, and Sweyn knows that you would not bother him with something trivial. The merchants who asked for trading rights with Ribe can wait. They did not put their bodies before the jarl to defend him and you did."

I saw that Agnetha was next to the newly promoted jarl and she looked queenlike. I thought then of those comments I had heard about Sweyn Skull Taker as a better king. Agnetha was certainly a better queen than Forkbeard's, Sigfrid the Haughty. "I am sorry to disturb you, foster father, and my request could have waited."

Agnetha smiled, "Modest as ever, Sven, and such behaviour endears you to all. Bersi and your mother brought you up well. What do you wish to ask your foster father?"

"I would marry Mary daughter of Steana." Even as they smiled, I went on hurriedly, "And we would be wed by a Christian priest."

Sweyn laughed as he stood to embrace me, "Many men might say that you were doing this to ingratiate yourself with King Sweyn Forkbeard, but I know you, my son, and it is because Mary the Christian asked you to do so. Of course, you have my permission and, on the morrow, when Lodvir and I travel to Ribe you should come with us and make the arrangements with the priest."

Agnetha came to hug me too, "Your mother would be happy. It is just a shame she is not here to see it."

I felt guilty, "Events conspired against me, my lady, the wars and …"

Sweyn nodded, "Do not apologise Sven for this is not your fault. Once again, we will have to go to war and have but a few months of peace and so we should make the most of it. When you are married in Ribe we shall hold a feast here. We shall celebrate the marriage and the fact that so many of us are still alive!"

And so, quicker than any might have expected, we were wed. The priest, happy to accommodate the new jarl, married us on the eve of the autumnal equinox when the seasons and the days were in balance. The jarl, Agnetha, Lodvir and Egbert were the only witnesses, and they were all that was needed and then we came back to the new mead hall where we could really celebrate. Unlike the last feast, I drank as sparingly as was allowed for many reasons, not least that I did not wish to miss a moment of the day. As was expected we were the first to retire and we entered a hall emptied of all but us two. The thralls and Egbert would return the next day but our first night was spent alone. I know not what I expected but the two of us found, to our mutual delight, that we were made for each other, in every sense of the word. The night seemed to last forever and was over in an instant, or so it seemed. To me that was magic, but my Christian wife said it was just a sign of true love.

Egbert and the thralls must have ghosted in for we did not hear them until it was almost noon. Egbert gave a discreet knock on the newly erected wooden partition between our bedroom and the main hall, "Lord, we have food to break your fast. Should we return later?"

Mary and I had been awake for some time and she lay in my arms. She looked up at me and said, "Perfect timing for I am hungry." She raised her voice, "Egbert, we will rise and eat at the table."

"Aye, my lady!"

In that moment order was established in my hall which was no longer mine, it was Mary's and that was as it should be. It had been my mother's and now it was my wife's. *Wyrd*!

It seemed that there were not enough hours in either the day or the night. Mary was enthusiastic about changing the hall as I was about the land and each day we worked with Egbert and the thralls to shape it to the way we wanted to. Although exhausted, each night was also a joy. By the time it was the harvest blót feast my shield brothers had had enough of my absence and forcibly took me to the mead hall for the celebration. Mary did not object although I was sure that she did not approve. I found that I needed the night of drinking, although in a more moderated manner than my two shield brothers and talking with the two men I trusted most in the world with revelations about the joys of marriage. Poor Hawk was bemused for One Eye understood it all, but Hawk could not. I knew that just as a first battle was a rite of passage that changed a warrior, so marriage made a man from a boy.

Just before I returned to my hall One Eye said, "But, Sven, as much as we all rejoice in this newly found happiness, remember that you are hearth weru and we have a duty to train the young warriors. I know we have skills, but they are nothing compared to yours. My one eye does not impair my skills, but I cannot pass on those skills to young men as well as you. Alf here is keen, but he is no swordsman and besides, they want to be trained by the warrior who wields Oathsword. Lodvir is now at Ribe and Griotard's wound means that he is slow and even novices can dance around him. Give us your mornings, eh?"

He was right and I had been remiss. The last time I had drawn a sword had been the Battle of Svolder and that had been three moons since. "I will give you the morning and I am sorry, brothers, you should have spoken earlier."

Hawk looked glum, "We would but our mother gave us the sharp edge of her tongue. If anything it cuts deeper than it used to!"

One Eye and I laughed.

There were just twelve young men who needed to be trained. One Eye and Hawk had chosen the harvest blót feast because until then the numbers who presented themselves for training varied with the needs of their farms and fishing boats. With the harvest in and days becoming shorter, all twelve were available almost every morning and that made life easier. The two most promising were Dreng Eidelsson and Snorri Sigmundsson. Every Dane we trained had skills, for their fathers and brothers had begun to train them from when they could stand, but these two had greater strength than the others and in Dreng's case quick reactions which were almost as fast as mine.

We used blank spear shafts and wooden swords to minimise the risk of serious injury. As I had discovered when I had begun training, a blow from a wooden sword hurt but it would not cause a life-threatening wound. As they would be fighting alongside the rest of the clan eventually, we made them fight closely together. It was harder that way but taught them to use shorter swings and to be aware of their comrades next to them. Having four of us to train them certainly helped for two were able to direct individuals while the other two could ensure that they stayed together. We used Dreng in the centre of one line and Snorri in the other. They quickly learned to command the others and that too helped. We used spears and shields followed by swords and shields. When we moved on to spear on spear and sword on sword it highlighted the difference between those who would be adequate warriors and those who would be good. I found that training the young men did me good and when Griotard the grim suffered a winter coughing spell and had to stay in the hall I took charge and that helped even more. I was able to hone the skills of the potentially better swordsmen.

Oathsword had done many things for me but the most important was to give me more confidence. I trusted the sword in battle and that allowed me to be subtle in the way I struck. I found that sometimes the edge would be the most effective stroke while at others the tip would be useful. I had even learned to use the flat of the sword for that would blunt the enemy sword and, sometimes, buckle it without making any difference to Oathsword. All of them wanted to best me even though I was using just a wooden sword. I had a reputation, and I was something of a legend. My defence of the drekar in the Seine was an oft sung song.

Dreng and Snorri tried everything they could to beat me but neither ever managed to strike a blow while they had to endure bruises from every encounter. As the winter equinox approached and we headed back to the hall Snorri asked, "How did you become so good so quickly, Sven, for my father said that you are still little more than a boy!"

I heard One Eye suck in his breath at the insult but I did not take it as one and I answered as honestly as I could. "There were boys in the clan who bullied me. It made me stronger and when I was thrown into battle, I found that I had to fight just to survive. Then I found Oathsword and the blade protected me. I know that I was lucky and not every man will find a dragon sword."

All the boys nodded as though it confirmed what they had heard. Dreng said, "Then you were chosen!"

Faramir was one of the Christians, "But is that not a pagan belief? God says that we should turn the other cheek."

One Eye said, coldly, "Do that in battle, Faramir, and not only will you die but, in all likelihood, the two shield brothers next to you."

This was an argument that often raged for those who converted to Christianity were conflicted by the pacifist nature of their religion and the need to fight to defend themselves. I took out Oathsword. As usual, it had a profound effect for every eye was drawn to it.

"This sword was ordered to be made by one of the most Christian kings, King Alfred of Wessex. He and his men fought our people and won. When they did so then King Guthrum was converted. They still fought for their land and their families. I am not a Christian, but I believe that the words, 'turn the other cheek', are meant to ensure harmony in a home. They are not intended to leave a people weak and defenceless." I sheathed the sword and said, "Sweyn One Eye is right Faramir, you cannot hold such views in battle. Better that you tell the jarl you would rather not fight in the shield wall. Not all men go to war and there is no shame in staying in Agerhøne."

He flushed, for we were nearing his home and he shook his head, "No, and you have explained it well. I see the difference." He turned to the others, "I will not let any of you down!"

It was the middle of Mörsugur when Mary gave me the news that she was with child. She had been a little unwell when the Christians had celebrated the birth of their Christ and I had feared she had some illness. She had consulted the wise women of the clan for advice. It was Mary who called them wise women, we called them volva or witches. The choice of the word made it easier for Mary to visit them.

When she told me, then I was happy beyond belief and then, immediately, fearful, "When will the child be born?"

She shrugged, "The wise women think that I conceived in the first month of our marriage for they said I was young and healthy as were you. They said the month you call Skerpla. I think that is the same as our May. I worked it out with my fingers." I nodded and my face fell. "What is wrong, husband?"

"I shall not be here for then I will be raiding with the king."

She gave me a sad smile, "And if you were here then what could you do? You would run around like a headless chicken and panic! Birthing is a time for women and not men!"

I shook my head, "I could be here and hold your hand. I could be at your side."

She looked suddenly shocked, "There when I give birth? Are you mad? It is a place for women who know of such things. Men know war, I accept that. Women understand other things. I know that you must go to war and it will give me time to become a mother. I can make mistakes, and none shall know it but I. There are some good women in your village. Since we have wed, they have shown me great kindness. Agnetha is a good lady and she said she will be at the birthing."

"Agnetha knows?"

Laughing she said, "Of course! There are no secrets between the women. When you sail away on your warship it is the women who rule Agerhøne and Agnetha is the queen. She is the one who keeps calm and order. She is the dispenser of justice and wisdom. It was your mother who taught me the order of things and of life in this stronghold. Go to war but come back soon and come back whole!"

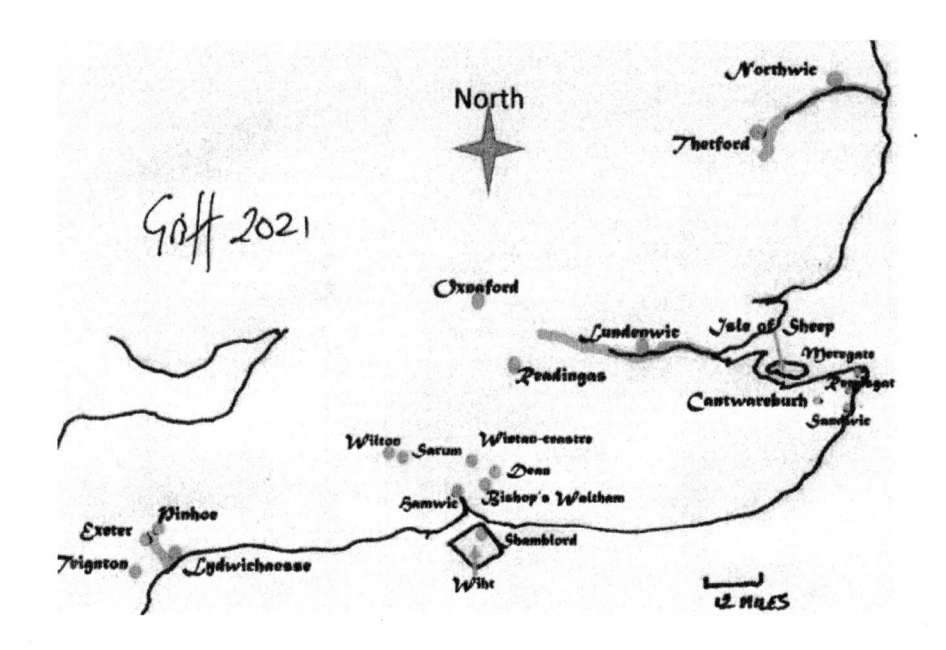

The English lands raided by the Danes

Chapter 3

We did not have to travel to the court of the king to discover our orders. Karl Three Fingers fetched them. Having delivered them and returned to the king, Griotard had given us the cynical reason for that, "The king does not like us and he would rather keep us isolated. I think he regards us as a sort of hunting dog. Useful for bringing down enemies but best kept on a steel leash and as far away from him as possible."

Perhaps he was right. To be honest it was better this way for we did not have to travel down the corduroy road and endure the false faces of King Forkbeard and his court. We liked Karl and away from the intrigues of Forkbeard, he was a different man. Lodvir was summoned from Ribe and we gathered around a table in Sweyn Skull Taker's mead hall. As I sat with my cousins in the room, which was normally dark and full of bodies, I was able to enjoy the intricate carving on the roof supports and the beams. One normally did not see them for at a feast your eyes were down but not up. As we waited, I saw all the detail: the tree of the stars, Yggdrasil and the creatures of the heavenly world such as the messenger squirrel Ratatoskr who to me also seemed like an animal version of Loki. The perching hawk, Veðrfölnir now had a real relevance of Alf. The Norns were there too, spinning, on one side was Sól, the sun goddess, and on the other Máni, the moon god. There was the goddess of the earth, Jörð, as well as Dagr, the god of the day and Nótt, a jötunn of the night. Not that she would be invited but Mary would understand none of this and might even be fearful of what she saw as blasphemy!

Karl, Lodvir and our jarl entered the hall and we stood. Karl's oathsworn were with him and they guarded the door. What was to be said was a secret but, Sweyn Skull Taker knew that he could trust all the warriors of the clan. The merchants were a different matter! After the usual pleasantries, Karl began, and he smiled at us when he said, "The king will not be leading this raid, I will!" That brought smiles to our faces and made the rest of the commands far more palatable. "Because we made war on the Norse last year the lands to the west were not taxed. King Aethelred did not have to send weregeld to us. He was foolish not to do so for now we will take payments from him in thralls and gold. King Sweyn was pleased with the efforts of the men of Ribe at Svolder and it is your ships and twenty I bring from Heiða-býr which will raid first Hamtunscīr and then Denshire. We shall use the island close to Hamtunscīr, the one the Saxons call Wiht as our base. There are no burhs there and we can control the mouth of the river. How many ships can you bring?"

Sweyn Skull Taker rubbed his beard and looked at Lodvir who held up his fingers, "Seven ships. We lost four at Svolder and with them, their crews."

Karl frowned and then shrugged, "We will have to do with quality then and not quantity."

Lodvir leaned forward, "And the profits from this raid, how will they be apportioned?"

"Two thirds for the king and his men and a third for you."

I knew that we would take more than that for the payment of which Lodvir spoke would be the coin the Saxons paid for us to go and that which we took from their churches. When we raided each drekar crew would keep what it took from houses, towns, villages and warriors.

Sweyn said, "When do we leave and how long shall we be away?" Karl frowned and Sweyn smiled, "I ask because my foster son is to become a father. Will his bairn be walking before he sees him?"

Karl nodded, "We sail from Ribe at the start of Einmánuður when the men of Wessex will be toiling in their fields and we return at the end of Tvímánuður when we can take their harvests."

"Half a year," he nodded, "and if we are away so long, do we need to pay taxes to King Forkbeard?" With no men working for half a year it would be an unfair burden. The Saxons had no such option and our raids would not only take coins from them they would have to pay more taxes to keep us away in the future.

"Ribe and Agerhøne will pay no taxes this year!"

We feasted that night but it was a muted affair for we did not have long to prepare. I told Mary, not the places we would raid, for that was too personal, but the time I would be away, and she accepted it. She had changed since my mother had died and we had wed. She seemed less argumentative and our life was more harmonious. The prospect of being a mother had changed her. Once more I wondered at my decision to delay wedding her. Hindsight is a wonderful thing. It is always perfect.

We had more work to do with our twelve new warriors. Training stopped as we helped them to prepare weapons. Their fathers and families had given them a sword of some description and some had bows but they needed spears. We had spears we had taken from our enemies, but a warrior liked to have his own. The best heads were taken from the shafts of the captured spears and we gave them to the youths. We took them to the woods where ash grew and they each chose a shaft that they would trim and polish. We showed them how to sharpen the spearheads and then each one finished them off themselves. The shields we had used had been training shields and each needed work for they would now be attached to a drekar. The four of us gave them advice as well as showing them our own shields. By the time we were ready to sail each of the twelve had a shield that was well painted and would afford protection in battle for they were double boarded, nailed and glued before having a cover of leather or sealskin.

While the unmarried warriors feasted and drank the night before we sailed, I spent the whole time with Mary. This time it was not my mother who fussed that I had taken enough with me but my wife. After I had returned from Svolder she had Egbert collect as much fruit as they could. Cooked with honey and suet and then sealed in waxed pots it kept well. She had one such pot ready for me. It was a thoughtful gift. When we were at sea and eating either raw fish or salted meat then a spoonful of the preserve tasted like nectar. The jars of pickled fish and venison were for my chest and would be my treat. That I would share them with my oar brothers was obvious, but they had been packed and prepared by my wife and that made them special. She had made my sealskin cape bigger so that I could sleep under it if I wished and she packed spare kyrtles and breeks. The squirrel hat might not be necessary, but it was good that I had it and the sealskin cap would be useful. The sea across which we sailed was often beset with squalls and storms. Being dry made it just a little more bearable. Finally, she gave me a jar of salve she had made up. It was my mother's recipe which Mary had adapted. The sea dried a warrior's hands and while they could bear the discomfort a scabbed hand could often become blackened and fingers might have to be removed. I had seen it happen to others. The salve was to ensure that we could row and fight.

"And when you come home there will be a child. I cannot promise you a warrior but I will do all in my power to ensure that the child is healthy."

"Boy or girl I care not!"

"And I will name the child which will be baptised as soon as they are born!"

There was finality in her words which told me that she would brook no argument. I gave her none. I knew the reason behind her vehemence; she wanted the child to go to heaven and for that it needed baptism. If it was a boy, it would not affect his ability to be a warrior. That would lie in my hands.

"Whatever names you choose will satisfy me. One Eye's son is like his father and grandfather, Sweyn. Calling out the name Sweyn will be a nightmare one day!"

For some reason that made her laugh out loud and after kissing me goodnight she was asleep. I lay awake for a short time. There was the slightest of bumps and, when I knew she was asleep and breathing steadily, I placed my right hand on it and spoke softly, "Child of mine, you are yet to be born and if the Norns have spun I may not return to see you. Know that even in the afterlife I shall watch over you. I shall be the thought which guides your hand and your eye. If I fail to return, then know I love you and I would have you watch and protect your mother for she is the dearest person that I know." I leaned over and kissed the bump. Mary's arm came over around my neck and that is how I fell asleep.

Mary did not come to see me off. I knew that she would cry, and she did not wish that. Instead, it was Egbert with two thralls carrying my chest who came to see me off, "Lord, Lady Mary will be safe while you are away. Lady Agnetha shows special interest in her. You and the warriors have made our home strong enough now and we will be safe. When you return there will be more animals and your crops will be ready to harvest. God smiles on your union and it has done my heart good to see the two of you together. It was your mother's dearest wish."

It was the longest speech I had heard from my freeman and I smiled, "And I never thanked you for watching both me and my mother when my father was away. Know that I appreciate all that you do."

He nodded, "The dark days were when I was first taken, and it was watching over you and your mother which brought joy and hope to me. I know now that God sent me here. You may still follow the pagan ways, lord, but in your heart, you are a Christian and I take some of the credit for that."

I did not believe him, and he had not seen me fight but I knew that I was different from many of the warriors with whom I would sail. I knew that I was kinder and more considerate. Perhaps he was right!

The jarl and his hearth weru were the last to board and as we set sail to head to the muster, the clan cheered. There were warriors left to watch our home. We had tried to persuade Griotard to be one, but he refused. There was also the next generation of young warriors who waved us off and I saw the regret on their faces. They would be the ones we would train the next winter. Life at Agerhøne was like a circle but the world appeared to be changing. A few generations ago there had been no kings and now they made decisions for us. How long would this circle remain unbroken?

More than half a year had passed since we had rowed. We also had twelve new warriors seated on their chests, and when we began to row we were ragged. Griotard growled and grumbled as we headed past the outlying islands north to Ribe. We used simple chants and it brought a little bit of order, but we knew that once we joined the other ships of Ribe we would all have to row better. When we reached Ribe the three of us would speak with the new crew and give them advice. Lodvir the Long had done so with me when I had first sailed, and I had a duty to do the same. Since **'Stormbird'** had been sunk we were now the largest drekar in the Ribe fleet. We had every oar double crewed and, in the case of the first three chests, triple crewed. It made for a crowded drekar but one whose warriors would lead the line behind the jarl and ahead of the men of the Ribe coast.

When we moored, the jarl had a berth reserved for him, we left Griotard to give the sharp edge of his tongue to the crew and headed for the jarl's mead hall. It was now Lodvir's home, but Sweyn Skull Taker was not precious about such things. He had chosen to live with the Agerhøne clan in their settlement and I knew that he did not regret his decision. Once we reached the hall he said, "I will be safe here with Lodvir. Until we sail then your time is your own." He looked at his youngest son and gave him what we knew was the serious eye, "Remember that you are the hearth weru of the jarl! Behave accordingly."

We all nodded but One Eye and I knew he was talking to Hawk!

The last time we had been in Ribe it had been Jarl Harald's town. Now it was Sweyn Skull Taker's and his hearth weru were accorded all sorts of courtesies and privileges I had never imagined. Those who sold items in the markets were desperate for us to take their wares. I knew why for they could then tell others that the hearth weru of Sweyn Skull Taker used their carved eating spoon or decorated bowl. Had we wished we could have taken enough drinking horns for the first two chests of rowers! We did not take from everything which was offered but we would have offended had we not taken some of the proffered gifts. The alewives happily filled up our horns for free and I saw that it was good business for as we drank other warriors came to buy ale and ask us about the Battle of Svolder or Oathsword. We had entered a different world! We had thought to buy food but we had no need. As we drank ale the alewives sent platters of choice pieces of meat, fish and cheese as well as warm bread covered in melting butter. Again I knew why; it was to make a profit for younger warriors thought to emulate us. They would spend their coins happily knowing they were in the company of veterans with names earned in combat. When we had been the hearth weru of a hersir we had not been as important. Men had asked to see the dragon sword but that was all. Sweyn Skull Taker's elevation had elevated us. Our names were known. Warriors used the names as though we had known them for years and yet they were complete strangers, and we did not know their names. By the time we returned to **'Sea Serpent'** we were almost dizzy with the changes which had been wrought!

The new warriors we had trained looked as though they had been used to clean the decks and had the look of chastened hounds. Griotard knew how to curse! We deposited our newly acquired wares in our chests and went to sit with them at the prow; the end reserved for novices. I remembered it well from my time with Siggi! I smiled, "Griotard the Grim let you know that you were not the best of rowers?"

Snorri nodded miserably, "We have not yet been to sea and no one told us how to row! Everyone seems to think that we know what to do without ever having been to sea!"

Faramir said, "I was a ship's boy for one voyage, and I had been to sea but I did not know that rowing was such a hard thing to do!"

I smiled, "You row in pairs." They nodded. "And which four are at the fore of you?" Dreng, Snorri, Faramir and Gandálfr all raised their arms. You four just watch the warriors in front of you and copy them, exactly. The rest can copy you. It is repetition, that is all. You slide the oar on the narrow side and then pull with the blade. When the others raise you do but you cannot be tardy nor delay for an instant. Today was an easy day for we sailed alone. Tomorrow or the day after, whenever we sail, we will be with a fleet and if we drop back then the rest of the Ribe fleet will too. If you thought Griotard was a grumpy bear awoken from his winter sleep too early, then make a mistake before the other ships and you will see a bear whose cub has been taken!"

One Eye laughed at the image and I knew that he would use it in a saga.

Gandálfr said, "But how can we row harder?" He showed me his hands. They were red raw already.

I shook my head, "Did you pack your own chests?" The looks they gave told me that they had not.

Faramir said, "I made sure my weapons were at the top, but my mother and sisters packed the rest."

"Each of you, open your chests and see what treasures the wise women of Agerhøne have hidden for their foolish sons and brothers."

It was as though they had discovered a chest of gold and jewels as they took out clothes, hats, capes and food. Then Dreng said, "What is this?" He held up a small pot.

"Open it." I saw others discovering equally intriguing items. Dreng opened it and wrinkled his nose, "Mother has given me some food which has gone off!"

Laughing, Hawk went over to him and took a fingerful of it. He smeared it on Dreng's reddened hands. Dreng's eyes widened, "It cools them!"

I nodded at the jar in the young warrior's hands, "So, Gandálfr, when we raid the Saxons find a good present to take back to your mother for she knew that you would need her salve."

Sweyn One Eye said, "And we will not tell them that their sons were too foolish to find it!"

It marked a change in the young warriors. After they had soothed their hands, they examined everything and then repacked it. It was a lesson learned.

Karl Three Fingers led the other ships into the harbour the next morning. His own ship, *'Firedrake'* was a large vessel; she had twenty oars on each side. Double crewed it gave her more than eighty fighting men. At least half of them were mailed and all were well-armed. It was clear that these were the best of King Sweyn's men. His very best would be with him, his hearth weru bodyguards but he was ensuring that Karl Three Fingers had men with him who could do the job. As the crews disembarked to visit Ribe's market I stood with Griotard. Hawk and his brother had gone to take Karl to their father and the two of us estimated the men we would have when we raided.

"We have three hundred or so, roughly. There is one snekke there and that shows Karl Three Finger's wisdom. You need a sneaky little snake to go places they would spot a drekar. I think that Karl had brought more than eight hundred warriors. This is not the largest warband the king has ever sent but we are enough to raid as well as any warband and we are led by a good man. I am hopeful, Sven." Griotard would not be sailing with us but he and some of our crew would join Lodvir. Griotard would be the sailing master. Griotard was rarely optimistic and it heartened me. Karl also showed that he would not waste one moment in port more than he had to.

The winds were in our favour, but Sweyn Skull Taker still made a blót before we sailed. Had the king been with us then we would not have been allowed to for it was not a Christian act. Karl just shrugged and we set sail in three fleets. The lithe little snekke, *'Adder'*, sailed ahead of *'Firedrake'* in the centre. We were the steerboard fleet and one of King Sweyn's other jarls, Eirik Mighty Fist, led the other. It was a wise precaution. If a storm came upon us then each group would be easier to reform and we had waypoints already decided where we would wait. We were heading due west by south to make for the river the Romans had called the Dunum. It lay in the land colonised by our kin already, Northumbria, and we knew that there were friends in Jorvik.

We would not necessarily land but we sailed there as it was the most direct route and there would be no chance of Saxon ships and warriors waiting to pounce. If we had rowed the whole way, then we could have reached the estuary in two days and nights. We would not row all the way. We would use the sails when we could and sail under reefed sails at night. We would row but that was to harden the crews and to make them one.

We reached the mouth of the river in five days. We spent a day there making minor repairs to some of the Heiða-býr ships. Thorstein the Lucky was less than complimentary about their captains for he knew that had they prepared for sea better then no repairs would have been necessary. While we waited, some warriors went ashore to hunt the seals which basked upon the sands there. We even had time to render down some of the flesh to make oil while giving us both fresh food and skins! The blót had been a good one! With all in good order, we sailed down the coast. Even our kin who lived there would be watching our sails warily as we edged along their sea. There were Danes who held the land all the way south to the Tamese but that did not mean that news would not be spread. Riders would already be heading inland to tell King Aethelred that a Danish fleet was close. The wolves were heading for the sheep pens!

It took just under four days to reach the Isle of Sheep at the mouth of the Tamese. Some captains questioned Karl's decision to land there for it told the Saxons where we were. Sweyn Skull Taker not only approved, but he had also been party to the decision. When, as we roasted some of the sheep we had captured, one or two of the older warriors wondered why we had alerted the Saxons our jarl explained as though to a child.

"We want the Saxons to know we are abroad and even now, in Lundenwic, they will be barring the gates and raising the levy. Further south, in Cent, the great churches will be ringing their bells to warn people that we are close. They will wonder where we will attack. They may even, although I doubt it, send ships and men down here to shift us. It matters not for on the morrow we shall have vanished like the morning mist and they will wonder where we have gone. Their burhs will be manned, and all will go about armed."

"Aye, but we still have to land, and they will be ready."

"Bergil, do you know where we will land?"

The older warrior looked shamefaced, "Wessex?"

"Perhaps, but if you do not know for certain then how will the Saxons know? They rely on their burhs to defend their people, but they can only stay there for so long. They have fields and animals to tend to.

We will disappear from view and they will watch the sea and see nothing. When we do reappear it will be from the south and catch them unawares. It will be like the shepherd boy who watches the sheep and shouts *'wolf'* too many times."

We left well before dawn and by the time the sun came up, we were well to the south and west of the easternmost tip of Cent. We sailed due south before heading directly west for a day across the sea and then we headed north to the island which lay off the coast of Wessex. Our strange route meant we did not cross the path of any Saxon traders and were as good as invisible. The gods smiled on us for it sent squally and wet weather. I was dry beneath my seal skin as we rowed north but with poor visibility and only those who had to be at sea then the Saxons would be blind to our approach. It was **'*Adder*'** which left us and then raced north to find the beach we sought on the eastern coast of the Isle of Wiht. The fire they lit to light our way ashore showed us that the landing site was safe and we drew the boats up on the sand.

The next part involved us. Lodvir had selected twenty warriors from the Ribe and Agerhøne contingent and our job was to make our way north, across the island. The snekke crew would also sail around the island and the intention was for us to head to Shamblord on the west side of the River Meðune. With **'*Adder*'** blocking the river we would destroy any boats we found and slay any defenders so that our ships could sail around and then hide in the river. We would be able to strike into the heart of Wessex and raid before the Saxons even knew we were there. The plan seemed to me to be flawless.

There was pride involved as we slung our shields on our backs and hung our helmets from our spears. We had to be at Shamblord before **'*Adder*'** to secure the tiny fishing port and I knew that the snekke would be equally keen to beat us. Lodvir let me lead and he brought up the rear. The warriors who had been chosen were all the best. Lodvir's hearth weru were with us as were some of the other hearth weru of the Ribe hersirs. It was dark but I knew that all I needed to do was to run north by west. When I reached a river, I would keep that to my shield side. The Allfather favoured us with a good moon. With cloaks over our mail, we would be hard to see and the moonlight meant we could see, in the distance, the shining of its light on the water. Every five hundred steps or so, I counted in my head, I would pause and glance around. Sweyn One Eye and Hawk were always close and as the light showed me that Lodvir had not fallen back I kept the same pace. I only stopped when I saw the two separate settlements of Shamblord. One lay on each bank of the river and between them lay their boats.

Our planning had been perfect, but it had assumed there would be just one settlement or that the boats would only be on one side. This upset everything. The Norns had been spinning. I waited for Lodvir to join me and he took in the problem immediately. "We will have to wait for *'Adder'* She can take the western village and we will take the eastern. Let us get into position." As we donned our helmets he said, "You did well, Sven. That was a good pace and none were left behind."

I looked up to Lodvir and his words meant a great deal to me.

This time he led and it was I who followed him. We could smell the woodsmoke from the houses which lay close to the beach. These would be fisherfolk and with no wall around the huts showed that they did not expect to be attacked. There was no reason why they should, but they were in for a shock. We would not need our shields and so we all left them on our backs which allowed us to have two hands on our spears. I had not used Saxon Slayer at Svolder but on the land, it was another matter. The spear meant that even if the Saxons fought back our weapons would be longer and certainly have a better head. Saxon Slayer was sharp enough to shave with and even a glancing blow would be deep. We would take no chances for the whole raid depended upon our success.

When we were just a hundred paces away there was a glow of light from one of the huts. Lodvir and I were on our knees so quickly that it would have seemed we had the same thought at the same time. We watched a fisherman come from his hut and make water in the vessel just outside the door. It would be used to kill lice on clothes before they were washed. We could hear his noise and it showed just how far noise travelled at night. I breathed a sigh of relief when he re-entered the hut. When we reached the huts Lodvir waved his arm to spread us out. There were ten dwellings, and he assigned the men he knew best first. Some huts had two of us watching them but the one I was given, the one closest to the beach had just me as a sentinel. Lodvir pointed to me to keep watch to the estuary as I was the closest.

'Adder' had made good time and I think that they must have rowed hard as well as using the sail. The sail was down when we approached the moored ships. There were four large vessels in the water and another ten drawn up on the beach close to me. The settlement on the other side of the river was smaller with just four dwellings and three boats. I waved my spear to attract their attention and Benni, the captain waved back. I pointed the spear towards the other side of the river, and he waved back. Along with Lodvir and the others I watched as the snekke rowed to the beach. Most of the crew disembarked and four men rowed the snekke back to the middle of the estuary. We were ready and

having done my part I turned to face the door of the dwelling. I had done my part and now we awaited Lodvir's command. I saw him wave his spear and I stepped towards the door of the hut.

The huts were all identical. There was a crude door hung on leather hinges and an opening in the roof to let out the smoke. Made of wattle and daub they were quick to make and easy to maintain. I pulled open the door and saw, by the glow of the fire a family of what looked like six. There was a man and his wife under a blanket made of sheepskin and four children under a second. Before I could say anything, the man flashed open his eyes and sat upright. Had I chosen to, I could have slain him there and then but Mary had changed me and as I spoke perfect Saxon I showed a more charitable side.

Pointing Saxon Slayer in his direction I said, "Saxon, if you wish to die then draw a weapon. If you wish to live, then stand and put your hands upon your head. You have my word that neither you nor your family will be harmed."

He stood and spat out, "And what is the word of a Viking worth? I would rather die fighting you."

"But that is not the Christian way is it?" My hand darted out and I scored a red line down his side with the spear, "My friend, I could have killed you then." He heard the cries of others and the clash of steel. Not all had obeyed us. "I am not alone."

His wife reached up to touch his hand and she nodded to him. He put his hands on his head.

"Woman, bring me his weapons and I will leave you alone."

She rose and, with the cloak around her shoulders to hide her modesty she went to the corner and fetched a seax and a short sword. As she handed them to me, she said, "You are a strange Viking."

I smiled as I took the weapons, "I married a Christian who was the daughter of a priest. I kill only those who try to kill me."

When I emerged, I saw that the sun was beginning to rise in the east. There were three dead Saxons. Lodvir looked up and I said, "I have the weapons of this one and they are within."

He nodded, "I am not sure that King Sweyn would approve but I cannot find fault with you."

We had done what was asked of us and we stood to watch until **'Firedrake'** edged around the headland. We now had our camp and it looked to me to be a perfect place for the fleet to wait. As the sun had illuminated the valley I saw that the twist in the mouth of the river meant that we could anchor the entire fleet and they would be hidden from the main channel by the fishing boats. The plan had nearly gone awry but Lodvir and Benni were both good leaders. All was well.

Chapter 4

Karl allowed us to rest while he and the other warriors secured the northeast corner of the island before taking all that there was from the island. There were no burhs and no great churches, but Karl ensured that there would be no warriors there to make our life difficult. We needed a secure base. Men were slain and every man woman and child were brought to the river where they could be watched. As soon as the island had been cleared of all threats we prepared to raid! Twenty Heiða-býr men were left to guard the drekar and the captives. The ships' boys and the captains would also guard the ships we were leaving. We had been forced to kill just a few from the village and the fisherfolk appeared grateful. We left half of the ships at anchor and double crewed the rest to row to the River Hamble which led into the heartland of Hamtunscīr. We left before dawn and Karl timed it perfectly so that we were rowing up the river just as dawn broke. We had light to see and surprised all of those along the river. We rowed three miles before we heard the bells tolling their warning. The river was still wide enough for us to land ships on both banks and we quickly moored and landed. Our two drekar were left under the command of Griotard, a few older warriors and the ship's boys. We landed on the steerboard bank and Jarl Sweyn, for the first time, led the men of Ribe and Agerhøne on a raid. There were more than two hundred and fifty of us who poured across the land. Keeping Lodvir's men with us the other captains each led their crews to attack the isolated farms and small villages.

We headed for the sound of the tolling bell. The crude map we had looked at suggested there was a small town or large village, too small to be a burh and it lay to the north and east of us. We ran towards it. This time my foster father led and as his hearth weru we dogged his steps. We heard cries from ahead and saw armed men hurrying to meet with us. Numbers were hard to assess but it made no difference in any case. Whomsoever we met we fought.

"Wedge!"

Even as we kept moving towards the Saxons who were improvising a shield wall, we formed our wedge. This time there was neither Lodvir nor Griotard and the new men would have to work out what to do for we had not trained them for this. Without even pausing to ensure that he had enough men behind him, Jarl Sweyn levelled his spear and we ran at the Saxons. Hawk held his spear above his father's head and mine was to the side. I saw now that there were thirty odd men in the wall. They had shields but poorly made ones and their spears were not as long as ours. Light glistened from helmets pitted with rust. The year we had not raided had made the men of Wessex careless.

The jarl increased his pace and we kept up with him. As he drew his spear back so did I. Hawk would keep his where it was. A few stones and arrows were thrown at us. An arrow struck the mail on my right shoulder, but it did not even penetrate the mail. A stone pinged from the helmet of the jarl and then my foster father and I struck together. Our spearheads were aimed at the faces peering from behind the worst shields I had ever seen. A short spearhead came towards my eye but by turning my head the metal merely scraped along the side of my helmet. I heard a cry as Saxon Slayer tore into the cheek and eye socket of a Saxon and then the sheer weight of our charge bowled over the four men before us. We stamped on their heads as we crossed over them and then we were through their line. As the wedge struck them then more men were speared and stabbed. The ones at the side and rear of the crude shield wall broke and ran.

I could see, as did the jarl, that the defence had been to slow us so that their families could escape. The Saxons were wise enough not to carry too much away with them; their lives were the most important thing. They would run towards the nearest place with a good wall. Hamwic was the nearest burh of any size and that was some miles away. As we reached the edge of the town, we saw the last of the families in the distance. There was little to be gained from chasing them as their speed meant that they carried nothing with them and calling a halt we turned to begin to take all that we could from the town. While others searched the churches and the houses, often digging in their floors for buried chests, Jarl Sweyn questioned the prisoners. They were all wounded and all but one looked unlikely to survive. He had me question the priest who had been stabbed in the leg. He would be crippled but he would live.

"What is your name, priest?"

I had learned that by asking questions that appeared harmless you could often be led to nuggets of gold. "John of Curbridge." He winced as he spoke, and I took my ale skin and offered him a drink. He shook his head, and I drank. When I offered it again he accepted. "And this is Curbridge?" He nodded. "Do not worry your people will make Hamwic for that is where they have gone, is it not?"

"It is and Eorledman Aethelweard who waits there is also the King's reeve. You will all die!"

I nodded, "All men die. And if the king's reeve is close by then so will Aethelred?"

"Of course for he would not desert his children in Aetheling Valley!" He realised he had said too much and shook his head. "No more!"

Jarl Sweyn had understood most of what had been said but I explained the priest's reaction, "Aetheling Valley suggests that the king's children are close. This cannot be the valley. We should send out scouts north to find it."

Jarl Sweyn was quick thinking, "Take my son, Alf, Leif and Lars, head north and see what you can find. We will use this as a base to raid. Be quick, foster son!"

"Aye, jarl, and I am honoured that you trust me."

"There is none I trust more!"

We ran along the road which led north and east. The river, whilst not navigable also went in that direction and I wondered if we were already in Aetheling's Valley. I hung my helmet from Saxon Slayer so that I could both see and hear better. I was not worried about an attack. The road twisted and turned until it eventually rejoined the river at a small, abandoned farm. We stopped to drink from our skins and take whatever food we could find while I got my bearings.

"We will leave the road and head along the riverbank for that way we will be hidden."

"We make better time on the road, Sven!"

"And we can be seen. If the children of the king are close, we do not wish them frightened into flight. If we take those as hostages, then think of the ransom we could demand. This is about cunning!"

When we left, I took a hunter's trail along the river and within half a mile I was rewarded. There, just ahead of us was a large town. This one did have a wall, but it was not made of stone and there was no ditch. More importantly, there was a huge church and what looked like a large hall. I turned, "We will head back. We have what we need. If this is not the valley the priest spoke of it is still a good target."

It was as we headed back that we came upon two Saxon warriors. We saw them because they were close to the road and obviously keeping watch for the likes of us. They would have information and using Saxon Slayer I signalled for Lars and Leif to go to my left. Hawk followed me to the right. We were within twenty paces before they saw us, and they ran. All the training I had done, running to the wood and back when I was a youth had made me a fast runner. The mail did not bother me, and I began to catch the one Hawk and I followed. When I was just five paces from him, I pulled back my arm and threw Saxon

Slayer, haft first. It smacked him on the back of the head and he fell face forward into a tree. When we reached him, I saw that he was not dead but was unconscious.

Lars and Leif arrived, "Sorry, Sven, we do not have your skill. We were forced to kill our Saxon."

"No matter, we have a prisoner. Bind him and hang him from your spears. We will take him back so that we can question him."

Food was being cooked when we arrived. The priest was hanging by his arms from a tree as Lodvir tried to get more information from him. I told the jarl of our discovery and he used water to rouse the young Saxon warrior. When he opened his eyes, I saw the terror in them as he saw that he was surrounded by fierce mailed warriors.

"The place with the wall and the church, it is Aetheling's Valley?"

Shaking his head he said, "No, it is Bishop's Waltham, and the Bishop has a home there."

"Where are the Aethelings?" He shook his head and was so scared that he began to wet himself. "Answer me truly and you will not die, I promise."

"I know not except that they are guarded by men of the king's bodyguard and kept in great halls to the north and east of here."

"Then this is the valley."

"Aye, it is!"

I turned to Jarl Sweyn, "That is all that he knows, of that I am certain."

"You have done well. Bind him, Alf."

As the youth was taken away and the priest lowered to the ground, for we could get no more information, Jarl Sweyn said, "And how far is this place called Bishop's Waltham?"

"No more than two miles."

"Then I will have Lodvir, when he has eaten, take two crews and cut it off. On the morrow, we take this treasure house!"

The four of us, the jarl and his hearth weru sat and ate together. As usual, Hawk was his buoyant optimistic self. I liked that quality for it was the best of my cousin. "If all goes like this then we can return home within a month!"

I looked at Sweyn One Eye who rolled his single orb. I continued to eat and waited for my foster father to speak. He waited until his mouth was empty and then said, "My son, it is good that you see every horn of ale as half full."

One Eye mumbled, "Over full if you ask me."

Ignoring his first born the jarl went on, "Karl Three Fingers has planned well. Our appearance at the Isle of Sheep and our disappearance means that the Saxons know not where we are. We have burst into their heartland and taken them by surprise. The Saxons are slow to rouse but they have a system. Each burh, town and village will now be ordered to supply warriors. They will be told to assemble and then, when they do, they will come to meet us in battle. The Saxons like the idea of hundreds and that is how they will be formed. There will be many bands of one hundred and they will gather together. If we faced them one by one then you are quite right, Alf son of Sweyn, we would be able to destroy them and we might be home sooner rather than later. That is not the way it will be and by threatening the children of the king we draw an army to us."

It was a patient explanation. I realised that I had known what my foster father would say before he did. There were no surprises in his words. The only surprise for me was that we were threatening the king's children. We did not need to take them, in fact, that was an unlikely occurrence but by threatening them we would draw them into battle.

"Tomorrow we attack a town with a wall. From what Sven says, there is no ditch, and the wall is not high but they will defend it. Now that I am a jarl I have to lead and that means we shall be the first over the wall. Others will place their shields so that the four of us can spring over the top." He smiled, "We shall see Alf the Swooping Hawk once more, eh?"

Before I lay down to sleep I took out the whetstone and sharpened Saxon Slayer and Oathsword. The virtue of a sharpened spear had been shown when a prick had made the fisherman acquiesce to my request. That done I said a silent prayer to the Allfather to watch over my wife and unborn child and then lay down at the feet of the jarl. To get to our leader the three of us would have to be crossed!

We did not take all the men of Ribe and Agerhøne. Men were sent to find Karl Three Fingers while others took our treasures back to the drekar and twenty men guarded the settlement. It meant we had just over one hundred and forty men with us as we headed along the road and the river. Our killing of the guards would have warned the people of Bishop's Waltham that Vikings were abroad, and they would be ready. I hoped that they had watched on their walls all night and would be weary. When we saw the walls another twenty men were sent to join Lodvir. His task was just to hold the road north. As Sweyn Skull Taker had explained, the Saxon army was slow to muster and we had a short time to take all that we could before a large army could be gathered to face us.

One advantage we always had was that we did not need a long time to prepare for battle. Even as we were marching north the captains and leaders were already instructing their men what to do. Saxons liked to be blessed by their priests and to have their sins absolved. They liked to sing hymns so that their God was with them. We needed none of that and as soon as we reached the wall Jarl Sweyn Skull Taker ordered Hawk to sound the war horn three times and we simply began our attack. Leif, Lars, Dreng, Eidel and the other experienced warriors using their shields held above them raced ahead to the wall and then stood, in pairs with their backs to the wall holding a shield between them. The four of us ran towards them. The same thing was being repeated all along this southern wall of Bishop's Waltham. Arrows and stones were sent at us and we had no shield to protect us. We had them over our backs. What we did have was speed and surprise. Our multiple attacks on the walls had divided the Saxon attack. Some sent arrows and stones at us while others tried to hit the moving mailed men who did not run in an obligingly straight line but jinked from side to side.

I ran to Lars and Leif. I had fought alongside them since my first battle, and I trusted them completely. I planted my right leg on the shield and even as I placed my left on the wooden boards I was lifted swiftly into the air. I felt as Hawk must have done on the Norse drekar. It seemed to me that I was flying. I had Saxon Slayer's head pointing down as I descended to the fighting platform. A Saxon looked up as the broad head of Saxon Slayer drove down into his shoulder. As he fell backwards his body broke my fall which was a softer landing than I might have expected. Withdrawing my spearhead, I rammed it into the side of a second Saxon who turned to face me. The others landed and I saw that we had cleared a patch of the wall ten paces long.

"Sven, Hawk, help the others to ascend the wall!"

The jarl and his elder son stood to protect us as I lowered Saxon Slayer over the wall. Lars grabbed it and as he climbed, I leaned backwards to counterbalance him. Once he and his brother joined us then we could begin to clear the walls. Dreng and Eidel followed quickly and when Galmr and Falmr joined us we had enough. Half of our men waited by the gate and Sweyn One Eye led us that way. I was to his right and Hawk followed. I had pulled my shield around once we had made the platform and its edge gave some protection to Sweyn One Eye's spear hand. Saxons faced us. I saw no byrnies, but the metal-studded leather and hide would afford some protection. They ran at us intending to sweep us from the walls. One Eye and I stabbed together with our spears. The Saxon spears came back at us but ours were longer and we thrust faster and with more power. The result was that the Saxons flicked up their shields and did not follow their spear thrusts with their eyes. We did. It had cost Sweyn his eye and now his helmet had a mask. My spear went into the thigh of the Saxon who was closest to the edge of the fighting platform. It was a narrow one and as Saxon Slayer grated off the man's thigh bone I twisted. The head of the spear was a large one and it tore a hole in his leg. Screaming he lost his balance and toppled to the town below. Sweyn One Eye had been even more accurate, and his spear had driven into the right shoulder of the Saxon he faced. As the blood spurted Sweyn swung his shield to smash into the side of the Saxon's head and the man fell before me and into the town like his comrade. Before the others could gather their wits we both stabbed so quickly that the warriors failed to bring their shields around quickly enough. A spearhead in the guts of a comrade makes a man think twice about standing and the Saxons who faced us turned and ran. We ran too and it was a foot race along the wooden fighting platform. They were running for their lives and not wearing mail. They won the race but instead of defending the gate, they kept running back into the heart of Bishop's Waltham and the church. We descended from the walls.

"Leif, Lars, open the gate!"

The four of us stood to face the town as the brothers descended the steps to unbar the gate and allow in the rest of the warband.

"Dreng Ebbisson, Eidel, open the north gate for Lodvir! The rest of you, form a wedge!" The two warriors ran to the other side of the gate and ascended the fighting platform. They would fight their way to the north gate and our reserves who waited there.

This would be an improvised formation. Leif and Lars would not be behind me but we had used it enough times for even the new warriors like Faramir and Snorri to know where to stand and against townsfolk it would suffice.

Folki Drengson's voice came from behind us, "We are ready, Jarl Sweyn!"

With such a mix of men behind us, Sweyn One Eye began a chant just to keep the beat and to put heart into the new warriors.

Our clan will beat you in the end.
Where is the bird? In the snake.
The serpent comes your gold to take.
We are the bird you cannot find
With feathers grey and black behind
Seek us if you can my friend
Our clan will beat you in the end.
Where is the bird? In the snake.
The serpent comes your gold to take.

It was hypnotic and I had a clear view of the Saxons before us as we moved slowly towards them. Knots of men stood with spears and shields but as our boots all stamped together and the last words were shouted out to strike like arrow heads, they turned and fled. They did not halt until they reached the church where two priests held aloft crosses and implored God to strike down the barbarians. The Saxons we had chased tried to join the shield wall but all they did was to disorder it. We did not stop but ran into them. Spears and mail are an irresistible combination. They had their faith to hold on to but that does not stop a broad-headed spear. The ones who stood were massacred and the rest simply fled. Many escaped by climbing the walls and dropping over the side to flee the town. They then ran as far away from Bishop's Waltham as they could get. Their fear saved many lives. When we piled the bodies before the church we found that less than thirty Saxons had been killed. Many more might have been wounded but they had escaped. We had lost just one man and his death had been avoidable. Running along the fighting platform he had slipped and broken his neck when he landed! *Wyrd*.

We had found a palace. The Bishop of Winchester was a rich man, and the town was both large and prosperous. We estimated that five hundred or more people had lived there. We found a huge amount of treasure and this time we found both wagons and horses. We began to ferry what we had found back to the ships. It was the next day when Karl Three Fingers and the rest of the army found us. They too had been successful, and men were already taking what we had found back to the ships. As hearth weru, we were there when Karl called a council of war.

"Our scouts report that the Saxons have raised the fyrd and the local levy are gathered to the north of us. We now have the chance to defeat them in battle and then we can raid this land unopposed!"

Jarl Sweyn Skull Taker was Karl's lieutenant and I saw that he did not like that idea, "Karl, we have not lost many men in battle, but half of our force is either taking goods back to the drekar or guarding them. We have less than five hundred men to face the Saxon army."

"Sweyn, this is not the king's army we will be fighting but the men of Hamtunscīr. We can beat them!"

Sweyn nodded, "In normal circumstances, I would agree but this is the Aetheling's Valley. They protect the king's children. That will inspire men, will it not?"

"Then we need to make them angry so that they fall upon our spears. We will burn the town before we leave and march north. Let us use their passion to destroy them!"

That was the moment I realised that Sweyn Skull Taker was a better general than Karl Three Fingers. The die was cast and the Norns had spun. When all had been taken and with full bellies, we left before dawn with a sky filled not with sunrise but the flames of the fire which devoured Bishop's Waltham!

The Saxons awaited us at a place we later learned was called Dean. There were more than fifteen hundred men of the Saxon fyrd and they outnumbered us by three to one! Nor did we have the number we expected. One warband, led by Guthrum the Greedy, neither arrived at Bishop's Waltham nor did they arrive at Dean. Karl Three Fingers was angry that forty-eight men were missing and that a hersir had led his men off on a separate raid. We had to face our foe with what we had. The Saxons formed a shield wall. The bulk of their warriors were without mail. Their thegns and housecarls were clearly identified by their mail, helmets and, in many cases, their two-handed war axes. They looked to me to be the stiffening of the line. They were like the pieces of metal I had hammered upon my shield; they minimised the damage I might take and for the Saxons were rocks of strength amongst the shifting sands of the bulk of their men.

"Sweyn Skull Taker, I would have the men of Ribe and Agerhøne on my right. Jarl Harald of Trelleborg will command the left. We let them blunt their anger on our spears and when their housecarls and thegns lie bleeding then we will advance, and we will take the field."

When the words dripped from Karl's tongue they sounded, as with all plans, like perfection. The reality is that the Norns, the battlefield, or men will change the outcome. It never works out the way it is planned but we could find no fault with it and so the mailed men of Ribe and Agerhøne formed the front line of the shield wall. The second line had a sprinkling of mail while the third rank was composed entirely of the unmailed warriors. Faramir, Snorri and the new ones were there. They had their bows and their slings. They would use those until spears were needed but I knew that if they had to fight with spears then we had lost the battle!

Hawk was happy for he was now in the front rank. He constantly badgered his brother and me to let him flank his father. He planted his father's standard between him and his brother. On my right, I had the brothers Lars and Leif. Five warriors down stood Lodvir and I knew that our section of the line was the strongest. We watched and listened as the Bishop of Winchester exhorted the Christians to slaughter us and avenge the dead of Bishop's Waltham. It was his treasure he wanted back and that was now safely on our drekar moored and guarded in the

Hamble. When his words had lit fires in their hearts, with spears banging on shields, they advanced.

Sweyn One Eye chose that moment to sing a song himself as the Saxons crossed the thousand paces to our front line. It was my song, the song of Oathsword.

> *When the clan of Agerhøne sailed the Somme*
> *When the warriors fierce were to Frankia come*
> *When Sea Serpent bared her bloody teeth*
> *Her crew were filled with blood-filled belief*
> *The Sword of the Saxons is strong and true*
> *With a dragon sheath bright and new*
> *The Sword of the Saxons is strong and true*
> *With a dragon sheath bright and new*
> *Skull Taker went to find monk's gold*
> *Hidden in a church, made of stone and old*
> *The Franks could not face his bloody blade*
> *All who came near were quickly slayed*
> *The Sword of the Saxons is strong and true*
> *With a dragon sheath bright and new*
> *The Sword of the Saxons is strong and true*
> *With a dragon sheath bright and new*
> *Sven Saxon Sword fought like a bear*
> *Three men were killed in the farmhouse there*
> *Then a jagged spear broke his skin*
> *Baring the bones and all within*
> *The Sword of the Saxons is strong and true*
> *With a dragon sheath bright and new*
> *The Sword of the Saxons is strong and true*
> *With a dragon sheath bright and new*
> *As the ship sailed home a trap was laid*
> *But Agerhøne clan were not afraid,*
> *They rowed and worked as a single man*
> *Determined to thwart the Frankish plan*
> *The Sword of the Saxons is strong and true*
> *With a dragon sheath bright and new*
> *The Sword of the Saxons is strong and true*
> *With a dragon sheath bright and new*
> *The Njörðr played a cruel joke*
> *The tide was turned, and their hearts were broke*
> *Then as Frankish ships loomed at their side*
> *A hero rose the battle to decide*

The Sword of the Saxons is strong and true
With a dragon sheath bright and new
The Sword of the Saxons is strong and true
With a dragon sheath bright and new
Sorely hurt with sword in hand
Sven Saxon Sword saved the band
He hacked and slashed at Frankish skin
Fuelled by the power which lay within
The Sword of the Saxons is strong and true
With a dragon sheath bright and new
The Sword of the Saxons is strong and true
With a dragon sheath bright and new
When Thorstein rammed the enemy boat
And Sea Serpent remained afloat,
Njörðr smiled and the clan had won
Saved by Sven, brave Bersi's son
The Sword of the Saxons is strong and true
With a dragon sheath bright and new
The Sword of the Saxons is strong and true
With a dragon sheath bright and new

By the time the Saxons were in the range of our bows and slings and had halted to send their own missiles at us we had finished the song and men banged their shields to drown out the Saxon shouts. We had raised our shields to bang upon them and they stopped the worst that the Saxon arrows and stones could do. It helped that our front ranks were mailed and the odd arrow or stone which penetrated the wall of shields did little harm. As most of the Saxons had no mail then ours did more damage and prompted a charge.

"Brace!"

Every mailed warrior had practised this. With the butt of our spears planted in the ground next to the right foot which was slightly behind our left, we locked shields and leaned into them. I had shields pushing in my back, but I did not know the warriors for they came from Ribe. I would have to trust them. Their spears were not planted in the ground but were held over our shoulders as were those from the third rank.

The Saxons ran but they did not chant and some fell. Others reached us before their comrades, but our section had the honour of a Saxon thegn and his six housecarls to face. They had recognised the superior mail and armour, not to mention the standard of Jarl Sweyn Skull Taker and they made for us. The housecarl who came at me held his axe in two hands. As he swung down at me, I raised my shield as did Lars and the jarl. I knew that I would have to take the blow and that it would hurt. The two spears behind me jabbed out as the axe struck my shield. Odin smiled on me for the head hit the boss of my shield. It dented it and it numbed my left arm but the axe head would be slightly blunted and my shield had done its job. My right hand jabbed forward and Saxon Slayer slid through mail links to score a wound in his side. His face, close to mine, showed the pain and I lifted the spear to ram it again before he could react. Even as he was raising his axe a second time Saxon Slayer tore through mail links and buried itself in flesh. This time it was his chest that was struck. Leaving the spearhead in his body I drew Norse Gutter and as the housecarl lifted his axe head I drove my dagger into his jaw and up through his skull. I saw the life leave his body and slipping Norse Gutter into my left hand grabbed hold of Saxon Slayer once more. The falling body freed my spear.

The one I had killed was the only dead Saxon that I could see and the sounds which filled my head were those of a weaponsmith and his workshop as mailed men exchanged blows. The second man who stepped into the gap vacated by the dead housecarl whose body lay between us was wary and, holding his shield defensively prodded and poked with his shorter spear. I blocked his blows easily and when my right hand suddenly darted out, I managed to drive it through his cheek. He turned and, with blood pouring from the wound, forced his way back through the other ranks.

Sweyn Skull Taker shouted, "Ribe and Agerhøne, forward!" He had seen the gap created by the dead Saxon, the one who had fled and the ones reluctant to face me. As one, every warrior either stabbed with his spear or swung his sword. The two spears behind me were able to strike the Saxons fighting Lars and the jarl. One slid to the ground as a spear entered his skull and the other reeled backwards. It meant we had an improvised wedge with me at the fore. I had the advantage that I was fighting men without mail and shorter spears. They fell back and soon our whole wing was marching forward.

I thought that we had won the battle until Karl Three Fingers roared. "Ribe, halt!"

Sweyn Skull Taker repeated the order and we stopped, watching the Saxons fall back in good order until they were one hundred paces away. I turned to my foster father, "We had them!"

He shook his head for he could see what I could not and he pointed to his left. Our line was now echeloned back, and our left wing had collapsed. There was a line of Danish bodies, some of them mailed and they lay ahead of our starting position. The plan had been a good one but the execution was flawed. "Karl was right and had we continued then we would have been surrounded and cut off."

We stood until the sun had passed its zenith. Karl called a council of war. "Stay here." He called out, "Lodvir, take command!"

I took out my ale skin and drank as Lodvir walked towards us, "That is why I hate fighting with other clans! I know the quality of our men but others..." He grinned at me and pointed back to the mailed man I had killed in the first attack, "A housecarl and he has good mail!"

Shaking my head I said, "Not good enough for Saxon Slayer pierced it twice! Still, I will take it back and his axe. It might be useful for hewing trees!"

Ramming Saxon Slayer in the ground and leaning my shield against it I went back to the body. Faramir raced forward to help me remove the mail byrnie and helmet. "Here, the helmet is yours." I handed it to the young warrior and I searched the body. I found a purse and a silver cross which I also took. I laid the axe on the byrnie and then took the housecarl's seax and sword. The sword was a good one, but I had two better. "Take these and give them to whoever needs them."

"But they are yours, Sven Saxon Sword; you took them."

"And before we reach Agerhøne I would hope to take more. I would rather the new warriors had a fighting chance of seeing our home again. Take them."

We left the field just before dark. We burned our bodies, we had lost eighty-six men, mainly Jarl Harald of Trelleborg and his men who had disobeyed orders and attacked prematurely. They had paid with their lives. Worse news was to come. Three miles from the battle we came upon the missing warband. Guthrum the Greedy and his men had been ambushed. Their naked and mutilated bodies showed the dangers of becoming isolated when raiding. It made up Karl's mind. As we reached our ships on the Hamble he said, "Tomorrow we return to Wiht. We will talk when we are there."

Chapter 5

Thorstein and Griotard had already packed our treasure below the decks. We had no thralls yet but we had gold, religious artefacts, weapons and food. If we had sailed home, then we would have deemed it a successful raid. We did not have to row down the rivers to the sea and as the wind was with us, we made the Meðune easily. Jarl Sweyn told Thorstein of the battle and we watched the land now illuminated by the fires of the burning dead. We were in a more sombre mood than we would have been before we had found the mutilated bodies. In a way, it was a good thing for the younger warriors for they saw the price of failure. I walked to the prow to speak with them and to ensure that none had wounds. Even a small cut could fester and kill. I was relieved that they had not even come close to suffering wounds.

"Thank you for the weapons, Saxon Sword. We are grateful."

I nodded at Snorri who, as one of the better swordsmen had been given the housecarl's sword. "You will learn that until you attain your full plumage and have a byrnie and good helmet you must be as a magpie or raven. Strip the dead when you can. Coins are useful back in Ribe but until we get there then a sword, shield, helmet and mail shirt are of more use."

"Will we go home now, Sven Saxon Sword, for we have taken treasure?"

"Not enough to satisfy the king and Karl Three Fingers will not like to leave with the bitter taste of a battle he did not win and butchered warriors. We will raid and now that you have been blooded then you have more chance of survival."

Gandálfr shook his head, "When I saw the axe come down, Sven Saxon Sword, I thought that you were a dead man!"

I nodded towards the shields along the side, "It took me a long time to make my shield. Lodvir and Griotard gave good advice. When we have the chance, I will beat out the dent in the boss but the time I spent was worth it, was it not?" They all nodded, "Instead of throwing dice the next time we are in camp see how you can improve your shield. Odd pieces of metal hammered onto the cover will add protection. The skins of dead animals will help soften the blow. Using seal oil or pine tar on the wood will also help. A mail byrnie is useful but, as the housecarl found, a shield would have been better!"

We returned to the Meðune and cooked the food we had taken. Karl decided to leave our next council of war until the morning and that was probably a wise decision as the dawn would bring the sun from the east and hope. I put my treasures in my chest before sharpening my weapons. The byrnie was valuable, not as mail but as metal. I did not think there was an immediate chance of needing my spear, sword and dagger but if they were dull then I could guarantee that I would need them. I also took the opportunity of putting dry sand in a sack to clean my byrnie. I shook it vigorously and then left it. We would not be leaving, if indeed we were leaving, before noon.

The captains and jarls were summoned to *'Firedrake'* first thing to be given their instructions by Karl Three Fingers. The majority of the crews were sent to shift cargo around. There were some ships with almost empty holds. All were distributed evenly. Of course, the treasures I had taken would remain in my chest. That was true of every warrior. I wondered what would happen to Guthrum the Greedy's ship, *'Ice Maiden'*. She would either need to be burned or to be crewed. She had remained on the Meðune but there were just her sailing master and ship's boys left from her crew. I had managed to not only finish cleaning my byrnie but also putting the housecarl's one in the sack by the time Jarl Sweyn returned. Clean metal was of more use than bloodied. My foster father and Lodvir joined us at the fire. We had relieved the Bishop of Winchester of a few barrels of wine and we broached one as we ate one of the pigs taken from his larder.

"We sail west!"

Lodvir smiled at me as Jarl Sweyn's statement sank in, "Back to the Fal and your sword, Sven. The Norns, it seems, have not finished with you."

I clutched my hammer of Thor, "And I never said that they had!" Lodvir laughed for we knew it did not do to disparage or to disregard the three sisters.

"Is there treasure there, father?" Hawk had thought we would go home and now he knew we would be away for much longer.

The jarl nodded, "The land we raid next has been attacked more times than the place they call Denshire. Even if we take little it matters not for we are already rich. We took no thralls here and I know that my foster son seeks those to work his fields. It would seem to me that this land far to the west is a better hunting ground and besides, the dead we left in the Aetheling's Valley seem to me a sign that this is not the place to raid."

Hawk said, "We could have won! When you ordered us forward then those at the rear of the men we fought began to flee."

"And had everyone done as they were ordered then you are right. Lodvir will tell you, my son, that such battles are rare. Some warriors will choose that moment for the chance of glory or some hersir will see a chance to make a name for his clan. We did not lose, and I will take that."

I waved a pig bone I was gnawing at the houses at the mouth of the Meðune, "And these people?"

"Will keep their homes and lives."

I finished off the sentence, "But lose their ships."

Sweyn Skull Taker nodded, "Aye, because we do not wish those on the mainland to know where we sail, and we cannot keep that too much of a secret. The longer the Saxons remain in doubt then the greater our chance of success. It is a sad fact of life, Sven. I can see that Mary has had an influence on you for you have a softer streak in you now."

There was veiled criticism in his voice, and I nodded, "The sea changes the land where it touches. I cannot go back to a time where my wife was not in my life nor would I wish to. She is bound up with me just as much as Oathsword. The Norns have spun, foster father, and I can do nothing about my circumstance."

"I know and those who are so chosen are to be pitied for they have little choice in the paths that they follow."

There was wailing and cries as we destroyed and burned the ships of the fishermen. There was wood enough to build new ones and the estuary lent itself to nets, but a man does not like to see his livelihood ruined and, as we sailed from the river, I knew that we had made enemies.

The wind and the currents meant we sailed to the west when we left the river. That could not be helped but Karl then took us due south until we were away from land. Once the Isle of Wiht disappeared we headed west once more. Sluggish winds from the wrong direction meant that we were forced to row. I knew that the sailing master of *'Ice Maiden'* would be glad of the chance to have his new crew, culled from other Heiða-býr ships, all learn to pull together. We had lost men but not ships and we kept the same formation. Two days from Wiht we endured a savage storm which found us spread across the western seas to the south of Syllingar. This was wild water and the walls into which we smashed were higher than the masts of our ships. We plunged into troughs and climbed cliffs. There was no order to the fleet and every ship looked to itself. When the storm eased and the sun rose we looked around and saw drekar scattered across the ocean. It took another two days to recover every ship and reform. We found that the snekke, *'Adder'* had disappeared. We found some wreckage and that was all. I was sad for I had liked her young captain, Benni. Two more ships were so badly damaged that they needed to be towed. The storm meant that the ships of Ribe and Agerhøne became the point of our seaborne wedge and we headed north to the coast of Denshire and the River Exe. Karl had decided that we would not try the Fal but virgin land we had yet to raid!

The coastline was a rugged one, but the Saxon strongholds appeared to be inland along the rivers. We beached close to the mouth of the Exe. There was a settlement on the far side of the river and so we landed on the sands to the west. Once Karl Three Fingers landed, he gave us the task of taking and destroying the settlement while he and ten ships headed up the Exe to raid the burh of Exeter. Our men were unhappy at the task as the twelve houses of what we later learned was called Lydwicnaesse, would yield little treasure. Our jarl showed his teeth and threatened to leave behind any who questioned our orders. In all the time we spent away from Agerhøne it was the only time he had to speak thus and it worked.

We crossed the river before dawn and took the houses without loss for the people had fled. They had left their animals and after burning their homes we returned to our new camp with animals we would keep to take back to our home. Mindful that this was not an island the jarl, now in command, had a ditch dug and stakes placed on the landward side. He was being cautious.

With Karl and his ships in the north, we raided the land to the west and the south. It was profitable and all were taken by surprise for they had no towers along the coast. The first they knew of our presence was when two or three ships' crews descended upon them, from the landward side in the early hours. This time we took thralls and they were secured, wailing and crying, in our new camp. We could almost have done this without drawn weapons for the sight of mailed Vikings inspired terror and few faced us with weapons. The ones that did were quickly eliminated.

Karl and his ships returned three days later and it was with empty chests and the air of defeat hanging heavily upon them. It was clear to all what had happened and as wounded were fetched ashore to be tended Karl Three Fingers met with Jarl Sweyn. We and Karl's hearth weru formed a protective barrier so that they could speak privately. We were a mailed human wall!

"Their burhs are too strong for us or else I am not the man to take them!" I had never heard Karl Three Fingers sound so low.

"Did we lose many men?"

"As many as we did at Dean. The men showed courage and obeyed orders but they had strong walls around Exeter and stake lined ditches. We did not have enough archers nor any war machines."

"And would the target have been worth it?"

"The target?"

"Exeter?"

"There were churches and the size of the place suggested it was rich, why?"

I knew that Sweyn was pointing without turning, "We have not lost a man and yet we have taken thirty slaves, sheep, cattle and treasure from three churches. All of that was within a day of here. If we moved a little further afield then who knows what we might find. You were right to come here, Karl Three Fingers, for it is a rich land but I wonder at the wisdom of attacking walls. Do we wish to rule their towns, or do we want to make coin and take treasure?"

I heard Karl laugh, "Wisdom drips from your tongue like honey from a hive! You are right. I will need a day for my men to recover. Tomorrow take your ships down to the River Teign for we took a prisoner who told us that it is a prosperous part of Wessex with the added advantage you can sail close to the best land. We will return up the Exe and raid the land around the burh but, for now, let the Saxons think that they have defeated us."

I know that the chance to sail with just the men of Ribe and Agerhøne suited the jarl for if anything went wrong then he knew who to blame, himself. We left nothing to chance and we emptied our holds so that we would be able to travel further up a river whose depth we did not know. We stepped the mast and relied on oars. It also meant that we would be hard to see. We left in the middle of the night and sailed the few miles down the coast to the narrow mouth of the Teign. It was a risk navigating at night, but Thorstein the Lucky was well named and once we were through then the river widened to, as we discovered later, almost six hundred paces wide. We sailed up the middle in the darkness. Dawn was not far off when, after rowing for more than three miles the lookouts reported that the river narrowed dramatically. I believe we could have still navigated a little further but, as we clambered ashore and smelled the woodsmoke, we knew that we were close to settlements. We had come far enough.

The jarl sent out four pairs of men to try to find places for us to raid while he organised the rest into three bands. We left twenty men to guard the ships and by the time the first of the scouts had returned the sun was up and we were ready to move.

Siggi Long Sight was the first back. he and his brother, Harald, were our best scouts, "There is a good-sized town just a mile away. It is not a burh and we smelled churches."

It was a simple report and it told us all that we needed to know. Leaving Ragnar Red Hair with the third group to take on any settlements the other scouts found, the jarl and Lodvir led the two largest warbands towards the town we later learned was called Teignton. Even as we neared it, we could see that it was bigger and richer than Bishop's Waltham. There were no walls, but we passed through a deer park which showed that nobles and royalty hunted here. Waving his spear to signal Lodvir to head east, we followed the river and headed west. We knew it was only a matter of time before we were seen but we were within two hundred paces before the inevitable shout rent the air, "Vikings!"

With the rest of our men, all fifty of them, behind us we descended like a plague on the town which was just waking up. There had been a town watch and it was they who gave the alarm. The four Saxons who ran at us were brave but deluded. They could not even begin to slow us up let alone stop us and their bodies marked the first Saxon deaths. There were, in truth, not that many. That was down to the planning of the jarl. We had struck them at dawn and with no walls for protection then they were doomed. By noon we had secured the whole town and had the time to select the best thralls and to use the town's own shackles to secure them. The river was too narrow for a drekar and so we used the townsfolk, even those we had not enslaved to carry all their goods back to our ships. As a royal town, it was rich, and our holds were filled with valuables richer than any I had seen thus far on the raids. We burned the town before we headed back, the next day, to our ships. By then Ragnar Red Hair had found other settlements which yielded slaves and riches. Exeter, it seemed, was the only place that was strong enough to defy us. We raided for a week before heading back to our camp on the Exe. We left behind burned towns that had people mourning their lost homes but no animals. It would be a hard winter in this part of the land. We left for the Exe even though there appeared to be little threat to us. As Sweyn Skull Taker said, it would not take long for the Saxons to raise an army to oppose us and we did not wish a repeat of the Battle of Dean.

Karl Three Fingers had not been idle, and he had built a second fortified camp on the other side of the river where we had destroyed the first settlement. It had enabled him to raid the eastern side of the Exe. We used the first camp we had made but then took a captured Saxon fishing boat to visit with Karl.

"Our holds are full, Karl, and we could return home."

Shaking his head Karl said, "The harvest is just being collected; we will wait until then to go back."

"But we have no room for it!"

Karl gave a sad smile, "I was given quite specific orders by King Sweyn. He wishes to punish the Saxons for their failure to send tribute last year."

As we had been busy in our own war the king had not demanded it, but I could see a method in King Sweyn's plan. If we hurt them badly enough then they would send money just to keep their crops safe.

"You and your men have done enough. Guard our camp and hunt. We will raid."

And so we had the strangest month I had yet spent as a raider. We wore no mail, and we hunted their deer and wild pigs. We caught fish and we ate well. The only raiding we did was just to take ale and the fermented apple juice. None of that even needed a sword. Oathsword had slept in its scabbard for almost the whole time we had spent in this part of the world. The enforced idleness just made me pine even more for Mary. We were not needed here, and I could be at home awaiting the birth of my child. I began to think of the words I would say to my wife and child when I returned home.

Some of the men had lain with the slaves we would take back and when he discovered this Jarl Sweyn Skull Taker became as angry as I had ever seen him. "These slaves belong to all of us who raided. If you have planted your seed in them then they are not as useful as if they were whole. All the men who have lain with slaves shall be given less treasure. The value of the slaves will be taken from your share." There were just twelve of the men who had done this but as we only had thirty female slaves then more than a third were at risk.

A messenger came from Karl and it proved that Sweyn Skull Taker had been proved right. An army had been gathered to drive us from their land and we were ordered to march north towards Exeter where Karl Three Fingers awaited us. The messenger gave us more information. All the captives were placed in one camp and the drekar all gathered together and guarded. With ships and slaves secure we led two hundred men north.

"Aethelred's High Reeve is a man called Kola. He has summoned a huge army and Karl thinks that he has taken so long as he wishes to ensure that they will win. He has raised not just the men of Denshire but those from the land further north, where we raided a couple of years ago."

I remembered that fight and knew that this might be a harder battle for they had fought well the last time we had been here. Karl's camp was not at Exeter but a couple of miles east. There was little danger of the men of Exeter sallying forth to join Kola as Karl's raids had whittled down their numbers when they had tried to stop our privations. The Saxon army was still gathering across the flat ground which Karl had chosen. There was a stream close to the Saxon camp and they had that at their back. When I went with Jarl Sweyn and Karl to view the Saxon position I thought that was a mistake. The stream was shallow and not particularly wide but if the Saxons had to fall back then it would hinder them.

"I think that there will be more than two thousand of them when they all reach us, Sweyn."

"And we have less than five hundred now." We had been forced to leave more than a hundred and eighty men guarding the camp and the drekar. Karl had to leave another fifty men to guard what he had taken. It struck me that my foster father had been right. We should have left when he suggested.

Karl nodded, "This time we use two blocks of men. Dean was a lesson to me, Sweyn. You have the right flank. It is a wide-open plain and they will try to turn us by outflanking us with their superior numbers. I intend to use that. We allow the enemy to push back. When they think that we are in their jaws then we strike, you and I, with our best men into their heart. We head for Kola, the High Reeve, and the priests."

"That is a risky plan."

"Aye, and had we tried it with the men we led at Dean it might have failed but the rotten wood has been shaved from the army and the ones who remain now know that you and I are good leaders who bring rewards. They will obey!"

In that, he was right although the men of Ribe and Agerhøne had always been dependable. It was ironic that the smaller army we now led was a better one than that which had fought at Dean.

We kept a good watch that night but as we heard men still arriving during the evening, we knew that there would be no night attack and the next morning we donned our war faces. Our clan did not go in for face painting and the like but some of the men led by Karl did and we saw warriors blackening or reddening their faces so that they would terrify the Saxons. We would just rely on our weapons and our resolve. It was strange but so long as we followed the jarl we were confident that we would win. As the Saxons arrayed and went through their normal ritual so Karl and Sweyn explained to each hersir and drekar captain what was involved. Lodvir would be with us and the men of Agerhøne would lead the right prong of the attack when Karl sprang his trap. Much depended upon the lightly armoured men on our flanks.

Lodvir used his shield and spear for effect as he told the leaders what their men would have to do. "Lock your shields and just poke with your spears. Our spears are longer and have metal heads. Some of the Saxons use narrow-headed spears or even spear hardened ones. Let them push you back, let them think that you are beaten. We stretch their numbers so thinly that it will be like an over-inflated pig's bladder and when it bursts then we shall reap the reward." Lodvir, despite his position in Ribe, was still Sweyn Skull Taker's lieutenant and his wisdom gave confidence to the warband.

Our formation must have encouraged the Saxons. We had a three-deep line and the third line was composed of slingers and archers. When our flanks turned, they would be in the centre. The Saxons formed a huge, long line three men deep. As at Dean, their front ranks were sprinkled with metal but there were fewer of them. Once again it was noon by the time they had prayed to God to help them and then they advanced. We just banged our shields as they advanced. We needed no chant for we were not moving. The Saxon battle plan was clear and they did as we expected. They used the flat fields to flank us.

Karl shouted, "Now!"

It was not the command to advance but for the second rank to echelon and angle themselves. It was like when we made a ship. The wetted wood was formed around a round object, gently so as not to break and to retain its strength. As the Saxons ran to surround us so our lines matched theirs. The slingers and archers, a third of our army, did what the Saxons could not do, they rained death upon them. The Saxons were so numerous that the deaths did not appear to shake their faith in their God, Kola, and victory.

It was their mailed men who first clashed with us. There were fewer axes this time and for that I was grateful. I had beaten out the dent, but I knew that I would need a new boss. The captured byrnie would give me the metal I needed when I returned home. We had no shields behind us and we could not afford to be pushed back. We had to hold firm and as the Saxon line collided with ours Jarl Sweyn Skull Taker shouted, "Thrust!"

With shield foot planted we all stepped forward with our spear foot and rammed our spears at the Saxons. The Saxons did not train as long as we did and they were ragged in comparison. More of our spears were bloody compared with the Saxons and our step forward meant that we had not conceded even a handspan of ground. My spear had found flesh, the housecarl's leg and when I used my helmet to butt him and then punch with the boss of my shield, the weakened warrior collapsed. "Go to your God!" Saxon Slayer drove down to pin him to the ground.

It was a mistake for even as I tried to withdraw my spear a second Saxon thrust at me with his spear. I pulled my shield around as I drew Oathsword. The spear struck my shield, but I barely felt the blow for my shield had padding. I brought Oathsword up under the spear and the Saxon was so busy looking for the wound he had inflicted that he failed to see the sword. I felt it slide and scrape along his ribs. I turned the blade slightly and the warrior screamed. Others had shouted and cried out, but the scream seemed to penetrate the battle noise.

As I ripped out the blade I shouted, "Oathsword! The Saxon sword has struck!"

It was not just my shield brothers who were heartened by the cry but all those who faced the Saxon mail. There was a collective cry of, "Oathsword!" It seemed to act as a spur. Perhaps it was the sword or the thought of the dragon sword which gave extra power to our weapons but as I brought it down to smash into the shoulder of another Saxon, it seemed that the enemy line took a step back and there was suddenly a pile of bodies before us. Jarl Sweyn Skull Taker stepped forward and that took our line across the bodies. I could now see that the Saxon line was much thinner and more importantly, I could see Kola and the priests. Kola was surrounded by his bodyguard and mounted on a pony so that he could better view the battle.

It was then that Karl shouted, "Forward!" and his hearth weru sounded the horn. It was the signal for every warrior to thrust forward. The slingers and bowmen sent one more missile and then dropping their bows and slings picked up shields and sharpened unused spears.

We did not run for that risked a fall; there were bodies littering the ground. Instead, we stepped forward as one. Others still had their spears but One Eye, Lars and Lodvir close by me also had swords. In a shield wall, there is no better weapon than a spear but when you are alone and not locked with shield brothers then it is a liability. The Saxon spears had no edge, and their wood was not protected with metal. As the Saxon thrust his spear at me I deflected it with my shield and then, angling my sword sliced across it to sever the weapon in two. I continued the stroke and even though the Saxon managed to raise his shield I knocked him backwards. He kept his feet and tried to draw his shorter sword, but I was on him and Oathsword smashed through his helmet and skull as though they were made of parchment. Some men broke and I saw that we were just thirty paces from Kola and the priests. A moment or two earlier they had seen their army surround ours and now, within a few strokes, they were under threat.

"With me!"

Jarl Sweyn Skull Taker was no berserker but he recognised the moment to strike and we ran. The pony Kola had chosen was not battle-hardened and as he tried to turn it and it fell when it refused to obey him. The priests ran and Kola's bodyguard formed a thin line around him. We did not pause. Hawk was the fastest and he ducked beneath the swinging axe of a housecarl to punch up with his shield and then to ram his spear into the neck and skull of the bodyguard. Sweyn One Eye deflected the spear and gutted his opponent. Out of the corner of my eye, I saw our jarl swing his sword to take Kola's unprotected leg as a housecarl's axe came at my head. I simply stepped forward and punched with my shield. It was not the axe head that struck me, but the wooden haft and I was so close that I was able to drive Oathsword into the neck and head of the bodyguard. Kola lay bleeding to death and the priests ran.

The Saxon command was gone and the whole army fled. They still outnumbered us, but we were between them and their camp. They ran and we followed. I saw that the younger warriors from Agerhøne were still alive and they pursued a broken enemy. As I had predicted the stream proved their undoing. Whilst some Saxons simply leapt it, others, like the priests, either hesitated or began to wade. The Saxons were stopped by a wall of their own men and they were butchered as they tried to escape the wall of metal which relentlessly pursued them. We did not stop until we reached the rich manors of Pinhoe and Broad Clyst. So confident had Aethelred's reeve been that he had not emptied them of their treasure. We emptied the two manors of all that they contained and then burned them. A week later we left the southwest. Our departure was marred for in the battle we had lost the first of the new warriors. Galmr Galmrson had been a solid enough warrior and it was not his fault that he had died. The Norns had been spinning. A dying Saxon had hacked through the back of Galmr's leg and before the bleeding could be staunched by warriors fighting for their lives, he had bled to death. Had we left before the battle he would be alive. We had treasure but treasure cannot buy young warriors. I was glad to see the back of the land and to head home to my wife and, hopefully, a child.

If I thought that it would be a swift journey home, then I was proved wrong. Karl stopped, once again, at Wiht. We refilled our water barrels and took more of the harvest they had collected but the real reason for our visit was for Karl to travel to Wintan-ceastre where he delivered a message to King Aethelred or those who represented him. It was a stark message. If the king wished to avoid a repetition of our raid he would send tribute before the raiding season. We waited on the island for a week but received no reply. Karl was not put out by the lack of response. He had not expected one and the fact that the Saxons had not said they would not pay was hopeful. For us it mattered not as, with decks filled with both animals and thralls we headed along the coast. We were going home and, with any luck, we would not have to raid for King Sweyn the next year.

Chapter 6

Agerhøne 1002

It took longer to get home than we hoped. The winds did not cooperate and we were heavily laden. We would need to clean the weed from the hull and replace sheets. The months away had taken their toll on the drekar. The men from Agerhøne who had sailed with Lodvir and the rest of the drekar came with us for our share of the treasure and thralls would take place at our home. For me this was a mixed blessing; whilst I would get home sooner there would still be a delay while everything was shared out equitably. There had been drawn weapons on Wiht when one captain felt he had been cheated. He had not. I hoped that we would not be needed here but until the other ships sailed away the three of us would be armed and protecting Sweyn Skull Taker.

My share of the slaves and animals were a shepherd, three boys and a girl, a ram and four ewes and a calf. The boys would be trained by Egbert to work in the fields and the girl would serve Mary. I could have asked for more, but I did not need more. I had more coins, silver and gold now than I knew what to do with. I could not spend them, but I hoped that when she recovered from the birth that Mary would be able to travel to the market at Ribe. It took until late afternoon for the wealth to be distributed. Egbert had come to take away the slaves and animals. I did not ask about the birth for that seemed unlucky. I would find out all when I entered my hall. The smiles I saw on the faces of Agnetha and the other women who greeted their husbands told me that Mary and the child were well and that sufficed. Had they frowned or wept then I would have feared the worst.

When all had left and we had bidden farewell to Lodvir, who was the last to leave, Jarl Sweyn Skull Taker spoke to the three of us. "Know that I am more than happy with how you behaved on this raid. Other hearth weru were too concerned with their own glory but you did all that was asked and more. Do not think I did not notice how you helped the new warriors and that we only lost one is down to the three of you. When time allows, I shall reward you and I absolve you of any duties until we are summoned to war again." He waved a hand around the village, "Although we are growing as a settlement I am safe here. Enjoy your farms and your families!" He pointed a finger at Hawk, "And you, Alf, find a wife!"

He flushed and we laughed. I headed back to my hall. The jarl was right, there were new buildings and new families. Soon we would have a market and then, perhaps, rival Ribe.

I took a deep breath as I entered my hall. I prepared to see my wife and child and I confess I was more nervous than I would have been before a battle. I was empty handed; slaves had already fetched my shield, chest, helmet, and weapons. I wore just a simple tunic with Oathsword at my side. I stepped across the threshold and as my eyes became accustomed to the firelit hall I saw my wife in the chair my mother had used. With curved wood at the bottom, my mother had rocked gently while she had spun. Now Mary rocked and at her breast was my child. I walked over and, kneeling next to her, kissed her hand, "You are well?" It seemed an inadequate thing to say but I knew not what else I should say. Mary looked almost saintly and I swear that there was a glow about her but that could have been the fire.

"Aye, husband and I see that you are whole. Come and greet your daughter, Gunhild. She was born three weeks ago, and she is healthy with a voice that demands food. You are in for sleepless nights!"

I looked at the babe whose head had turned from the nipple to look at me. She had blonde hair and blue eyes. She was beautiful. I had not enjoyed the company of babies and I knew not what to expect.

Mary said, "She hears more than she sees but she is whole. It will take time for her to get used to you." She smiled, "I knew none of this, but the women of your clan are kindness itself and they have told me what to expect. They did not lie to me about the birth and whilst it was painful, I am happy to try to make you a son next time."

I laughed, "Let us enjoy our babe first. You chose a good name and mother would be happy."

"I was named Mary after the Virgin and my mother. Gunhild has been christened but a Danish name seemed appropriate. I am happy living here in Agerhøne."

I stood and kissed the top of her head, "And now I will go and bathe and take the stink of damp, sweat, saltwater and blood from me. I thank you for not mentioning my pungent smell."

She laughed, "Do not worry, husband, some of the smells our daughter makes will turn your stomach too. I am less fussy than I once was."

That day began the most idyllic of times. My days were filled with work on my land and the training of the slaves as well as spending time with my wife and daughter. The nights were joyful too as I was able to watch Gunhild as she slept. I also spent time, as the days grew shorter and colder to melt down parts of the Saxon byrnie. It had not been the best of mail but by melting it down in the weaponsmith's workshop I managed to make a new boss for my shield and some metal pieces to add strength to it. I still had enough of the byrnie to use as replacement rings for my byrnie. The younger warriors now trained by themselves although I knew that after the winter solstice there would be another eight new warriors to train. My life developed a pattern that was so predictable as to be comfortable. I did not have to worry about what to do; there were tasks ready for me each day. The ewes were all serviced by the ram and that was a relief. We would soon have a flock. I did not think that we would be raiding the next year. Unless King Sweyn wished every Dane in his land to cross the water then it would be someone else's turn. Galmr's death had made the young warriors realise that they had been lucky. They still trained for war, but they did not need war; there was a difference.

    As the winter solstice drew close the jarl held a feast in his mead hall. Mary had instructed the new girl and the other thralls to make me a tunic that represented my status. She had not understood the term hearth weru when she had first been brought to the village but now, she saw it as a sort of minor nobility. I had to dress appropriately. She also had the girls plait my beard, moustache, and hair. I found it tiresome but it pleased Mary and so I endured it. The new seal skin boots I had ordered made from the seals hunted at the mouth of the Dunum meant that I looked smarter than I could ever remember. Perhaps this was another side effect of marriage for when we arrived at the mead hall Sweyn One Eye was as well presented as I was. Hawk looked as though he had dressed in the closest clothes he could find at the top of his chest!

    I was looking forward to the feast as Sweyn would reveal his new song, the Song of Svolder and I would be able to see those who, like Siggi, my first oar brother, lived a little way out of Agerhøne. Although we three were seated close to Sweyn Skull Taker I knew that men would rise to come to speak to us. Our mead feasts were not as formal as some I had heard of. As usual, the feast began sombrely with a recounting of those who had died since last we had feasted. It was a shorter list than the ones which would be taking place in other mead halls. That done we sat, and Sweyn Skull Taker spoke. He mentioned those who had performed particularly well on the raid. Those who had not distinguished themselves were not highlighted for that was not our way. He then singled out the three of us and I felt embarrassment as every warrior banged the pommel of his dagger or seax on the table. Agnetha would not be happy and her thralls would have to spend the next days repairing the dents, scratches, and dints.

"I could not ask for three better hearth weru and the fact that they are all of my blood is particularly pleasing." He gave a smile at Griotard, "I remember when they were appointed by me there were some older warriors who questioned my choice!" Everyone knew to whom he referred and Griotard, to his credit, gave a mock bow and a shrugged apology. He had since recanted his opposition. "They showed in Wiht, Hamtunscīr, and Denshire, that they are the best of the clan." There were more cheers. "To that end, I have had made for them, by the goldsmith in Ribe, three herkumbl for them to wear on their helmets. I have chosen the design as the bird that is the sign of our clan with the dragon sword, my foster son's blade, Oathsword. Since the blade came to the clan we have gone from strength to strength and I wished these devices to commemorate the event."

He passed one to each of us. They were beautiful. The sword was picked out in gold as was the surround and the sword lay on a sea of silver. It was very effective. The goldsmith had already drilled holes so that when we attached them, they would not be damaged. I was touched beyond words for the gift must have cost him much of his share from the raid.

"And now on with the feast!"

I spent as much time admiring the herkumbl as drinking for the first part of the speech until my cousin stood to sing his new song.

The king did call and his men they came
Each one a warrior and a Dane
The mighty fleet left our home in the west
To sail to Svolder with the best of the best
Swedes and Norse were gathered as one
To fight King Olaf Tryggvasson
Mighty ships and brave warriors blades
The memory of Svolder never fades
The Norse abandoned their faithless king
Aboard Long Serpent their swords did bring
The Norse made a bridge of all their ships
Determined that King Sweyn they would eclipse
Brave Jarl Harald and all his crew
Felt the full force of a ship that was new
Mighty ships and brave warriors' blades
The memory of Svolder never fades
None could get close to the Norwegian King
To his perilous crown he did cling
Until Skull Taker and his hearth weru

Attacked the side of the ship that was new
Swooping Hawk leapt through the sky
To land like a warrior born to fly
Mighty ships and brave warriors blades
The memory of Svolder never fades
With such great deeds the clan would sing
They cleared the drekar next to the king
Facing Olaf were the jarl and Sven
Agerhøne and Oathsword joined again
Mighty ships and brave warriors blades
The memory of Svolder never fades
The bodyguards of the King of Norway
Fought like wolves in a savage way
It mattered not for the dragon sword won
Stabbing and slaying everyone
The king chose the sea as his way of death
And Long Serpent was his funeral wreath
Mighty ships and brave warriors' blades
The memory of Svolder never fades
Mighty ships and brave warriors' blades
The memory of Svolder never fades

While it was not exactly the way it had happened it was close enough to meet with the approval of the clan. The newer warriors saw that if they were as courageous then, in some future battle, they might be named. It was the perfect start to the best feast I could remember. Sweyn One Eye and I carried Hawk to bed. I knew what he had to look forward to for I had been there too.

I fitted the herkumbl myself. I wanted it to be perfect. Mary could not understand the fuss. "It is a small piece of metal. How will that help you in battle?"

"It is what it represents, my love. Men will know how highly we are thought of and that can give a warrior an edge in battle."

She did not understand but then my mother had never understood, and she had been Danish!

By the time the days lengthened a little, a fortnight after the winter solstice, Mary consulted the women of the clan and gave me the news that she was with a child once more. The babe would be born at the start of Tvímánuður and as we had no plans to raid then I would be there. The Saxon girl we had brought from Denshire, Anna, had proved to be a natural when it came to looking after Gunhild and Mary happily entrusted our daughter to her care. It meant that my wife could now attend to more of the duties of running the farm and lands. That was a relief to me as I had little interest in them. She and Egbert got on and enjoyed discussing the mating habits of animals and which fields to leave fallow. It was as though they were speaking a different language!

Jarl Sweyn Skull Taker was often in either Ribe or, occasionally, visiting with the king at Heiða-býr. It was through such meetings that we learned what was happening in the outside world. It was winter and few ships traded. They were our usual means of discovering news but in winter it was through the king and we learned that the Saxons had paid twenty-four thousand pounds of gold to buy off King Forkbeard. That we only received a small amount for our trouble made men like Lodvir and Griotard angry, but the jarl was philosophical about it. "We made coin and we benefitted. That it cost us but a few warriors is something to thank the Allfather. With the gold safely in the king's hall at Heiða-býr, we will not be going to war!"

People across the water, in the land they now called England, assume that we are a warlike people. We like war but we do not need war and the news that we would not have to wear our byrnies nor sail across the seas to raid brought smiles to our faces. The young still trained for war and Sweyn, Hawk and I joined them, but it was a time for honing skills. We would need them but not for some time.

I visited Ribe too, with Mary and we took Hawk with us for company. Leaving before dawn we had two thralls and a wagon for Mary was anxious to spend some of my horde of coins. The thrall, Anna, was excited to be visiting somewhere so big. The village in Denshire we had raided had been just four houses and when all the men were slain we had taken the rest of the village. She sat on Hawk's second pony as we rode to Ribe. We were well wrapped for the weather, but it was not as cold as it had been. It was a sure sign that spring was not far away. It did not do to speak of such things, it was considered bad luck. Hawk made Anna and Mary laugh as we rode along. He thought he had a good life. With no responsibilities, he hunted most days or just sat drinking with the other young warriors. I did not envy him and even before Mary had come into my life, I had not enjoyed such a life. It suited Hawk.

As soon as we reached the town we went to the jarl's hall. Lodvir lived there and it would have been rude not to speak to him. He accompanied us to the market, and it guaranteed that none would try to cheat us. That was an unlikely event. From my belt hung my dragon sword and it ensured our safety and that we would be treated well even by those merchants and traders who were new. Ribe market was a large one and there were many who travelled to it; our success had encouraged others to come here to live. There were some visitors from Norway. Since Svolder that kingdom was jointly ruled by Denmark and Sweden. There was more trade between all three lands. There were warriors who still resented us but not merchants and ordinary folk. There were merchants who visited the market to see if they could sell their own goods in what was seen as a peaceful land. The harbour was full of their ships for there were empty berths. Our drekar were hauled on the beaches having been cleaned and repaired and kept from their biggest enemy, the sea!

While Mary examined every item presented as though it contained a viper, I spoke with Lodvir and Hawk. Hawk had made an effort for the visit and looked every bit the dashing young warrior he was in battle. I saw some of the unmarried women of the town cast him admiring glances. He preened!

Lodvir and I stood apart and spoke, "Ribe has become, since Svolder, a much busier place. I know that Agerhøne has grown Sven, but so has Ribe. It is not just the Norse merchants who take advantage but the Swedes too, now that they have parts of Norway, come here. Some merchants are building homes and warehouses here." He nodded to Hawk, "Your father will be even richer soon for there is a tax on new buildings and on ships using the port. It is not a large amount, but it builds up."

I nodded, Hawk was beaming at a particularly pretty young woman who was at the same merchant as Mary and looking at the same items. Three Swedes were with her. "It is the same at Agerhøne, Lodvir. Since we returned from Wessex, I am amazed at the numbers who live close to the town now. I can see a problem in the future."

Hawk had drifted off and Lodvir ask, "A problem? How so?"

"Mary has told me that we are privileged and I know what she means. We have land and a fine hall. What of the sons of Lars, Leif and Dreng? When they are ready to be men where will they farm? Where will they build their halls? If these merchants come to build bigger halls and warehouses where will be the land for ordinary warriors? If they leave Agerhøne and Ribe then who will crew our drekar?"

Before Lodvir could answer Hawk approached us with the three Swedes and the pretty young woman, "Hersir, this is someone who seeks a meeting with you. I said I could introduce you."

Lodvir and I smiled for he had not done this for the merchants but the young woman.

The well-dressed Swede spoke, "I am Aksel Østersøen and I am a successful merchant with land and ships. Since our kings have rid the seas of Olaf Tryggvasson, I have begun to look for places I could use

83

closer to the west for that is where lies the best trade. England is a rich place and there are more of your people living there than before. I see a way to make more money. Hersir, I would build a hall in your town."

Lodvir nodded, "I am hersir, but this is the town of Alf the Swooping Hawk's father, Jarl Sweyn Skull Taker."

Hawk had been using his eyes to dance with the maiden and had not been listening. Aksel said, "This is the warrior who broke the Norse line? I have heard of you, young man and I am honoured."

"What? Oh, the leap? It was nothing and we warriors do what we must do to win. It is in our blood." This was not like Hawk who was not known for his false modesty. He was trying to impress the young woman and from her fluttering eyes, he was succeeding.

Aksel turned back to Lodvir, "Would it be possible to meet with you and discuss the matter?"

Lodvir had learned to be the counsellor when my foster father had made him hersir and he knew his responsibilities, "Aye, you can come back now. Sven, will you be offended if I leave you?"

I laughed, "I have some hours yet for my wife has yet to make her choices. We will see you again Lodvir for my wife will wish to return home this night." I looked at Hawk, "And will you be returning with us, cousin?"

He looked at the young woman and then Lodvir, "I think I will spend the night in Ribe. I have yet to decide upon what I will spend my coin. You do not mind, do you?"

Shaking my head I said, "No. It is good." Lodvir rolled his eyes for, like me, he knew the real reason.

When Mary had made her purchases and the thralls were taken to the wagon she asked, "Where is Hawk?"

"He went to Lodvir's hall with a merchant."

Mary brightened, "And that pretty young thing?" I nodded. "It is good, husband. Agerhøne is too small for Hawk and he needs a larger sea for his net. Come we have yet to finish. I have heard of a wood carver not far from here. We need a better table!"

It was not dark when we reached our hall, but it was very close to it. Gunhild was asleep and poor Anna could barely keep open her eyes. I was glad that we did not have such a journey to do every week. Mary was happy for she had spent wisely. The table would be delivered when the last details were finished and that would take another month. It would give my wife the chance to have more building work done on the hall. She wished it changed to suit her and our growing family. Being the daughter of a priest she had lived in a home that was theirs and they did not have to share. She wished my hall to be like that. She envisaged a great hall, as she termed it but then there would be smaller rooms. When I pointed out that building walls would make them colder for it would hide them from the fire, she pointed out that we could have other fires and there was enough stone to make the fire safe. She also told me that she wanted wind holes putting in the walls. She believed that the movement of air was healthier. She pointed out that we now had wall hangings and they could be used to keep out the cold in winter. She was my wife, and I went along with her. In the end, we found we just needed one more place for a fire and the hall was still warm.

Hawk did not return for a week and when he did, he came with Lodvir. They passed my land and Lodvir gestured for me to accompany them. Although Hawk's absence had been noted it had not caused concern for he was in Ribe and there the son of the jarl would be safe.

Agnetha examined him as he entered, "And where have you been gadding, my son?"

He bowed and said, "In Ribe with Lodvir the Long."

Sweyn Skull Taker was still one of the cleverest men I knew, and he had an ability to detect things which were yet unsaid, "And yet you return with Lodvir and have asked Sven Saxon Sword to join us. I think there is more here than a young man enjoying himself carousing. Sit. Lodvir, I would have you tell me what has happened."

I could understand my foster father's concern. The last thing he needed was a wild son causing problems in his town. Ale was fetched and I saw the frown on Agnetha's face. Alf was her youngest and, I think, her favourite.

"As Sven will tell you, Hawk asked to stay in Ribe when we met a Swedish merchant and his daughter; his youngest daughter." I saw Hawk suddenly stare at Lodvir as though willing him to be silent. Lodvir smiled, "I will speak honestly, Hawk, as is my way and tell the jarl what I believe happened and why." Even I was becoming concerned. "Aksel Østersøen is a very rich man, jarl. He has ships taking amber and timber from the east and he trades for jet from the west. He has ships that sail to Normandy and trades with the Franks. He intends to build a hall in Ribe."

"All that is good, Lodvir, but I cannot see how it concerns my family."

"Nor did I, Jarl Sweyn, although as Sven will attest, Hawk and the young woman, Frida, were attracted to each other. I was not concerned with that but it became clear, as I spoke with the merchant that he sought an alliance with Denmark. He encouraged Hawk and his daughter to spend time with one another." Agnetha stiffened and Lodvir held up a hand, "All was done well, my lady. Aksel brought his daughter to Ribe in order to secure a husband but not just any husband, he wished one who had influence. The Norns must have been spinning for they put Hawk in their path."

My cousin burst out, "It is not like that! Frida and I love each other and wish to be married! Her father saw that we were made for each other. You make it sound as though it was planned, Lodvir!"

"Peace, Hawk, Lodvir always speaks the truth. Sven, you were there when they met and you, too, are honest. What say you?"

"They looked at each other and I saw that they were attracted to each other. She is a pretty little thing, foster father, and Hawk looked handsome. As for her father's intentions, all that I can say is that he was keen to speak to both Hawk and Lodvir."

Agnetha said, "Alf, come here and give me your hands." Agnetha, like many of the women in the clan, was something of a volva and she stared into her son's eyes and held them. He did not waver and she nodded, "He believes that this is the woman for him and as this is the first time he has shown any interest in marriage, Sweyn, then I think we encourage it."

Hawk beamed but his father's words wiped the smile from his face, "Lodvir, where is the merchant, now?"

"In Ribe. He has taken over an inn and he is having a hall and warehouses built. The man is rich, jarl, and there are many men working on his home. If I am to be truthful, I am sorry Hawk, I think he came to Ribe not just seeking any husband for his daughter but looking for the unmarried son of Jarl Sweyn Skull Taker. He had heard the story of the battle of Svolder."

Agnetha did not seem put out, "And perhaps the Norns have spun and trapped my son in their web but that is *wyrd*, is it not?" She nodded to her husband.

"Lodvir, return to Ribe and invite Aksel Østersøen and his party to visit with us here. My wife and I will speak with him and I will make a decision."

"That is not fair! I have made the choice!" Hawk reverted to the reckless warrior he had once been.

His father was patient and Sweyn said, "Alf the Swooping Hawk, when Sven Saxon Sword wished to marry, even though we knew his intended, he came to me to ask my permission." That was all he said, and I saw Hawk's shoulders slump in resignation. It would happen the way the jarl intended.

This would be a different sort of feast than the ones we normally enjoyed. It was rare for men and women to share the table in the mead hall. Normally it was reserved for warriors. This would be different for as Agnetha and Frida would be there so the other wives would be invited. It marked the beginning of a change for us. Mary thought it wonderful for she disliked the men only mead hall and thought women exerted a moderating influence. She might have been right and I for one did not mind but older warriors, like Griotard, did. He could not understand it and it took Sweyn One Eye and me a whole afternoon to persuade him that it was not changing the old ways but, perhaps, making a few changes. Agnetha had chambers erected for her guests. The jarl had the biggest hall in Agerhøne and Agnetha sought Mary's advice about making chambers. My wife and Agnetha were now close and that could not have been predicted when I took her as a thrall.

The merchant came with his two bodyguards and his daughter as well as his servants. Lodvir had told us that the merchant's wife lived in Norway. Frida was the youngest of six girls. The gods it seemed, had not granted Aksel sons and his desire to make a good marriage made sense. He brought gifts for Sweyn and Agnetha. For Agnetha he had a necklace made of jet and amber; it was a beautiful gift and even though we knew that the raw materials had not cost him much, the craftsmanship had. For Sweyn he gave him a Saami bow inlaid with silver. It looked almost too beautiful to be used in war. The biggest surprise was Frida. She looked stunning and her golden hair was coiled like serpents. I could now see that she was slightly older than I had thought and was, indeed, of an age with Hawk. That they were smitten by each other was obvious and understandable. Hawk was a hero of Svolder and what young woman could not be swayed by that thought. Frida looked like a princess. The looks I saw on the faces of Agnetha and Mary showed that they approved but the test would be Sweyn who would not like to be used by this Swede.

Frida was seated between Agnetha and Frida and Hawk between Aksel and Sweyn, I was seated next to Sweyn One Eye and we were able to enjoy ourselves as we watched Hawk squirm as Aksel and Sweyn spoke over him. Frida was also subjected to a volley of questions, politely asked, of course.

One Eye laughed, "Who would have thought my little brother would have succumbed to the first fluttering eyelashes he spied."

I shook my head, "He has been seeking a bride for some time. I saw him looking at the slaves we took on the last raid. He was seeking a beauty and the Norns have spun him one."

It was only after the Swede and his party left, having arranged a marriage for the summer solstice, that I realised how little the arrangement had to do with love. That there was love was clear but that did not concern Aksel. Unlike Mary and I, the two had been attracted from the moment they met. Mary and I learned to love. It was the Swede and our jarl who made it more of a practical arrangement. Aksel had money to spend and he wanted the safety and security of a powerful warrior. The men of Ribe and Agerhøne were perfect. Jarl Sweyn also wanted something from marriage and Aksel agreed to fund a threttanessa. It was also agreed, to my great surprise, that Hawk would take over from Lodvir as hersir in Ribe at some time, unspecified, in the future. Lodvir was happy about the matter for he had only taken on the role to please Sweyn. He agreed to stay on for half a year and act as adviser to my cousin. I knew it was a risk but I knew how marriage had changed his brother and me. It might do the same for him. Sweyn One Eye was happy as he would now inherit Agerhøne and that pleased him.

As we returned from the wedding on the shortest night of the year my foster father spoke with me, "Sven, I hope that you are not envious of your cousins."

I frowned for I did not understand the question, "Envious?"

"Your foster brothers will inherit power and titles and I am unhappy that I can do nothing for you."

I laughed, "And I want nothing, jarl. I am happy with my hall, my family and my life. I am pleased for Sweyn and Alf and there is no envy harbouring in my heart."

He looked relieved, "Agnetha said that was how you would feel but I needed to know. I love my sons, but we all know that in battle it is to we two that warriors look. When I cease to go to war it is you who will lead the clan to war, as Lodvir predicted all those years ago before Oathsword found you."

I was both surprised and flattered for I had not known that.

My son was born on the first day of Tvímánuður and he was a healthy child who was heavier than his sister had been and was born with a shock of brown hair. The birthing had tired Mary out, but she was happy for she had borne me a son. I had been in the hall during the birth and found the cries of pain hard to bear. I was glad that I had missed the first birth for the second saw me shaking with fear at the thought of losing my wife. We named the boy Steana after Mary's father. It pleased me for there was not another Steana in the village and he would not be confused with another. There were Svens and Sweyns aplenty! Perhaps if we had another boy, he might be a Bersi but I was not certain I wished to put Mary through such pain again.

With every warrior at home, we had the best harvest ever and our animals produced more young than any could remember. Perhaps that was because we now had more animals to start with. My only concern was that all the decent land within three miles of Agerhøne was now farmed and it was not just the animals who had been fecund. Being at home for so long meant that the wife of every warrior was with child. Where would they farm?

Those problems were for the future for Sweyn now had a second son and Frida was with child. The blood of Sweyn Skull Taker would flow through another generation!

Chapter 7

Denmark 1002

King Aethelred was not my king, but I knew that he was a bad one. He had paid us gold early in the year but, and I know not why, on the last day of Gormánuður, the day of the Christian saint, St Brice, the king ordered every Dane living in his lands to be killed. Even now, many years later I can find no sense in it. To make matters worse two of the victims were King Sweyn's sister, Gunhild, and her husband, Pallig. The payment of gold Aethelred had made meant nothing to King Sweyn, he would have vengeance and Jarl Sweyn and his hearth weru were summoned to his court for a counsel of war. We had enjoyed a year of peace but that would now end! We had thought the gold ensured peace. It did not.

That there was anger amongst the jarls was clear but, as I stood listening to the debate, I sensed that King Sweyn Forkbeard was not as upset by the death of his sister as he made out. It struck me that he now had a pretext to go beyond just raiding and bring large swathes of King Aethelred's kingdom under his control. I am not sure that he thought at the time that he would be king of that land, but having taken large parts of Norway the ambition must have lurked in his head. The king's two sons, Harald, the younger and Cnut, the elder were at the assembly and I wondered what they thought of it all. The princelings were heirs to what might turn out to be an empire. That Harald was seen as the heir was down to the fact that Cnut's mother had died and Harald's mother, Sigfrid the Haughty, still lived. They showed in their faces and their build that they had different mothers and, as I later learned, their characters were different too.

The assembled hearth weru were spread around the hall. There was no hint of danger to our charges from weapons but each jarl, with the exception of Jarl Svein Hákonarson, the Norseman, and our jarl, had ensured that their hearth weru wore shining mail and gleaming helmets. They were making a statement. We did not need such adornments for our achievements spoke for us. I also had Oathsword hanging from my belt and I saw every warrior's eye drawn to it. Thralls brought refreshments to the room, but they were served by us, the hearth weru. We tasted each jug before pouring it into horns. There would be no treachery in the hall, but the refreshments and the ale came from outside. We took no chances. There were many Norse who resented the defeat at Svolder and while they might not have the courage to face us in battle there were other means to achieve their ends. It was when King Sweyn spoke of Aethelred's new wife, Emma of Normandy that we all paid close attention for this was news. The sister of the Duke of Normandy suggested an alliance with warriors who would give us a harder fight than the Saxons. The Normans came from Viking stock and were renowned as fierce fighters. There were even a few who suggested we go to Rouen to fight them. Wise heads prevailed but it was decided that we would attack England in the next campaigning season. The question was where?

I knew that his failure to take Exeter still rankled and it was Karl Three Fingers who suggested that we fall upon that burh. As part of his argument, he said that King Aethelred had given the land to his wife and she had garrisoned it with some of her kinsmen. A new nunnery nearby also suggested a rich haul. When Karl said that we had a ready-made base on the Isle of Wiht, it was decided. We would return to the scene of our great success. The difference would be that the fleet we would take and the warriors who crewed them would be able to defeat any army that the Saxons sent to defeat us. I thought that we would return to Agerhøne directly, but we did not. While other jarls and their hearth weru left we were summoned to a meeting with the king, Karl Three Fingers, Jarl Svein Hákonarson and the two princelings.

King Sweyn was smiling and that always made me suspicious. He positively beamed and addressed Sweyn Skull Taker, "Karl here has told me of the great deeds you did when you raided for me and know that I am grateful. You helped to fill our war chest and that will bear fruit when we raid. You too, Jarl Svein Hákonarson, have been no less successful in putting down the rebellions fermented by those who lost at Svolder and cannot face the consequences of their defeat. I would like the two of you to act as foster fathers to my two sons. Harald will go to Norway with you, Jarl Svein Hákonarson, and Cnut will join the Jarl of Ribe and Agerhøne. I would have them learn the art of war from the best that we have. Both are of an age where they can learn the art of war. They have been shown how to use a sword but as the future leaders of Denmark and my lands in Norway, they need to learn the skills of leadership. I would, of course, train them but I have other demands upon my time. What say you?"

There could, of course, be no refusal and both jarls nodded their agreement and their thanks for such an honour. My heart sank for we now not only had our jarl to protect but also the heirs to the crown! Surprisingly, to me at least, they came alone and without either servants or guards of their own. Cnut would live in the jarl's hall and be brought up as I was, as a foster son. I wondered at the arrangement and its purpose. Trying to see into Sweyn Forkbeard's mind was like trying to unravel the coils of a snake! Cnut did have his own pony and he could, thankfully, ride. He was no longer a child but he did not have the frame of a youth of Agerhøne the same age. The farewells were perfunctory, and I saw none of the affection which Sweyn Skull Taker had for his own children and, indeed, for me. This could only be a good thing for the princeling. We could not comment on the task for the simple reason that while we were at the court, we did not know who was listening and it seemed both rude and offensive to Cnut to talk about him as though he was not there. Instead, while my foster father wrestled with the new duties, Sweyn One Eye and I spoke with the boy.

"Agerhøne is not as grand as Heiða-býr, Cnut."

"I know. You are Sweyn One Eye?" My cousin nodded, "Did it hurt when you lost your eye?"

"The wound hurt, and I did not know that I had lost the eye until later. It has taken me time to grow accustomed to fight once more, but my cousin Sven helps. He guards the jarl's right side and I the left."

The young Dane was a serious-looking youth, and he did not smile. It must have been hard for him to be thrust amongst strangers with barely a goodbye. "And you are the warrior with the dragon sword." I nodded, "You let me touch it when I was younger. That was kind and I have never forgotten. Often warriors ignore me because I am young but one day, I will be older, and they will take notice."

Hawk asked, "Will you miss your brother?"

"Not really for he hits me when others are not looking and his mother protects him when I try to fight back. I will have my revenge."

I felt sympathy for him then as I remembered the blows I had received until I had stood up for myself. It made me determined to make his life as pleasant as possible.

We were nearing Agerhøne when Jarl Sweyn spoke for the first time since we had left the king, "You will be treated the same as my sons were and as my grandchildren are. My grandson, Sweyn, is but a little younger than you. You may follow him for a while and do the same duties as he does."

"You will teach me the sword?"

To my surprise, he was looking at me and not his foster father. I nodded, "The three of us train the young warriors so, aye."

"No, I would have you teach me. In Heiða-býr when men spoke of the Battle of Svolder and of the Battle of Dean, it was your name was mentioned more than any other. Karl Three Fingers says that you are the best swordsman he has ever seen. My father said anyone who wielded a dragon sword would have an advantage. Karl did not agree but he said nothing."

His foster father said, without turning his head, "You will do as the other boys do. Sometimes it will be Hawk who trains you and sometimes Sweyn One Eye. If you are lucky then Sven Saxon Sword will teach you his skills. It will be many years until you need to use them! When we go to war, next year, you will be with the boys who use slings and bows. Can you use either?"

"No."

"Then before you use a sword, we will show you how to be useful in battle and harass the enemy. You will also fetch ale skins and, if the battle appears to be going against us you will take my banner to the rear."

Cnut was silent for the rest of the journey as he took in what would be a starkly different life than the one, he had enjoyed in Heiða-býr. Two miles from Agerhøne, Hawk was sent to warn Agnetha of our arrival. That he should have done so sooner showed that Sweyn Skull Taker's mind was elsewhere. He had much to think about. The result of Hawk's ride was that the servants and thralls were well presented when a possible King of Denmark dismounted. The jarl handed his reins to me, "Stable the pony and then you are done. I fear you and my sons will now have less time with your families and we have a princeling to watch."

It was clear that he was not happy.

"Aye, jarl. He seems a malleable boy. It may not prove as difficult as you imagine."

He gave a wry laugh, "I fear it will prove much harder than I imagine. There are problems I have not even considered. Taking a boy to war is hazardous enough, as you well know, but taking one of the king's sons has no good side to it! The best we can hope is that he returns from the Exe whole! Tomorrow we will meet to work out a routine for him."

When I reached my home Mary had heard the noise of our arrival. I told her of our new charge and, almost as an afterthought, about the attack planned for the next year."

She looked wistfully at our sleeping son, "At least we have enjoyed a year without war, and I wonder at King Aethelred. Why does he poke the wolf?"

"I know not but you are right it was a foolish act, and it will bring more tears to the hearths of his warriors."

Winter was not as bad in Denmark as it was further north but, as we settled down to train Cnut and the other young warriors for war and to prepare ourselves for battle, it was hard to face the morning with a wicked wind coming from the east, often bringing sleet and snow showers. It encouraged us to be active. Jarl Sweyn gave each of us one day a week when we would not be needed and that was more than I hoped for. Cnut was the youngest warrior we trained by some margin. Boys his age would normally have been used as ships' boys, but we could not do that with Cnut. He was the king's son and it would be too late for him to learn the skills. He was, in any case, slightly bigger than most who scurried up the lines and ropes. I gave him lessons with the bow and Hawk with the sling. When we went to war then the boys would often face the greatest risks and have to stand before our battle line to weaken the enemy. If that was Cnut's fate, then he risked a short life!

Faramir, Gandálfr, Falmr, Snorri and the other warriors we had trained still attended when they could, and they joined the new warriors who had to endure all that they had. We knew that this time we would be attacking Exeter and so we practised making a moving wall of shields that would protect warriors who could hack at a palisade with an axe. The younger warriors were expendable, and it was they would have this duty. The hearth weru would be likely to be the ones who hacked and chopped at wooden walls. I was not looking forward to taking the town, but I knew that it would be the richest prize we had ever taken. Why else would Aethelred give it to his new bride?

Sweyn One Eye saw Cnut not only when we trained the new warriors but also each night. His own son was used to show Cnut his duties. It was a test of him as a future leader. He could have done as his own brother had done and made the life of Sweyn Sweynson a misery, but he did not. He was aware that the boy was in awe of him and treated him kindlier than one might have expected from the son of King Forkbeard. Lodvir spent much time visiting too but that was nothing to do with Cnut and all to do with the preparations. We had ten ships we would be taking including the new threttanessa, **'Aksel's Gift'**. I was not sure it was an appropriate name for a drekar, but all the correct ceremonies and rituals had been in order and it was his money. Lodvir would sail it and Griotard would be promoted from sailing master to the captain of **'Hyrrokkin'**. I feared for my old friend for I was not sure that he would stay out of the fighting! When we trained the young warriors, I found that the old man had slowed and all but the most inexperienced could best him.

It had been more than a year since we had sailed and so every drekar was hauled from the water and we cleaned their hulls. That was a chastening experience for Cnut but as every male, including the jarl, was so occupied, he had little choice. This time we not only rid ourselves of the weed but applied a concoction that appeared to kill the worm which might otherwise eat out the keel. Finally, the wood was protected with pine tar. Although the most necessary of tasks it was the one we all hated. Whatever clothes we used would be ruined and the tar would still be found in our fingers a week after the work was done. It was as we did it that Thorstein gave the jarl the bad news that **'Sea Serpent'** would not have many more voyages left in her for battle and age had both taken their toll.

On the day I had to myself I found that Gunhild was becoming more of a person and less of a mewling babe. She would recognise me and smile. The joy that brought was indescribable and I found myself surprised that I liked it so much. If she did not smile and reach for me I felt as though a Saxon had stabbed me with his seax. I know it was foolish, but she was my first born. I would walk with her, holding her two arms until I thought my back would break. She would giggle and laugh when we did so. I looked forward to the time that Steana would be old enough to do the same. I was gentle with Gunhild, but I knew that I would be rougher with my son. He would grow up in the harder world of boys. Gunhild would be protected and that was as it should be.

As we prepared to set sail, I sharpened my weapons. This time I would take the good sword I had captured before I had married Mary. I realised that I had the skills to use two swords. My long dagger, Norse Gutter, had been a revelation to me and, in some circumstances, of more use than a shield. I had made a second scabbard and Mary had woven a dragon design for the outside. I wore that one over my back. I packed my chest a week before we sailed so that I knew I had all that I needed. This time it would be hard for Hawk to leave for he had a wife and that wife was with child. He had entered the world of his brother and me. It showed for he was more serious and, when we trained the new warriors, he laughed less and chastised more. Frida would stay with Agnetha and she would be well looked after. Her father was off trading. He did not know exactly where we would be raiding but he knew that we would raid, and he could profit from it. He was not a warrior and he fought his wars with coins and knarr! When we returned then Hawk would take over as hersir of Ribe.

We had a farewell feast in the mead hall. It was all the warriors we would be taking. This time our ship would be fully crewed as would **'Aksel's Gift'** and **'Hyrrokkin'**. Agerhøne would have two hundred warriors when we fought the men of Exeter. Cnut did not sit and eat at the feast but joined the other ship's boys who waited on us. It was a good way to be. That none of us abused our position showed what a wise choice King Forkbeard had made.

Cnut brought another large piece of cooked pig and the others were busily chopping hunks off it. As he stood to wait for the platter to be emptied, he chatted with me. I was happy for him to call me Sven rather than my full name and he and I often chatted easily. The Oathsword connection made that easier. "Sven, what do we eat on board a drekar? I have sailed on one but never for long. We cannot cook, can we?"

I smiled, "Not unless you wish a burnt boat! Let me see, we will have bread for the first few days. It will become staler but salty seawater makes it softer. We have pickled fish and dried meat and, of course, you and the other boys will have lines trailing astern and you will catch us fresh fish which we eat raw. Believe me that is the best of food! We will sail down the coast of Northumbria and Mercia. We can scavenge for shellfish. You will get used to the food and then, when we land, we eat whatever we can take!"

He took away the platter and returned with a dozen small fowl called pullets. I was fond of them and I took two. As he waited for the platter he asked, "And where will I sleep?"

We had discussed this, and the jarl wanted the princeling protected, "The three of us will use our chests and capes to make a den and you will sleep there with us. I do know it will not be as bad as it could be. Those who sleep close to Griotard the Grim will have to endure his snores and, even worse, his foul farts!" It made the boy laugh as I knew it would. I believed I had put his mind at rest.

It was Agnetha who had his chest made up. It was small enough to fit between Hawk's and the gunwale. He would not be wearing mail and had no helmet so it could be smaller. He would not need to sit on it and Agnetha ensured that it had a sealskin cover to keep it dry. She was a caring woman.

At the feast, there were no songs and few drank to unconsciousness. It was just an opportunity in the peace and calm of the mead hall for men to tall of things other than war; their land and animals, their families; their hopes for the future. It was a time of reflection and once we left we would all adopt our war face the next time we met. Then would be the chance for bold songs and for a warlike demeanour. When we faced the Saxons and, possibly the Normans, then they would feel our full wrath. For us, it was nothing to do with avenging the dead of St Brice's Day Massacre; we did not know those people. We were going to fight an enemy we despised and to take all from him so that we would be richer and they would be poorer. None of us might like King Sweyn Forkbeard but at least he was a proper king, one who led. When we assaulted Exeter, he would be there with us. I doubted that Aethelred would leave his fortress city of Lundenwic!

That night Mary lay in my arms. Steana had been satiated with the breast and slept. Anna lay in Gunhild's chamber and my wife and I could whisper and cuddle. "As much as I do not like that you go to make war and to make war on my people, I cannot help but think that this weak king, what was it one of your jarls called him, a driveller? He has brought this upon himself. He has a choice with an enemy like you, he either fights or submits. It seems to me that he has done neither but, husband, and I know you will do as I implore, be not cruel. Do not kill for the sake of killing. Kill if you must but kill warriors."

I kissed her, "And you know that is my way but do not try to make a Christian of me. Our children can be brought us so but when Steana is old enough he will stand in the shield wall and he will defend himself. To do anything else would mean his death."

She kissed me back and there was a silence, until Mary's words cut like a knife, "He could be a priest."

"And if that was truly his choice then I would accept it. I would not be happy for I believe that our children will have the strength of us both within them and a priest would not be world enough for either of them. You enjoy the life of a lady do you not?"

"Aye, of course."

"And your parents enjoyed such a life too?"

Her silence was eloquent, and she did not answer. Soon her breathing showed me that she was asleep. It was rare that I had the last word and I tried to remember how I had managed it.

Chapter 8

Cnut was not to be given sea duties. Firstly, it was too risky and secondly, he did not have the skills the other boys did. He had not had the experience of scampering up ropes and lines like a squirrel. He had not balanced atop the yard to peer out to sea with a deck pitching back and forth. He had not been brought up to race along a strewn deck with heaving oars and a storm sent by Njörðr. He would wait by the steering board and act as a messenger for Thorstein the Lucky. He would fetch our horns of sea ale and if a storm blew cover us with our capes. In short, he would become a servant but, when he ruled, it would help for he would know what the lowliest of his subjects did when they went to war. That he was slightly older and a little bigger than the other boys would also be a spur for him to avoid making a mistake.

As usual, the first part of the voyage was the easiest. We sailed to Ribe to meet with the other drekar. There would be too many ships for the port when the king came and so we would await his arrival aboard our drekar and sail out to meet him when his fleet arrived. We had been told that there would be one hundred or more ships and that mean five thousand warriors. Our king was taking the vengeance trail and he was taking no chances. Even Jarl Svein Hákonarson and twenty Norse ships would be joining us. Cnut and his brother would be in the same war but in different parts. Their experiences would be different and would make them different men.

The fleet arrived three days later, and they appeared as dark dots on the horizon and then, as the sails grew larger, we saw the size of the fleet. It was formidable. Although it was not as large as the one from Svolder it would be harder to keep together for we had more open sea with which to contend and we would not be able to simply wait for an enemy to appear. As soon as the dots were seen we readied for sea and rowed out in good order to wait a mile or two off the coast. We had not received orders about our position, but Sweyn Skull Taker had told his captains that we would adopt a three drekar wide formation with ours at the head. Pots had been made to contain oil we could burn at night so that we did not become separated. The responsibility of keeping the pot filled on our ship was given to Cnut. That first row to the meeting point was our easiest one and we just sculled to exercise muscles that had not had to do this for some time. Even so, when we hove to and awaited the fleet I turned and saw some of the new men at the prow rubbing their hands. I saw Faramir speaking with them. The advice I had given would be passed on!

The usefulness of *'Adder'* must have been mentioned to King Sweyn for there was one attached to the fleet and *'Blue Tongue'* headed towards us. "King Sweyn asks that your ships take position to the larboard of the ships of Heiða-býr."

"I will do so."

Thorstein nodded his satisfaction. They were the ships Karl had led on the last raid and we knew their captains and the quality of their seamanship. The problem would lie with the unknown ships which would follow us. A poor lookout could result in a collision.

It took an hour or more for the ships to be positioned to the king's satisfaction and then, with a breeze from the northeast, we headed due west to the estuary of the seals. I wondered, as our backs heaved and we rowed with purpose if the king intended to emulate entirely Karl Three Finger's raid. If he did then our predictability might be our undoing. We did not have to row for long and as the sun began to set ahead of us then oars were stacked on the mastfish and the sails were reefed a little. Our lights were replicated on other ships and our tiny glowing dots continued to sail through the night. It was not just the ship's boys who stood a watch. A quarter of the crew also kept a sharp lookout for there were ships to our steerboard and behind. We knew there would be no land until we saw Northumbria, but ships could be wrecked, and an upturned hull could seriously damage a ship.

The second day found a stronger wind which helped our progress, but the swells and troughs made a rougher passage and some of the new sailors found it hard to retain the food they had consumed. Part of it was the change of diet. Cnut looked a little green, but he managed to hold on to the food he had devoured although I noticed that it was a whole day before he ate again! The wind continued during the night and Jarl Sweyn had us as the night watch. Cnut was happy to join the watch but we sent him to our fur lined nest. He had eaten little and there was little that he could do. We needed experienced eyes.

The next morning one of the new ships which had been behind us had disappeared. We did not even know her name but that she had a red and blue dragon prow. Speculation was idle for anything could have happened to her. We knew that she had not collided with our ships for none had damage but another sort of collision or a weakness which had been aggravated by the weather could have caused her to disappear. It was one ship and the king did not waste one moment in searching for her. We pushed on. Once again, we used the Dunum to make minor repairs and to hunt the seals. Those who had been there the first time knew where to look and we ate cooked seal that night.

Karl Three Fingers had helped the king with his plans, and we did not land at the Isle of Sheep. In fact, once we neared the Tamese we headed out to sea so that we would not be seen from the Cent coast. We headed south and then turned sharply north-west to arrive at Wiht once more. This time we landed on the south coast and three smaller drekar were sent north to retake the fishing village we had occupied. If the fisherfolk remained, then they would not fight. They had learned their lesson. We made a camp and King Sweyn called his council of war. It was almost a Thing for there were more than a hundred captains, hersir and jarls who listened to the king and his lieutenant as they explained their plan. Cnut was with us and I saw his brother Harald. The two did not even exchange a look and standing with their respective foster fathers did not have to speak!

It was Karl who spoke and that was reassuring. He had made mistakes but not many of them and we were confident that if he spoke then the plan had his approval, "We return to the Exe but this time we shall take Exeter. My oathsworn and I have warriors to avenge." The king looked indifferent, but I knew that the men they had lost in their failed attack rankled with Karl and his men. "We shall sail up the Exe and camp on both sides of the river. Jarl Sweyn Skull Taker and his men will seal off the town from the northeast. They will raid as far as the burnt-out hall of Pinhoe before joining the rest of the warband to surround the burh. Every crew will make their own ladders to assault. We spend a day identifying the key parts of their defences and then when we sound the war horn five times, we attack."

That was the plan of attack but there were other elements that concerned the campaign.

"Once we have taken the town, and take it we will, we ravage the countryside until they send an army to meet us. We cannot count on a leader as poor as Kola was but whomsoever they send we will defeat them. We then march east. The fleet will follow, and each captain will need to leave a crew so that our ships can return to our camp at Wiht."

It was then I saw the cleverness of the plan. It had just enough differences from the original raid as to throw off any Saxon plans they might make. When we returned to our drekar Lodvir and the jarl joined with Griotard to choose which crews would stay aboard. In the end, it was a mixture of experienced and older warriors who might find the march across Wessex harder and the younger warriors who were untried. As we would all be involved in the assault on Exeter then every warrior would have the opportunity to be blooded and to take treasure. We would march east with a pared-down warband.

Cnut was a clever youth and as we settled down to eat, he asked us questions that showed he had a military mind already. "We will lose men when we attack the walls and ditches of this burh?"

He had never seen one, but we had told him what they would be like.

I nodded, "It is inevitable for it will be heavily defended and even a farmer or a merchant who hurls a rock or throws a spear has the ability to cause a wound or a death. Men who know they are going to be slaughtered fight hard and there will be their families inside the burh. It is why your father sends us to cut the burh off from the northeast. When our ships are seen then many will try to make the walls. This way we ensure that there are as few men inside the stronghold as possible."

He nodded, "And then we put some men in our ships, and they sail east?" We all nodded and ate the food which had just been ladled in our wooden bowls. "Then the further east we go the more chance we have of facing an army which is greater in number than ours."

I was impressed with the way he had worked out the problems we would face. "Aye, Cnut, but we are usually outnumbered in any case when we face the Saxons. Know this, they fight in a different way to us. In the times of King Alfred then every man in the land would be raised to fight us. That is how they defeated King Guthrum." I unconsciously touched the sword the great king had used. "Now they do not use every man and each hundred has to supply a certain number. That is their weakness for the ones who fight know that there are others who are not. They have fewer mailed men than we do and so if the battle goes against them then the weaker ones will break. That is what happened at the Battle of Dean. Of course, it does not guarantee victory, but we win more than we lose."

Hawk wiped his mouth with the back of his hand, "And you, young Cnut, will be at the battles we fight. You will hurl your stones at the enemy and hope to kill or hurt at least two. That way the odds are lessened the closer they come to us."

It was as though he suddenly realised the danger he would be in, "And they will be trying to kill me?"

One Eye laughed, "For sure and that is why Karl Three Fingers ensured that you had a leather jerkin and cap. You may still be hurt but they lessen the chance of death."

"And," I advised, "you will need quick feet so that when the order comes to return you race back and hurl yourself beneath our shields and crawl to safety!"

"That does not sound dignified!"

We all laughed, and I shook my head, "Forget dignity and think of life. When you emerge unscathed behind our rear lines then you will be alive and there is nothing more dignified than life!"

Our previous raid had prepared us well and we negotiated the mouth of the Exe just after dawn. It was as we neared the head of the river that we heard the tolling of bells. Karl's plan made it easier for us as we kept to the steerboard side of the river and had no other ships to navigate. As soon as we reached the sand, the hearth weru leapt ashore and waited while the ship was secured to the shore. We left our spears aboard. It was unlikely that we would have to face a shield wall and our swords would be better weapons. Some of the ship's boys would remain aboard with Thorstein but half, including Cnut, would be coming with us. Each crew would operate alone, and our endpoint would be the ruined hall and village of Pinhoe. Each crew had a horn and if there was a serious threat then a blast would summon help. The tolling bells told us that we did not have long if we were to do as Karl Three Fingers wished; they knew we were here. We disembarked quicker than I had ever known and our crew, all sixty-six of us, raced off through the fields.

We had four miles to run for Pinhoe was north and east of Exeter. Our speed was rewarded when we saw hundreds of Saxons running towards us and heading for the burh. We were two miles from our ships and the nearest crew to us was that of Lodvir, two hundred paces from us. The people were heading for the herepath, the road which had been built by King Alfred to connect the burhs. As we drew swords to run at the Saxon men who were trying to make a barrier between us and their women, the jarl shouted, "Sven, watch the boy!"

Even as I acknowledged the order, I saw that Cnut had run ahead with the other slingers and was whirling his sling above his head. I cursed his speed for he was forty paces from me.

The four slingers struck Saxons and I heard a whoop from Cnut as his stone pinged off the helmet of a Saxon who dropped to his knee. Cnut looked around for another target and I saw, to my horror, that the Saxon had risen and was nocking an arrow. The range was less than forty paces, and he could not miss.

"Cnut!" My words were in vain for there was so much noise, screams and the sound of feet pounding on the ground that he did not hear. I ran as though my life depended upon it and I watched the Saxon begin to draw back the bow as Cnut hurled a stone at another Saxon. I saw the bowstring touch the Saxon's ear when I was just ten paces from the boy and I did the only thing I could, I ran between the arrow and

Cnut, turning my back as I did so. Cnut looked up in shock as I appeared and then the arrow struck. It was as though someone had smacked me hard upon the back but my cloak, shield and mail protected me.

"Stay behind me! When I turn, I want you there!"

He nodded and drawing my second sword ran towards the Saxon who had, foolishly, decided to end my life with a second arrow. He was too slow, and I was twenty paces from him when he nocked the arrow. His eyes were on the nock and not me. As he looked up, he saw his death as Oathsword swept across his unprotected neck and half severed his head. I looked for another threat and saw that there was none close by. I turned and said, "Take the Saxon's bow, arrows and seax. They are yours."

He nodded as he obeyed, "You have an arrow in your back!"

"Pull it out and keep it, Cnut, for it will be a reminder of how close you came to death. Had the arrow hit you then you would be dead, and I would have to explain to your father why I failed to protect his son."

It was a chastening experience for the youth who had been caught up in the moment. He now dogged my steps and I had to be careful, as we carved our way through the Saxon men, not to catch him with my sword when I made a wide swing. There were more warriors and men than I had expected and, as the women and children realised the futility of getting through an increasingly large warband and headed north, away from Exeter, Jarl Sweyn led us to Pinhoe. Another of our crews was further north-west and they would deal with the Saxons. We saw the reason for the large number of men. They were rebuilding Pinhoe. There was a hall and a church as well as some houses in the process of being built. The Saxon camp had animals tethered there and there were tools scattered around.

"Lodvir, take the animals back to the ships. The rest of you take what is of value and then burn everything, the buildings, the camp and the tools. Let us show the Saxons that we have returned!"

By the time we had finished a pall of black smoke rose in the sky. There was no hurry as we headed to Exeter which lay just a couple of miles away. Already it was surrounded by a ring of campfires. The fires were there to help our warriors identify where they could camp, and they were also a threatening message to the Saxons; they were going nowhere. There would be no attempt to ask them to surrender. King Sweyn wanted a victory for he was in command. Svolder had shown him that he had to lead. Then he had been tardy and had missed out on the glory enjoyed by Jarl Svein Hákonarson and Sweyn Skull Taker. Our king would have songs sung about him.

We were directed to our camp by one of Karl Three Fingers' oathsworn, "You have this three hundred pace section of the wall!"

Almost absent-mindedly Sweyn nodded and then took off his helmet to assess the walls. Sweyn One Eye shouted, "Make a camp here! Cnut, find us ale!"

"Yes, Sweyn One Eye." Cnut was still subdued after his brush with death. I knew that when he slept, he would find it hard for he would imagine what would have happened had I not managed to reach him.

The three of us went to stand with the jarl and we took off our helmets. Hawk laughed when he saw the hole in my cloak. When I explained how I had acquired it he said, "Sven Saxon Sword, perhaps we should name you, Sven, Princeling Shield!"

"One name is enough for me. I cannot blame the boy for he hit a warrior with his first throw, but I could do without the responsibility."

Without turning the jarl said, "And yet my son is right in one way, Sven, you have been chosen as the boy's protector. For the rest of this raid, I will make do with my sons for protection."

I did not like it, but I always obeyed orders.

The defences were indeed formidable. There were stakes before the ditch and while I could not see the bottom of it, I knew there would be stakes there to catch us as we crossed it. The part nearest us would be deep, what men called an ankle breaker and the slope on the other side would be equally dangerous. The wooden walls were built atop what looked like Roman foundations and there was a fighting platform. Towers were at each corner and over the gatehouse which also looked Roman. To reinforce the gate the bridge over the ditch had been drawn up to protect the wooden gate. The walls were lined with men. We knew that they would not all be warriors but that did not matter. They would have stones, arrows, boiling water and spears to hurl at us as we crossed the killing field before the walls.

"We cannot risk the ones without mail. We will have to use those who have byrnies."

Sweyn One Eye kept such numbers in his head, "We have eighty of those."

"Then make sure that the others all have a bow. They cannot assault the walls, but their arrows can make life hard for those on the walls. We have the night to prepare for I know that King Sweyn will order the attack as soon as he can."

Hawk said, "We found many arrows at Pinhoe. I will have those distributed and I will set the boys to collecting river stones. It will keep them occupied." Marriage had made Hawk more responsible in many ways and his brother and I did not need to constantly ask him to perform his duties.

When Lodvir returned with the carcasses of some of the animals they had slaughtered at the ships he was informed of the plan. As the meat began to cook, he sat with us while Jarl Sweyn ensured that the others knew what they were about.

"I do not like this, Sven Saxon Sword. I do not mind facing a Saxon sword to sword but here we have to watch our feet lest we are speared by a shit covered stake and then climb a ladder while men are dropping stones on our heads."

"Why climb the ladders at all?"

Hawk laughed, "And how else do we enter the burh? Fly? I can do so but the rest of you…"

That made us all smile but I shook my head, "I have looked at the walls. See how they have used Roman walls for the base."

Lodvir nodded, "Aye and we all know how well the Romans built."

"It is almost a thousand years since they did so. Look closely, that is moss growing in the mortar. I see ivy too."

Hawk frowned, "And?"

Lodvir grinned, "I see what you mean, Sven. It means that the mortar is old and weak. We dig out the mortar and pull out the stones. So long as we are protected from the falling stones it would be easier than using axes."

"And without a support then the wooden palisades would be easier to bring down."

Sweyn One Eye said, "Or we could use fire. Once we have a stone removed, we light a fire and let that do our work for us."

By the time Jarl Sweyn Skull Taker had returned we had improved our plan and Lodvir presented it to him. He beamed, "Well done, Lodvir!"

"'Twas not me, Sweyn. It was the boy I trained. His mind is as sharp as his father's was!"

"Well done, foster son. Your father would be proud of you. We will still use ladders for that will keep those on the walls occupied. Sven as this was your idea you choose the men you will use."

I had thought of this too, "We will need every mailed warrior on the ladders. I will use Faramir, Dreng, Snorri, Siggi and the other young warriors. They have good shields and that is all that is needed."

Amongst the tools we had taken from Pinhoe were some hammers and some chisels. I chose the best of each and then went to see the eight warriors I had selected. I presented it as an opportunity rather than an order.

"The jarl would have all those without mail using slings and bows on the morrow." I saw their faces fall. "You eight, if you choose, can come with me and protect my body with your shields. I intend to bring down the walls of Exeter."

They all shouted their agreement and then Snorri asked, "How will you do that? Magic?"

Faramir said, "Or will you use Oathsword!"

"Oathsword will be there but I shall use hammer and chisel. Dreng you will need to bring fire in a pot and Snorri, kindling. We shall need Thor's help when we do this."

That evening, while we ate, I said to the jarl, "Foster father, I cannot watch Cnut while I light the fires!" Cnut had gone to fetch water to clean our bowls and was not present.

"I know. I will put the boy with the other slingers. Bergil the Brawny managed to hurt his ankle today and I will leave him to command the others. He is not happy about having to remain here and he will ensure that the princeling does not move!"

He was right and neither Cnut nor Bergil were happy about their task.

We were all prepared before dawn. We had eaten well and were as prepared as we could be. It felt strange to have a hammer and a chisel as my weapons of choice and I knew that once we were within two hundred paces of the walls then a host of missiles would be hurled at us. Lodvir had reminded us that the Saxons sometimes used darts. My young warriors would all carry their shields whilst mine would be across my back. I had already kissed the hilt of Oathsword and asked the Allfather to watch over me. I prayed that while the Norns had spun a strange future for me that they would not cut the thread so early. Once I reached the walls then I felt confident that the wall of shields above me would protect me.

Dawn had barely broken when the horns sounded five times. The ones attacking from the west, Jarl Svein Hákonarson and his Norsemen, would have the advantage of the last hint of night's cloak to protect them. The ones attacking from the east would have the advantage of a new sun in the eyes of the defenders. We had no advantage for we attacked from the north.

The jarl raised his sword and our slingers and archers closed to within range of the walls. Some would be wounded, and some would die. I saw that Bergil the Brawny had his shield protecting Cnut! I knew the boy would not like that. Following my young warriors, I walked towards the stakes. The stakes would do little to stop us for they were spaced far enough apart to allow us through, but they would catch the unwary if any did not present their shields to face the enemy. We made the edge of the ditch successfully although I had heard the arrows and stones slamming into the shields of the young warriors before me. Eidel had an arrow wound to his leg but it had been a glancing blow and would not stop him. We all stopped at the edge. The other mailed warriors had their shields before them. I saw that the stakes were far enough apart to allow us to tread a precarious path through them. The danger would come if we slipped and I saw that they had used water to make the slope more dangerous.

I shouted to my companions, "Treat the slope like winter ice! Spread your feet and keep your balance." That was easier said than done and, for the first time, I would lose the protective shields. I had to do as I had advised but faster than they did. Jarl Sweyn Skull Taker and his hearth weru led the advance and that drew arrows and stones to them. I stepped down and used my left heel to dig into the soft mud. I found it easier than I had thought. If I had used the flat of my boot then I might have slipped but I was, in effect, making my own steps and I reached the bottom upright. As a stone clanked off my helmet, I disobeyed my own orders and used my quick feet to dance through the stakes which were covered in human and animal dung, A wound from such a stake could prove to be fatal. When I reached the other slope, I did not stop but used the hammer and chisel to dig into the bank and to pull myself up. A dart hit my right shoulder but my cloak, sword belt and mail meant it barely penetrated to my padded undershirt. I reached the wall as Faramir and Erik Red Hair put their shields above me.

While time was of the essence I needed to find a weak spot and I sought the thick strand of ivy which had embedded itself in the mortar. The mortar had been put there by the Romans. I saw the crushed seashells they used and when I pulled the ivy, I was rewarded with not only ivy root but also great chunks of mortar. Some were as thick as my finger. More shields appeared above me and my world darkened. It did not matter for I could feel where I had to dig. I smashed the hammer against the head of the chisel and each blow brought out more of the mortar while it sounded like hailstones as the Saxons dropped stones of increasing size. Once I had done the bottom of the single stone, I began on the sides of the block of masonry. I did not need to make a hole big enough to enter but it had to have a space for the firewood.

It was then that I heard Dreng shout, "Oil! They have oil!"

The boiling oil was dropped onto the shields. I heard Erik cry out as his arm was burned by a splash of boiling oil, but he was a warrior and he endured it. The shields had absorbed most of the damage, but it was a warning for me to hurry. When the last piece of mortar was removed,

I said, "I am about to pull out the stone. Be ready with the fire and the kindling. We will have to drop back into the ditch so watch the stakes."

They chorused, "Aye, Oathsword!" It seemed I had a new name, amongst these warriors, at least. I saw a crack in the stone I was about to pull, and I took a chance. Placing the chisel end in the crack I gave an almighty swing and not only did the stone crack a little more but a piece the size of my hand fell. It meant I had something to grab and I pulled. The stone came away and I hurled it into the ditch. I saw that the palisade had been embedded in the stone and I could see another stone on the far side. That stone would face the inside of the burh.

"Kindling and fire!"

Even as the kindling was ignited, we were slipping down the slope and my foot was arrested by the stone I had removed. The Saxons had helped us with the oil as most of the oil was impregnated in the wood of the palisade and with a whoosh, a wall of flame leapt into the air. I heard the screams as those who were above us were either burned or jumped out of the way. Shielding my eyes from the brightness I saw that while we had not yet made the fighting platform the rest of our men were duelling with the defenders but in front of us there were no defenders. The fire had taken hold and driven them away.

Turning I cupped my hands and shouted, "Bergil, send axes!"

"Aye Saxon Sword!"

My small band were, largely, whole. Eidel and Erik had wounds, but they could still fight, "When the axes come, we will climb again. We will take the wall to the left of the fire. It will be hot work but the wood will be all the weaker. Shall we be the first in Exeter's walls?"

They roared, "Aye, Oathsword!"

I was tempted to draw the magical weapon but then it came to me, I might still need my hammer and chisel! Gandálfr brought the first axe and three boys brought the others. Gandálfr grinned, "I am a better axeman than an archer."

We ascended the slope. The smoke and the flames made it a much easier journey the second time and as the four with axes hacked at the wall closest to the flames, I found another ivy-covered stone. I had a better idea of what to do this time and I found the crack before all the mortar was removed. As I pulled it out, I heard a creak from above.

"Gandálfr, fetch your axe!" I pointed to the base of the wooden palisade and the stone. "Strike the wood and then see if you can push out the stone." I laid down my hammer and chisel as I stepped back and the young warrior, in three blows, smashed through the wooden stake. The other wood was weakened already and there was an alarming crack. I heard a scream as a defender fell to his death and then as the internal stone was removed the air rushed in and fanned the flames. The wall of fire seemed to spread quicker than a cloud could move. I saw some of our warriors begin to descend the ladders before the inferno engulfed them too.

Our other axes had made a gap and the wind took the flames to one side. I saw that there was almost a gap and drawing my two swords, climbed to the top of the bank and putting my shoulder to the weakened and blackened wood smashed my way into the burh! I felt the heat and my beard and hair were singed but as I stepped into the burh, I heard the screams and shouts of shock. Four Saxons ran at me. None were mailed but each had a sword and a small round shield. I did that which they did not expect, I ran at them and used both swords at the same time. While Oathsword found a bare neck my other sword deflected a blade that was aimed at me. I felt a Saxon sword smash across my back as I passed the first two surprised defenders. My shield and mail did their job and I heard a scream from one as Gandálfr's axe ended his life. I blocked another sword and rammed the sharpened tip of Oathsword up under the jaw of the Saxon.

I had been foolish enough and taken all the risks necessary, "Shields!" I had trained the young men and they formed a shield wall on me. Behind me, I heard Bergil the Brawny ordering the charge as he led the rest of our men through the gap we had created. Their walls were breached, the wolves were in the sheepfold and the end was inevitable. This was a strong burh with a good garrison strengthened with Normans under the command of Count Hugh, the Frenchman but they had expected their walls to do what they had done the last time we had come and keep us at bay. They had thought to make us bleed upon them until the nearest two burhs, Bridport and Lydport could send warriors to their aid. They had failed.

Jarl Sweyn joined us and he was beaming, "Well done my foster son. The new blood of Agerhøne is strong! Now let us advance through the burh to the other gate. King Sweyn will be anxious to take the riches of this place." He waved his sword to Gandálfr and the others, "This is work for mailed men. Take what treasures you can and secure this wall."

I could see that they were disappointed and wished to come with us, but they obeyed, "Aye, jarl." Raising their weapons they saluted me, "Oathsword!"

As they trooped off Sweyn One Eye said, "Another name! You are like our clan and hard to pin down!"

We formed a wedge and headed down through the straight streets of Exeter. Designed to allow warriors to rush from one part of the burh to another, they were now a dagger to the heart of the stronghold. We had moved just fifty paces when Count Hugh and his forty Normans came to face us. We outnumbered them for Lodvir and his men had joined ours, but they were a formidable foe for they were alike enough to us to make the outcome questionable. Like us they had byrnies, but they all wore the helmet with a nasal, ours were less uniform. Some of the Normans had spears but most had swords or axes. They made a shield wall and both bands of warriors advanced towards each other. We headed for the Norman Count who had scale armour and a domed helmet. His shield was that of a horseman and covered his left side. There was not enough room for a heavy charge, and we met at a fast walk. I had no shield and the Norman who faced me thought to take advantage and he rammed his shield towards my face in an effort to distract me while he brought his sword from on high. I fooled him by ignoring the shield and while my second sword blocked his swinging sword, Oathsword darted out to slide into his left orb. Such a wound makes a man scream, not because he is less of a man but simply because of the pain. It was curtailed when Oathsword came out of the back of his skull showering the next Norman with blood, bone and brains. The shield did not hurt me for by the time it struck the strength had gone from the blow.

  The street was only wide enough for twenty odd men and there was a huge press as men sought to bring a weapon to bear when there was no room to swing. Warriors used heads and helmets to butt and knees to drive up under byrnies into unprotected groins. Even so, it might have been a bloody stalemate had not Jarl Svein Hákonarson brought his warband to attack the side and rear of the Normans through the street which ran east to west. With Vikings on two sides, the Normans died. None asked for quarter and all died well but died they did. Count Hugh lasted just four strokes longer than the man I had first slain, his lieutenant. It was after noon by the time the last defender was slain for some hid in houses to try to ambush us as we cleared them. It ensured that none were left alive and, the next day, when the treasury, churches and granaries had been emptied and the dead stripped of everything of value, we burned the town to the ground. By the following morning, there was no sign that there had ever been a burh at Exeter for the only remains were the foundations of the old Roman fort and Karl Three Fingers was satisfied.

Chapter 9

The king left us to mop up the villages and towns within twenty miles of the ruined burh. We loaded our drekar first and then the king took his warriors to rob the abbeys, monasteries, and nunneries which the burh had protected. His Christianity was conveniently forgotten! The best slaves had already been taken and so we just took animals. The ram I had chosen the last time had proved to be popular with farmers and we found another one to take home. We also gathered eight ewes. If we had to then we could use them for food but, in a perfect world, they would be added to our flocks. We spent three weeks taking all that there was to take and then King Sweyn ordered the fleet back to Wiht. The army would not board the ships, instead, we would march east, plundering as we went. Raiding parties had headed as far west as Om Walum and we had many ponies and horses. Those who had been wounded or considered too old were sent on the ships to join the warriors who guarded what would become our camp. As we said, when we were told, this was a bold move. From Exeter to Wintan-ceastre was more than a hundred miles. There were at least five large burghs between us and the capital of Wessex. The Saxons would have time and opportunity to gather a huge army to face us. We had not lost as many men in the taking of Exeter, but we had lost men and with those now aboard the ships heading to Wiht we were a pared-down army, but everyone seemed confident. I knew why. The enemy had a weak king.

The fleet sailed but we stayed in camp for the last feast. The fleet's movement would confuse the Saxons. Had we left? We had devastated the land close to Exeter and not a Saxon remained there who was alive. It was different at the mouth of the Exe and the Teign. Word would be sent to the east and the king that the Viking ships had left.

King Sweyn was in an ebullient mood when he addressed us. I knew that there were some Saxon advisers. I later discovered these had served his brother-in-law, Pallig and defected to King Sweyn after the massacre. They brought detailed knowledge not only of the land but the men who might face us.

"Warriors, you may wonder why I have sent our wave stallions to Wiht; I will tell you. We will ride stallions ourselves, albeit the four-legged kind and we shall head east. We will take all in our path. The nunnery at Wilton is but newly built and filled with treasure and that shall be ours. Sarum has a fine cathedral and is a rich city. That too will fall. Now I know that some of you will wonder what the Saxons will be doing while we are relieving them of their treasure. The answer is simple; they will gather every warrior that they can and face us in the field. They will outnumber us but as Karl Three Fingers will tell you that does not guarantee that they will win. The men who face us will be led by Eorledman Aelric and a more spineless creature does not exist. If he does face us then I fear him not and would happily send Cnut and Harald, young though they are to do battle with him!"

That brought laughter and cheers. The two boys were popular for neither had shirked in the assault.

The king revelled in the cheers and went on, "And what of the driveller, King Aethelred? I have it on good authority that he will squat like a toad behind Lundenwic's walls where the rabble there will support him." He shook his head, "He can squat all he likes. Sven Saxon Sword has shown us that a burh can be taken by brave men who are resourceful and well-led!" That brought a cheer louder than the earlier one and the ghost of a frown flickered over the king's face. He dismissed the thought with another smile and more bravado. Tomorrow we head east and take Yeovil. We will be swift and strike so quickly that they will have no idea where we will strike next. I want our path to Wintan-ceastre marked with the bodies of Saxon warriors and the burned and blackened remains of their towns. This king thought to kill our people. He will now pay the price!" The smile returned as the greatest cheer thus far rent the air.

We left in the middle of the night aided, ironically, by the Saxon herepath which had been designed to move the Saxon army quickly around. Yeovil was not a burh and our ponies and horses took us there to arrive a couple of hours after dawn. We had not raided as far east as this and the word must have spread that the Viking fleet had gone. The gates of the town walls were open, and we were inside them before they even had time to react to the warband which materialised with the sun. Perhaps they had not expected us to ride. They fled leaving all behind. Those who were at the fore, Karl Three Finger's men, had warriors to fight but by the time the rest of us reached the town, there were no more to fight. We took everything that there was to be had. We had taken the town so quickly that we even captured more horses and for the next week King Sweyn ravaged and raided the land which lay close to the town. With many ponies and horses that was a distance of fifteen to twenty miles. We lost not a man and took so much treasure that I wondered how we would be able to carry it to our ships waiting along the coast for us.

Cnut showed his hard side as we raided the small town of Glestingaburg. There was a hill with a tower, but our attack was so swift that the Jarl and ten of his best warriors reached it and took it before it could be manned. We burned it and then headed back to the town where the rest of our warband was busily taking all that there was to take. When I let families go, some of them with youths of fourteen or so, he questioned my judgement. "Sven Saxon Sword, they will become warriors one day. Why not kill them now and then there will be fewer enemies in the future?"

I did not tell him of the promise I had made Mary, but I tried to give him a reason which, I hoped, might appeal to his Christianity, although I was coming to realise that his family's adherence to the White Christ was merely a way of gaining credibility, "You could be right but think on this. They might not. They might become merchants, farmers or priests. They bring us more profit and if the ones I spare do become warriors, do you think they will have any confidence when they face us again? They will be more likely to run. Do not be so eager to spill blood for there is a time and place for such things."

I was not convinced that he believed my arguments, but I felt honour bound to make him as good a man as I could.

We heard, perhaps through spies once more, that the Saxons, under Aelric were heading for us and that they had an army which outnumbered ours. We headed east to meet them. We would not fight from horseback but the army which would meet them would not be as tired as they were for we had ridden whilst they had marched. We tethered our animals and left some men and the boys to guard the treasure we had taken. Of course, every warrior had a purse on his belt, hidden beneath, if he wore it, his mail. That way none would leave a war poorer. If we were alive when we stopped fighting, we would have coins! The two exceptions were Harald and his brother Cnut. We faced the Saxons over open fields and, as usual, the Saxons spent some hours exhorting their God to smite us. When darkness fell, they had still to attack. Many of us wanted to initiate a night attack but King Forkbeard assured us that it would not be necessary and, sure enough, by noon the next day the army had headed east, unwilling to fight us. Cnut was particularly disappointed and he had envisaged a real battle with shield walls and heroic deeds.

We rode quickly to Wilton where we surprised the nuns at the nunnery. It was indeed rich as was the village which had grown around it. The nuns were made thralls and both the dwellings and the nunnery were burned to the ground. Such was the speed of our attack that Sarum, which had an old ring defence and earthworks was simply abandoned and the people there fled to Winchester. We burned the town after taking all that there was to take. To Cnut's great disappointment that was our last action and we headed back to our fleet. The reason was simple, we could not carry any more. Our ships would be heavily laden on the way home. There would be no half-empty vessels. We marched south without any hindrance whatsoever. I believe we could have stayed there and spent the winter feeding from our enemies. I did not want to and I for one was glad when the fleet set sail at the end of a very successful campaign season to head back to Denmark. King Aethelred had been taught a lesson and King Sweyn now knew that we had the beating of the Saxons.

The voyage home was as slow as ever. Laden ships whose decks were covered in animals and thralls meant that we could use fewer rowers and were more reliant on the wind. The winds were usually in our favour at that time of the year and had been one of the reasons for our return. As hearth weru, we were spared any rowing and the rest of the crew kept men at the oars during the daylight hours, and once King Sweyn had left us to head north, at night too. We landed at Ribe and that was because we had sprung a strake. *'Sea Serpent'* was old, the oldest in our fleet and we would not take her to war again. We left her at Bolli's shipyard, and we walked back to Agerhøne. A few of the younger warriors and ship's boys ran the whole way to warn the town that we were coming. We had been a village but now we were a town.

The wailing thralls and the awkwardly minded animals slowed us, and it was almost dark by the time we reached our home. The thralls were put in the thrall hall without food as a punishment for the noise they had made. I just went directly to my hall. Gandálfr and Faramir happily carried my chest of treasure. They each had a suit of mail taken from the dead Saxons and Normans. They were grateful to me and, had I been able, would have happily been my oathsworn. A hearth weru cannot have oathsworn.

I think Cnut was a little unhappy that he would be in the jarl's hall once more. He still saw me, of course, but that was just on the days when I helped to train the young warriors. Cnut felt he owed me his life. Just the two of us and Hawk knew of the incident for I had not been loose with my tongue. The secret nature of the event seemed to draw us closer together. We had certainly been closer on the way back across, first Wessex and then the sea, than he had with my cousins. I was impressed with the way he dealt with it. I knew, from our conversations that he was more than happy to learn how to be a leader and Sweyn Skull Taker was a better model than his father. Cnut had seen how Sweyn had taken the time to speak to all his crew, as well as each of his captains. In contrast, the king spoke only to people to give them orders. His speech to inspire us had been a rarity. Cnut would learn while he was at Agerhøne, but he missed my friendship. For my part I was also learning; I was discovering what it was to deal with the young. I had not had younger siblings and my brothers had not had time to become fathers. Cnut was a chance for me to prepare for the time Gunhild and Steana became children and not babes.

The two had changed in the months I had been away. Gunhild could now toddle and her babbling took the form of words. She spoke both Danish and Saxon, but her Saxon was better. That was Anna's influence. I knew it would be the same with Steana and I determined to make his Danish at least as good as his Saxon. I would remedy the bias shown by his mother and his nurse. Mary was just pleased to have me home, although she had been kept busy. Frida had given birth to a son and he had been named Aksel. It was a good choice and Hawk, who had been born Alf, was happy with the name. His wife had not enjoyed an easy birth and she rarely left the hall. Agnetha would care for her but there would be no second child for Hawk for some time. It delayed the departure of Hawk for Ribe.

Mary and I had some time alone for Anna had taken the children to bed where she would tell them stories. I suspect they were stories from the Bible, for she and Mary often spoke of the stories they had been told, but I did not mind. Stories were stories and when they were old enough, they would hear Sweyn's sagas.

"Poor Frida showed me that I have been blessed and a little lucky. We should try for a third child while I am still healthy."

That pleased me and I squeezed my wife's hand, "We shall be home for the winter again and I think that many warriors will be doing as I do."

"Yet, husband, the land which the younger warriors wish is not there. Gandálfr, who married not long before you left, and his wife have to live on his father's farm. It is not large and there is no privacy. Bertha, his wife is with child and she worries that when it is born, next month, then there may be problems with her husband's mother."

I knew that there was something behind her words but, as usual, discovering what they were was too hard a task for me, "And what is it that you wish, my love? Speak plainly."

She smiled, "We have a thrall hall which is now almost empty. Gandálfr and Bertha could live there. Now that Egbert is a freeman and has his own home there is no one to supervise the thralls. I fear that without supervision they may get up to mischief."

I could not see a problem with that so long as Gandálfr was happy about it. When I spoke to him the next day, I saw that my wife had already mentioned the idea to Bertha for Gandálfr eagerly accepted my offer. He took on the role of thrall master happily and I knew that there would be no mischief. It proved to be the start of a new way of life, for the young warriors I had trained envied Gandálfr and his wife. While some who married had fathers whose land was large enough for them to have some portion of it, others did not and, as they married, they asked my permission to live in the thrall hall. I acceded, of course, for my wife was kind.

Winter was approaching and we all knew that King Sweyn would return to the rich land which had yielded so much treasure that his warriors were finding it hard to spend. Some foolish warriors chose to have helmets inlaid with silver and gold. A nonsense as it added little to the strength of the helmet and yet attracted an enemy. I knew that from the herkumbl. Although there was not a great deal of gold when we had fought the Normans at Exeter, I had seen warriors' eyes widen when they spied it. For us, it was a badge of honour and not a measure of our wealth. We spent our coins more wisely and we went to Ribe to order a new drekar. It would be named *'Sea Serpent'* for by the time it was launched we would have buried, with dignity, our old drekar. We had coins to spend and so it would be larger, nineteen oars a side and as we wanted it quickly, we paid Bolli to employ more men. There were more men in Ribe seeking work for the town had now blossomed, as had Agerhøne. It was not just Aksel the Swede who had made his home there. Many Norse merchants had come and there were even some Northumbrians who had seen the potential for profit.

Lodvir surprised us all by taking a wife. She was the widow of a sea captain whose ship had failed to return from a winter crossing to Norway. They had begun to become friends before we had raided, and the absence had thrown themselves into each other's beds. He was to be a father and the hall now had a woman's touch. The Norns had been spinning but I was pleased for Lodvir deserved a family. That he would find it strange amused me. I visited Ribe often either on the business of the jarl or on Mary's and I saw him more frequently than I had. It was good for I missed the warrior who had made me the man I was. When Hawk became hersir then Lodvir would live in the hall he had built with his own profits.

Our new table had been delivered and I was instructed by my wife to order two similarly carved chairs for us two. Another expense but I could afford it. I was also asked to buy fine cloths and fabrics for she wished to sew a tapestry to hang on the walls. I knew it would have a Christian theme but that mattered not for there was increasing pressure from King Sweyn and his wife to convert to Christianity. It was not yet a command and I found it hard to reconcile with the way we had enslaved nuns and destroyed churches. It was a political gesture and, in the eyes of our king, made us, he thought, less barbaric. I knew the Saxons did not agree with that!

Our clan was growing. When my father and his crew had been killed, all those years ago, then we had shrunk but the dead men had left children at home and now that crop had ripened. With the influx of settlers, we would be able to crew the three Agerhøne drekar easily as well as supplying more men for the Ribe boats. We buried **'Sea Serpent'** on the spring equinox when her replacement arrived. We had taken the mast, oars and steering board from her. We used fishing boats to tow her out to the end of the harbour for she would be used to make a breakwater. Even in death, the drekar would serve us. She was filled with rocks and her gunwales were barely above water. The jarl and the hearth weru, along with Thorstein were the crew who went with her on her final voyage. We had with us a large fowl for the jarl would make a blót to ensure a safe journey for the drekar. When it was in position we made the sacrifice and Thorstein and Sven Skull Taker said farewell. We left the drekar and then the fishing boats loaded more sacks of rocks and pebbles on top of her decks so that the drekar sank ever lower until, suddenly, with a flash of bubbles both sides slipped beneath the waves and she went to the bottom. The water was not deep, and we could still see her. The blót had been a good one and gradually the sea would reclaim her. Worms would eat the wood and creatures would move into the rocks to make a home. Sands would pile up on the seaward side and as we added more stones, each year, so, eventually, a stone breakwater would appear. I did not know if I would be there to see it but I hoped my children would and I would tell them of what we did. The story was every bit as valuable as Noah and his Ark or Jonah and the Whale.

We then had two weeks in which to fit out the new drekar and give her sea trials. It was preparation for my family. Soon I would be away again. The island to the west was still a happy hunting ground for us. As men had died or suffered wounds which meant they could no longer go to war so the newer warriors moved up the drekar, closer to the steering board. It was seen as a place of honour. The new drekar could accommodate more men and so the first day of the sea trials was spent in the harbour with Thorstein balancing the weight of the warriors with their experience. Cnut was older too, indeed had he been one of the clan then he might already occupy the oar closest to the prow for he was now almost a man and shaving. Thorstein used him to race up and down the centre to move men until just after the sun had passed its zenith he was ready for us to row out of the harbour. He would not risk the sail on the first day. The ship's boys would not have to scurry up sheets and risk life and limb on the new yard. Instead, he took the drekar through its paces. It was good for the new warriors to have a much easier time than they might have had if this had been a raid. By the end of the afternoon, he was satisfied. The next day would see us sail to Ribe and return. That day would see the sail unfurled and the oars would be pushed to the limit. We would not have shields and so we were all in for a wetter time! The sail had been made by Agnetha and the women of the clan. The volvas had woven spells that they had sewn into the design. It was a coiled sea serpent, and the red eyes were two spells which the volvas had spent many hours spinning. Their hair was incorporated so that when we were at sea they would be there with us. Mary, of course, had had nothing to do with the pagan ritual. She was not the only Christian, but she was the most prominent. The volvas and the other women accepted that for they knew that her heart was in the clan.

I wore my cape as we took the new drekar to sea. Both the wind and the waves would give us a better test than had we sailed the previous day. We would be close to the coast but there would be troughs and swells. The wind would be with us when we sailed north and against us south. It was as though the Allfather had arranged it for we were able to line the gunwale and see the sea as it flicked from our hull. The wind made us fly and it was exciting to be the first warriors on a new drekar. I felt honoured and wondered at those who had first done the same with the original **'Sea Serpent'**. Were they watching from Valhalla?

I was at the steering board with the jarl, Thorstein and Cnut, "She is well made, Jarl Sweyn. Let us see how she turns eh?" We were a mile out of the harbour, and, as we had already passed the nearest island, with open water before us, he pushed the steering board to larboard. We seemed to spin and the phrase wave stallion came to mind. It was like a good horse that responded to a rider's heels. Some of the warriors were almost caught out by the move and I heard laughter as they were hauled back aboard. It was a warning that we were aboard a ship and a warship at that. She was more like a sea creature. The waddling knarrs were safer, and slower, while we were on a dangerous creature. Handled badly then disaster could ensue.

Lodvir had seen our approach and he awaited us on the quay, "A fine drekar, I envy you. Bolli makes good ships but he told me that he was lucky to find a single tree to make the keel. It is a good sign."

"Aye, and when we return to Agerhøne this afternoon we shall see what we can do with oars. The crew did well yesterday, and I hope that this morning has shown them what we can do."

It went better than we could possibly have hoped and although the new warriors had red hands at the end none wished to go ashore. It was as though we were all desperate to go raiding just so that we could see what our drekar could do on the open ocean! We knew that we would be raiding and so, after the sea trials Jarl Sweyn asked for the crew to give another afternoon to train for war. We hearth weru had trained young warriors but it had been some time since we had trained as a clan. With a larger and newer crew, it would be needed and so we practised. For Cnut, this was something new. He had seen his father's warriors, but they had just practised their fighting skills and not their fighting formation.

We used the shield wall first as that was the most basic of our formations and the one we used the most. Using four boys to stand in for us Sweyn and I chivvied and pushed the newer warriors into position. We were training and so we did not wear mail but we knew which warriors owned mail and our front rank was determined by those men. We had some younger warriors who also had mail and we put the biggest of those behind the boys who represented us. The last rank was given the most attention of all. We alternated those who had been to war with those who had not. Once Jarl Sweyn was happy with the formation we showed the newer ones how to press their shields into the backs of those before them. Then the boys left, and we took our place.

We used our clan chant to get the beat. Every warrior knew it having heard it from when they were boys.

> ***We are the bird you cannot find***
> ***With feathers grey and black behind***
> ***Seek us if you can my friend***
> ***Our clan will beat you in the end.***
> ***Where is the bird? In the snake.***
> ***The serpent comes your gold to take.***
> ***We are the bird you cannot find***
> ***With feathers grey and black behind***
> ***Seek us if you can my friend***
> ***Our clan will beat you in the end.***
> ***Where is the bird? In the snake.***
> ***The serpent comes your gold to take.***

Marching with spears held over shields was a hard skill but after half an hour we had managed it. It was then that Jarl Sweyn revealed a new formation. I had expected us to go into a wedge, but Sweyn Skull Taker realised that we had more men and, more importantly, men who had fought in a sea battle as well as two major battles against Saxons. We used the Boar's Snout formation and, although I did not know it before I learned that I was to be moved from the jarl's right shoulder.

The jarl addressed us all but looked at me, "We will use two wedges. I will lead one and the warrior you all call Oathsword, Sven Saxon Sword, will lead the other." Every eye turned to me. "Cnut, you shall be me. Stand here and Hawk, stand where Sven usually stands." The warriors who were usually placed behind us were split up. Once there were ten men in the wedge, four at the back, three in front of them, Sweyn One Eye and Hawk behind Cnut, then the jarl placed a rank of men behind them. Four overlapped them. He addressed us all. "I will put the other ranks in place when we have made our second rank. Come, foster son." He took me, eight warriors from the first wedge and placed me parallel to Cnut who looked quite interested in what was going on. "Leif and Lars, you have fought with Sven since his first battle. Stand behind him." That was comforting for one or the other had always been behind me. "Gandálfr, Faramir and Dreng, you have also fought with Sven. Stand behind the brothers. The last four were also from the men I had led at Exeter. Jarl Sweyn was clever and knew that the fire we had created that day was not just a literal fire. There was a fire burned in our hearts as shield brothers and he was using it.

Replacing Cnut, he had the king's son and the other boys to act as an enemy. With shortened ranks behind us, we began to march.

We are the bird you cannot find
With feathers grey and black behind
Seek us if you can my friend
Our clan will beat you in the end.
Where is the bird? In the snake.
The serpent comes your gold to take.
We are the bird you cannot find
With feathers grey and black behind
Seek us if you can my friend
Our clan will beat you in the end.
Where is the bird? In the snake.
The serpent comes your gold to take.

It was harder than when we had marched as a shield wall for I had to keep pace with the jarl and my cousins. However, the advantage of the two wedges, the boar's tusks, was clear. As we neared Cnut and the boys, I saw that we would penetrate an enemy line first. With two such wedges, we would tear great holes in an enemy shield wall and when our line moved up, we would be able to punch a wide hole in an enemy line. We stopped when darkness descended. We had not had a perfect practice, some men had fallen but the novelty meant that every warrior was buzzing as he spoke to his shield brother on the way back to the town.

I went back with the jarl, the hearth weru and Cnut. "Jarl, I am pleased with the honour, but it puts you at greater risk for you now have just two hearth weru."

"I saw, at Exeter, that you, my foster son are also a leader. Men followed you and Oathsword. That is too powerful a weapon to keep just for my protection. I know that this puts you at greater risk but both Lodvir and Griotard agree with me. We have spoken of you and your skill. You were chosen to find the sword and since it has come to the clan we have seen nothing but victory, treasure, glory and growth! You are still and will always be, hearth weru, but now you will draw those enemies who would come to me, to you. It is I who will be grateful to you. Perhaps this will give Mary cause to curse me, I know not but I believe that Oathsword will protect you and, as the whole clan knows, you are now the best warrior."

We had reached his hall and I had to make my way back to my own hall, "Me?"

Sweyn One Eye laughed, "Cousin, in the last battles we have fought the first enemy to be killed by the clan was struck by you. At Dean, it was your movement forward that broke the Saxons. Do not be unduly modest. I know that with my one eye I can never be the warrior you are but even with two eyes I doubt that I would have the natural killing skills which you have."

Hawk nodded, "My brother is right. There was a time, before Svolder when I was jealous of you but now I see that you cannot be jealous when the choice was made by others. You did not choose this path, Sven, the Allfather, the Norns," he shrugged, "some higher power made the sword come to you and at that moment you changed. In your heart, you know it. I would not be you for you have been noticed and you could become a plaything of the gods and the Norns. I am happy just to watch my father's back. I have had my single moment of glory and I would not change it. For you, your life will become a series of such events."

With those wise words from Hawk, I headed home. There would be little point in explaining to Mary this new formation and the danger it would bring. She would not understand my words and all that it would do would be to increase her fear. Instead, when I was greeted by my family, I babbled on about the new drekar but inside my mind was a maelstrom!

Chapter 10

Agerhøne 1004

It was spring when we next sailed to war and this time King Sweyn had chosen to raid the Land of the East Angles and the most important city on that coast, Northwic. The city had many Vikings living there as well as Angles and Saxons but they had all chosen to support King Aethelred. They would regret that choice. There were other reasons why the clever Karl Three Fingers had suggested the raid there to the king. It was a shorter voyage; we could simply sail south and west, and the English would have no warning. We had not raided there before, and they would not be expecting us, but the most important reason was its riches. With more than twenty churches and many warehouses, it was a major port on the east coast. Lundenwic and Jorvik each had a long river journey for ships wishing to land their cargoes. Northwic was closer to the coast. Even Jarl Sweyn agreed with the choice. The flat land in the east suited us and meant that there were few burhs. The many rivers afforded opportunities for us to use our drekar for support. The river, Yare, was wide enough for our drekar and we could surprise them by attacking at dawn.

We would be sailing with fewer ships as the Norse would not be with us. They would be raiding Northumbria. Uhtred the Bold ruled Northumbria and had recently defeated the Scots. With their eyes on the north the Norse thought that they could raid Northumbria and weaken it for King Sweyn now, clearly, had his eyes on the crown of what men now termed England.

There was great excitement in Agerhøne as we prepared to meet the fleet, this time off our coast. We had a new ship and many new warriors. Our new formation gave more warriors the chance for glory and, thanks to our successes we had many more mailed men than most other clans. The bird after which the clan was named might not have fine plumage but we did. Gunhild was now old enough to know that her father was leaving, and she wept. It touched me. Steana was too young to know too much but I knew that there would come a time when he wished to sail with me and that would, in turn, bring tears from Mary.

Lodvir brought the ships from Ribe and the ten drekar in our fleet waited close to the port for King Sweyn and the sixty ships he would be bringing. While we waited Lodvir told us what he had learned from Aksel. Hawk's father-in-law traded with not only Frankia and the

Empire but also England. He knew the leaders and gave us information about their defences. We had no need to worry about his tongue being loose as he knew he would benefit from our success and he ensured that none of his ships would be anywhere near the east coast while we attacked!

"Ulfcetel Snilling, some men call him the Bold, is the local lord and while not an eorledman we have heard that he is a good leader and he will not develop a sudden sickness as did Aelric. This man will fight. It is said he is descended from the Saxon hero, Byrhtnoth, who fell at the Battle of Maldon. Whatever the truth of his heritage, he is not to be underestimated. So long as Karl advises the king then all should be well."

We had become used to weak Saxons and I wondered if this might be a stiffer test of our new warriors. Cnut felt himself to be one of those new warriors. When Karl had come to tell us of our raid he had brought a byrnie and helmet for Cnut. He had grown over the winter and broadened out. The training had made him stronger and he had skills. None of us wanted him to be in the front rank of a shield wall but he could now defend himself and use a spear and a shield. I was curious how he would be used but that was as far as it went. With my new responsibilities, should we use the Boar's Snout formation, I could not afford to be distracted by worrying about the king's son. At least he now knew his way around a drekar and what his function was. He was Thorstein's assistant and he commanded the ship's boys. He did not have to do as they did but he had sailed enough to give commands especially to the four young boys for whom this would be their first raid.

Lodvir had also found a Saxon who worked for Aksel the Swede, Edgar. He knew the river and when the rest of the fleet hove to we passed on the information to Karl Three Fingers. The result was that we would lead the fleet to assault the city. It meant that once we reached the coast of the East Angles then we would follow Lodvir. We had now sailed enough times with King Sweyn and his fleet to be more confident about the way we sailed. We were no longer wary of a drekar suddenly appearing at night to ram into our steerboard. I did not realise, until that voyage, the advantages such confidence gave. It meant that when we were not on watch we were able to sleep soundly rather than with half an ear for the sound of a collision. We made the crossing in four easy days. The new *'Sea Serpent'* had seemed eager to show us what she could do but Thorstein restrained her. The time would come when we would be able to unleash her full potential. We did not need it as we sailed to Northwic.

When we saw, to the west, the smudge that was the coast, we hove to for we had mail to don and a mast to place on the mast fish. We wished to be invisible. In addition, one or two drekar were a little tardy and the sun had yet to set. We would begin to row and head west as the sun dipped towards the horizon and use our oars. Lodvir would lead and we would be close behind. Cnut was given the unenviable task of sitting astride the prow and giving hand signals to avoid us ramming *'Aksel's Gift'*. Once we were ready, we began to row. It would be in silence to avoid alerting the countryside and it would be steady for we did not need speed. We had miles to row and a steady rhythm would help us. Those of us close to the steerboard had a great responsibility for the rest would take their cue from us. We had to keep steady and maintain a regular pace with Lodvir. To that end, the Jarl stood close to us and slapped his thigh to give us the beat. He, in turn, was guided by Cnut. As we rowed through the flatlands and Fens of the land of the East Angles I could not but reflect that we worked well together. The days of Thrond and discord were gone. The entire crew were in harmony, even with the addition of an outsider, like the princeling, Cnut. Thorstein too kept an eye on Cnut as the steering board edged us around the bends in the river. That they were not severe was good. We caught the whiff of both woodsmoke as well as animal and human waste as we ghosted along the River Yare. People in the small settlement at the mouth may have seen us as we sailed along the river but as no church bell had tolled it meant they either had no church or had decided not to risk our wrath. I suspected the latter. Even without sails, our drekar would have been seen as grey shadows on the water. Our guide had told us that there were neither towns nor villages between the mouth of the river and Northwic. That was confirmed as we sailed down a silent river. Only the oars striking the water and hulls as they slid through the Yare made a sound.

This was the time of year when the days were becoming longer than the nights, but not by much, and the first hint of false dawn must have appeared ahead for we were ordered, by Sweyn Skull Taker's slaps, to row a little faster. Lodvir's guide must have recognised that we were close. When Thorstein began to put over the steering board and our jarl instructed us to raise our oars then we knew we had arrived. Our fleet would tie up first and the rest would use us to make a longphort. We would fill the river and our drekar would become a bridge into the heart of Northwic.

A shout from the shore and the sound of a tolling bell let us know that we had been seen. Our ship's boys were fast and we were secured to the wooden quay before we had finished stacking our oars. I did not bother with Saxon Slayer and I slung my shield from my back. I had practised more with two swords and found that I could manage the weapons easily. With a newly acquired pair of seaxes tucked in the top of each seal skin boot, I was confident I could deal with the warriors we found in Northwic. It was not a burh and there would not be a large garrison! The nearest burh was more than a hundred miles to the southwest.

    We three were the first off the drekar and our feet landed on the wood quay before Lodvir's men. Jarl Sweyn Skull Taker took command, "On me!" We needed to clear the drekar so that King Sweyn and his men could cross and follow us. Our job was to secure the wooden gates to the town. We would have a short time to do so as the town watch would be our only opposition. Of course, the tolling bell would rouse the men of the town and they would dress for war. That all took time and we raced towards the gate. The ones who had given the alarm were already racing through it and a few arrows came our way from the fighting platform. I guess that the Saxons were petrified for even as they slammed the gates shut, I heard someone curse as the bar was dropped. The four of us, with men close behind us, ran as fast as we could, and we simply hurled our mailed and metal covered bodies at the gate. We were lucky or perhaps the Saxons were careless and they had not quite locked the bar in place. Our weight burst it asunder and when it cracked open, we almost fell as we stumbled over the watch who had been knocked to the ground. Leaving the five men to be dealt with by those behind we ran towards the sound of the tolling bell. It would be either a church or a tower but, either way, would be the rallying point for the defenders. If we could get there first, then the town would be ours! We did not try to stay together but ran along the stone made streets swinging our weapons at any who looked like they posed a threat. After we had struck six men the rest fled before us. At our backs came the rest of the crew and, as I glanced round, I saw that Cnut was flanked by Faramir and Gandálfr. I had not asked them to do so but they knew it was the right thing to do.

    The bell was tolling from a large church and while the lower part was stone, Roman by the look of it, the upper parts were wooden. Men were forming ranks before it, but they would be too late and without breaking stride, we threw ourselves at them. A spear was jabbed at me but I partly deflected it with the sword in my left hand and the head of the spear scraped along my mail. Had I not worn mail I might have been hurt. Oathsword came down from on high to slice into the neck of the unfortunate Saxon. Our sheer weight had driven us through the thin line of Saxons, and we burst into the door of the church before they were able to close it. Had they done so it would have been of little consequence for we would simply have burned them alive. Their church might be a sanctuary if we were a Christian army but despite the crosses worn by our king, we were still what they deemed to be barbarians.

A priest raised a cross before me and said, "God strike you dead, Viking!"

Hawk shouted, "Kill him!"

I could not do so for Mary would be unhappy. Her father had been a priest. I pulled back Oathsword and smacked it into the cross with such force that it broke his nose and knocked him unconscious. He would have a reminder of this day but he would live. I do not think that Jarl Sweyn relished slaughtering women and children for most of those in the church were not warriors. He roared, "Flee! If you stay, then you die!"

We did not need slaves and their flight would make others run too. We wanted the riches of the city and not its people. They saw the barbarians with bloody swords, and they ran. There were four doors in the church, and they used them all. We had been the first inside the walls and so there was no one in the north part of the town. That was the way that they fled.

"Lodvir, secure the church and its treasure. Agerhøne with me."

It was a clever move on the part of the jarl. He knew that the rougher parts of the city would be close to the river where there was trade. The better homes and the houses of the merchants would be in the north part of the city where it would be quieter. Our pursuit made those who thought about collecting treasure from beneath their floors think twice and just run. By the time we reached the north gate, the sun had risen and, so far as we could tell the only ones left in in the walls of Northwic were Danish. With the gates in our hands, we systematically went through every house to dig up treasure and take the other valuables that they had within their homes. We had a rich haul and by the middle of the day, we had returned to our drekar to store what we had. Bolli had made the ship so that we had two holds to use and it was the forward one we filled with the treasure. The ships of the longphort were largely empty as the warband was busy doing what we had done and looting.

It took two days to empty the town by which time the Saxons had raised an army to face us. They arrived at the south side of the longphort. They outnumbered us but that did not worry us. Their leader was indeed, Ulfcetel Snilling and he looked like a warrior who could handle himself. He had scale armour and a good shield and sword. He took off his masked helmet, a sign that he wished to speak. He came forward with his oathsworn and we went with King Sweyn, Karl Three Fingers and Jarl Sweyn Skull Taker.

"Danes, do we fight, or will you leave?"

King Sweyn smiled, "There is still much to take in this land. England is rich and Denmark is poor."

Ulfcetel the Bold snorted, "I doubt it for you bleed this land dry. We will fight you."

King Sweyn nodded, "And many of your men will die, more than we will lose for my men are mailed and powerful. Yours are farmers with bill hooks. Do you really want your people to be slaughtered?"

Even the oathsworn who faced us were not all mailed in contrast to us who each wore a gleaming mail shirt.

After looking at our numbers the Saxon gave a resigned nod, "Then can we have a truce while we collect gold to pay you to leave?"

With a magnanimous bow, the king said, "Of course. A week?"

"Ten days would be better."

"Ten days then."

As soon as he said it then I knew that King Sweyn had no intention of honouring a truce. Ulfcetel made the mistake of not asking for an oath. King Sweyn purported to be a Christian and had the Saxon asked him to swear an oath on a cross then the breaking of the truce might not have happened. The Saxons left but not without leaving five hundred men camped just half a mile south of the river.

Once we had crossed to the longphort King Sweyn called a council of war. I was there to watch Cnut who stood close to his father. This was, I think, the start of a change in their relationship. He now saw his son as a potential heir. He might not be the one who would become King of Denmark, but he definitely saw him as a potential leader of some sort.

"We have some days to empty and then burn this town. We wait until the wind is blowing from the south to do that. Tomorrow I want Jarl Eirik of Heiða-býr to take the horses we have captured and find another place we might raid. I want the rest of you to raid the land close by and take what food you can. As the Saxons are camped south of the river then it will, perforce, have to be the north side."

Lodvir asked, "And the truce?"

King Sweyn laughed, "Means nothing. If they bring the gold within a couple of days, then I might honour it, but I think that they are simply raising a larger army." In that, he may have been right for the Saxon general did not look afraid of a fight, just afraid of a fight he knew he would lose.

It told us much about our king. As the Saxons were close to the south bank of the river it was decided to move the ships of the King to that bank. That pleased us as it meant we no longer had a bridge over our drekar, and we could use the whole hold. Thorstein would be happier about that for he liked a balanced ship.

We found little food and, from those we found it seemed that the land had a famine. Perhaps God had abandoned the English and the lack of food was a sign. Whatever the reason, we did not enjoy the normal feast we usually did.

Jarl Eirik returned so quickly, within a day and a night, that we knew he had found a target worthy of breaking a truce but it was better news than we expected. "Almost thirty miles south of here, King Sweyn, is Thetford, not only does it have fine churches the king's mint is there. They make all the coins for this part of the world. It would make the treasures taken thus far seem like nothing."

He made an instant decision, "Tomorrow, before dawn and hidden from the Saxon camp, we take the crews of my ships and raid Thetford. Jarl Sweyn Skull Taker you will remain here and I will leave four of my crews to watch my ships. If the wind changes tomorrow, then fire Northwic. It should attract the attention of the Saxons. We will return in three days." He turned to his son, "Would you like to come raiding with us?"

Cnut was much taller these days and whilst not as tall as his father he was closer in height than he had been when the king had sent him to us. He was able to look directly at his father, "Will there be a battle?"

The king looked at Jarl Eirik who shook his head, "There is no wall and we only spied thirty warriors and their thegn."

Cnut shook his head, "Then I will stay here for I have not seen a wooden town burned."

That was not quite true for we had burned Exeter, Wilton and Sarum. It told me that he was making an excuse and wished to stay with us. I wondered how his father would take the rejection. He dismissed it, easily, "Your loss and I doubt that we shall see a battle. This Ulfcetel must be like Aelric and will not have stomach for a fight."

From what I had seen and heard, I thought him wrong. Of course, if the king took the mint and all its coins then that treasure would go to him. He might share some but there was no compulsion for him to do so. Jarl Sweyn was philosophical about the matter, "We were the first in Northwic and we took more than did the king. We are saved a sixty-mile march. We eat well here and the wind, I think is changing. Tonight we might be able to light the fire the king wishes."

We descended once more into the city to see if we had missed anything and Cnut came with me. I noticed that Faramir and Gandálfr also followed. "I was surprised, Cnut, when you did not go with your father. You would gain riches."

He smiled, "When I inherit, I will gain all that belongs to my father, or half at least. Besides, I think that there is more chance of a battle here."

We all stopped for he seemed so confident in his words. "Are you now fey? Do you have the ability to see into the future?" I deliberately avoided using the word Norn and especially not Verðandi, as I did not wish to invoke their enmity.

"No, Sven, but I think that this Saxon will have us watched and if he sees more than two-thirds of our men leaving to head south knowing that they break the truce, then he might break the truce himself and attack us."

There is a phrase my mother had used, *'out of the mouths of babes'*. What Cnut had said made perfect sense. The Saxon camp had five hundred men already in their camp. Ulfcetel the Bold could quickly reinforce them and perhaps the king was right. It could be that the Saxons were raising a better-armed army to fight us. At the very least they could cause mischief to our ships and King Sweyn had conveniently now moored most of them on the south bank of the river. As soon as we returned to Jarl Sweyn I told him what Cnut had said.

He nodded, "That makes sense and explains why the back of my neck is itching. Lodvir, have two ships used to bridge the gap between the drekar in the middle of the river so that we can cross to the other side. Choose drekar we can burn if we have to. When I fire the city take half of our men to reinforce the south bank."

We had something to do and we set about the arson eagerly. By burning the town with the wind now blowing from the south-west it ensured that the north bank would be safe and there would be no places for an enemy to hide. We used every man and boy to light the fires and we worked our way south so that the last place we fired was the wooden wall of the town. As we stood on the quay all that remained were the warehouses and the quay. They would be burned when we left if we left!

The jarl was in control and his mind had already planned the next steps, "Thorstein, I give you command of all the ships. I want the boys and the captains ready to defend these drekar and, if they are threatened to sail them into the middle of the river. We dare not lose these ships or we cannot get home. We would die the richest Danes in England! I will sound my horn five times if you are to abandon us!"

That made Thorstein smile, "Do not worry, Jarl Sweyn, they shall not get their hands on our new drekar."

The fire we had lit made the night day. King Sweyn and Karl Three Fingers might even see the glow in the eastern sky and wonder. If all had gone well, they would have taken the town and the mint by noon. It is in the nature of men who enjoy a victory to celebrate. They would be in the town enjoying the food and ale there but they would have men watching the land. The fire would be seen and King Sweyn would know that his orders had been obeyed.

By the time we were ready Lodvir had secured two drekar so that we had a narrow bridge. It was not a longphort and by the severing of the ropes which attached the two ships then the bridge of boats would be broken. We might lose half the fleet, but we would still have ships we could use to sail home and, more importantly, treasure in our holds.

Lodvir had organised the men who had been left to watch the Saxons and we four, along with Cnut joined him. "Falmr Flame Bearer says that the Saxon camp is quiet. He and his men were about to go to bed when I came."

The jarl nodded and smiled at Falmr, who was an older warrior, "Do as you planned, Falmr, but have your men ready to rise and fight."

"Aye, Jarl Sweyn."

"And us?"

"We too, sleep, Lodvir, but without fires."

Cnut said, "But I might be wrong! I am young and if no one else thinks this…"

My foster father smiled, "I should have thought of this as a possibility and all that you did, Cnut, was open the wind hole in my mind to see it. If we have to endure a cold night sleeping on the ground in mail then so be it but, before you sleep, Cnut, find a good horse. If you are right, then I want you to ride to Thetford and fetch your father and his army for if they do plan mischief then they will bring far more men than we have at our disposal."

"Aye, foster father!" He seemed pleased at the prospect of doing something so noteworthy.

As he went the jarl nodded, "I have hopes for that one. He may change but I see in him a strong man with a sharp mind!"

Although we lay down to sleep, we had four or five men in each group of sleepers watching. It would not matter if they dozed for they would be sitting and you can never have a sound sleep like that.

It was Dreng who shook me awake, "Sven Saxon Sword, we have spied movement towards the Saxon camp."

I stood immediately and listened. Sure enough, there were sounds and although dawn was not far off the sounds were not of men waking and lighting fires. There was the jingle of mail. I roused the jarl and Cnut, "Jarl, the Saxons are coming. Cnut, ride to your father. If they leave as soon as you reach them then we might be saved."

Cnut just nodded and ran to the horse which he had left saddled and tethered. It was thirty miles to Thetford and if he did not spare the horse or himself he could be there not long after dawn. I doubted if the whole army could reach us but even a couple of hundred, force-marched or using the horses and ponies they had taken, might prevent us from being massacred.

We roused the men silently. The movements we had heard did not suggest an imminent attack. That would be improbable anyway. Ulfcetel Snilling would have heard of Sweyn's treachery by noon then he would have had to gather his men and march to the camp. We had time. The fires of the burning city had died but there was a pall of smoke behind us. It would disguise us from the rising sun and slow down the arrival of dawn. If Cnut and the jarl were right then the Saxons might seek to win this war by destroying our ships. To do that they had to approach silently or else we might simply sail downriver.

It was dawn and the sky was a little lighter when we saw the movements of the Saxons. We had not stood to make a shield wall but men crouched, with weapons ready. The only ones the Saxons would see, and they would be solitary shadows, were the sentries they expected to see. We saw the Saxons because we were looking to see them. Our men, and the four crews left by the king, were in a half-circle with each end anchored at the river and the extreme of our drekar. The centre of our line was held by the crew of '***Sea Serpent***'. Even our new warriors were trained so well that the jarl could be confident that they would hold. To our right was Lodvir and his crew. Even if the flanks crumbled then we could fall back to the drekar.

Obligingly the Saxons did not move until dawn had broken. We saw their line as they began to move towards us. We four were standing but the rest still crouched, laid down, or were seated. There were at least two thousand of them. Ulfcetel the Bold had raised the local fyrd and brought more mailed men than when he had first come to the aid of Northwic. I saw the mail of thegns as they led their farmers and townsfolk towards us. We had few archers but the ones we had were here in the centre behind us. There were no slingers for they were on the drekars.

"Archers, be ready!" We watched the Saxons move forward steadily and already I was impressed by this Ulfcetel. He had not indulged in the normal practice we had seen before. There had been no ceremony exhorting God to strike us down. His men advanced behind a wall of shields and spears. There were not as many mailed men as we had seen at Dean but there were enough to stiffen the Saxon line. The jarl waited until they were two hundred paces from us and then shouted, "Rise! Shield wall! Hawk, the horn!"

As every man rose and we faced the Saxons with our shields and spears, five clear notes rang out. Thorstein knew his business and the captains and boys would have been ready but what they were about to do took time and we would have to buy them that time. The payment would be dead warriors. He would have to untie the drekars from their moorings on both sides and then move them so that they were in a long double line in the centre of the river. They would have to be far enough from the banks to prevent the Saxons from getting close to them and they would need to be anchored. They would give us support if we found our backs to the river but I hoped it would not come to that.

As soon as the horn sounded the Saxons stopped and looked at the Danes who had risen like wraiths from the ground. As they were in range the jarl shouted, "Archers, loose!"

There were just a hundred arrows and some struck mail, helmets, and shields but many were hit because they were not expecting it. I heard an order shouted and a wall of shields covering both the front and top of the Saxons appeared. The next shower of arrows merely rattled off wood! They began to advance but it was a slow march for these were the fyrd. The seasoned warriors, the thegns and housecarls, could move faster but these were farmers and villeins who were unused to marching in time to their neighbours. All this suited us for it gave more time for Thorstein to save the ships and increased the likelihood that Cnut would find his father and bring reinforcements.

"Lock shields!" I was not next to the jarl for I was with Leif and Lars in case we had the chance for a Boar's Snout formation. It felt strange to be going to war without my family close by. This would be the first time since that raid in Wessex when I had found Oathsword. *Wyrd*!

The men around me pressed close to my side and my back. Lars said, "Do not worry, Sven Saxon Sword, we shall not let you down. The Oathsword will not be lost while one of us lives. We swore an oath."

I glanced at his brother who nodded. When had they made this oath? Leif held up his right hand and I saw the fresh scar along his palm. They had sworn a blood oath and recently. It made me more determined than ever that they would survive.

I shouted, "We will all live! These are Saxon farmers we face, and we are the warriors of Agerhøne. We will teach these easterners the lesson those in the west learned to their cost, that we are the best of the best!"

It was the right thing to say and the men around me all cheered and shouted, "Oathsword!"

With the Jarl to my left, a few warriors away, and Lodvir the same number to the right I knew that I would be as safe as any Danish warrior, but this was no Aelric who came towards us and Ulfcetel the Bold was living up to his name!

I know not if it was planned but the men who faced us were not led personally by Ulfcetel. He attacked our line to the right of Lodvir. A thegn led his people towards me. I commanded the men around me and I shouted, "Thrust!" I knew the importance of all our spears striking at once. The thegn apart our spears were all a foot longer than the Saxons and I could see that our shields were better too. Our spears smashed into the Saxons. Some of our spears deflected theirs while the ones which came at us were either blocked by our shields or mail. The thegn's thrust was a good one. We both hit the other at the same time. The only difference that I could tell between the weapons was that Saxon Slayer had a narrower tip and while his broad head hurt when it struck my byrnie, Saxon Slayer burst first one and then another six mail links on his. I pushed harder and the broader part of my spear enlarged the hole and then found flesh. I twisted the head to aggravate the wound and was rewarded with a spurt of blood. We both withdrew our weapons. Gandálfr and Snorri were behind us and their spears had darted out too. As the Saxon line was pressed close to ours by the mass of men behind them so those two spears found flesh. Gandálfr's drove through the cheek of the thegn while Snorri's found the eye of the oathsworn next to him. The thegn was hurt but I could not bring another weapon to bear for we were too close together. I used the only weapons I had, my head and my knee. I pulled back my head and butted the thegn. He had a nasal on his helmet, but it mattered not for I still managed to break his nose. At the same time, I drove my knee up hard between his legs. He could not control his actions and his head jerked forward which allowed me to ram the edge of my shield under his chin. The combination of blows rendered him unconscious and it was only the press of men which held him there. I took the opportunity, as the weight of his mail dragged his body down, to turn Saxon Slayer. I had enough space to drive the spearhead into his throat as he lay at my feet.

I quickly turned the head up and before the man behind could react, I stabbed upwards with Saxon Slayer. It found flesh beneath his jaw and the spearhead entered his skull. As he was dying his hands grabbed the haft of the spear and locked on. A Saxon sword hacked down at the same time and bit into the ash of the spear. I let go for I knew I could not rely upon the weapon. Drawing Oathsword I could not resist saying its name, "Oathsword!"

The name acted like a spur and with a roar and a cheer the men I led stabbed and stepped forward. Thanks to Snorri's thrust and the warrior wounded by Lars we had space and we moved up to stab at those who were without mail. They were also not warrior trained and we were. Oathsword slashed across the neck of the first Saxon and gave him a quick and merciful death. The spears of those around me were still whole and they either found flesh or forced back the fyrd who faced us. We were becoming, almost unconsciously, the Boar's Snout.

Lodvir shouted a word of warning, "Sven, do not advance! The Saxons are close to our right flank. You will be surrounded."

Was this to be like the Battle of Dean again? We were winning but others were not. I nodded and shouted, "Agerhøne, hold. Let us make these East Angles bleed!"

The Saxons might not have understood my words, but they recognised our action and that we had stopped. They hurled themselves at us. It was futile for their weapons were not good enough to penetrate the mail we wore and our shields were all superior to theirs. When Oathsword smashed down on the shield which was made of boards nailed together I broke the shield and his arm. When I punched him in the face with my metal boss he fell to the ground where his fellows trampled him to death. In their eagerness to get at me they struck blindly and with spears protruding from behind me and Oathsword darting like the tongue of a snake they either died or were so badly wounded that they were out of the battle. The pressure ceased as they stood to face us.

Jarl Sweyn Skull Taker shouted, "The flanks are collapsing, Agerhøne, fall back!"

I knew that the river was a good one hundred paces behind us, and we had space to walk but I did not like the move. The Saxons took heart and, as we stepped back, they ran at us with renewed courage. The result was the same. We had yet to lose a single man from those around me, yet a wall of Saxons lay before us. The fact that they were poorly armed and protected explained their deaths but as I looked to my right and left, I saw that our frontage had shrunk. Of the crews left by King Sweyn, I saw not a single warrior. It was just the men of Agerhøne who were left and that meant the odds were even more in favour of the Saxons. Had they continued their advance then we would have been pushed into the river and many of us would have perished, drowned by our armour, but Ulfcetel the Bold also halted his men. We had paused in the middle of a battle. He was reordering his lines.

"Archers!" Jarl Sweyn took advantage and more of the Saxons who wore no mail died before they could raise their shields. Only fifteen or so were killed and wounded but it halted any movement towards us. It took almost half an hour for the Saxons to reorganise their lines so that Ulfcetel and his best warriors, all mailed, moved to face Jarl Sweyn, Lodvir and me. He had recognised our strength and intended to break us once and for all. Our wounded had been moved to the river and without looking I knew that Thorstein and Griotard would have ferried the wounded back to the ships in the river. It would give them more men to defend our ships if we all died. We expected to die.

Sweyn One Eye began a chant. It was to put heart into the warriors.

The king did call and his men they came
Each one a warrior and a Dane
The mighty fleet left our home in the west
To sail to Svolder with the best of the best
Swedes and Norse were gathered as one
To fight King Olaf Tryggvasson
Mighty ships and brave warriors blades
The memory of Svolder never fades
The Norse abandoned their faithless king
Aboard Long Serpent their swords did bring
The Norse made a bridge of all their ships
Determined that King Sweyn they would eclipse
Brave Jarl Harald and all his crew
Felt the full force of a ship that was new
Mighty ships and brave warriors blades
The memory of Svolder never fades
None could get close to the Norwegian King
To his perilous crown he did cling
Until Skull Taker and his hearth weru
Attacked the side of the ship that was new

We did not finish the song for the Saxon leader recognised what we were doing and he ordered the charge. It was premature and they were not all locked together. This time it was a mixture of swords and spears which came at us. I could see Saxon Slayer still sticking from the dead Saxon. The housecarl who came at me had a two-handed axe and his shield hung over his back. He ran at me so that he could swing it in an arc. Gandálfr and Snorri's spears still flanked me, but they would not stop him. I looked at the swing of the axe head and estimated where it would strike. That would determine if I used my shield or my sword. I guessed it would be my shield. I did the unexpected. As the axe came down, I dropped to one knee and angled my shield to take the blow. At the same time, I drove up with Oathsword. My movement made him mistime his strike and while he still hit my shield the blow was not as hard as I had expected. Although he wore a long byrnie my sword drove up into his unprotected groin and when I felt flesh, I rammed harder and twisted. My hand felt his breeks, they were wet and when the axe fell to bounce from my shield then I knew he was dead.

As I rose, I found myself face to face with a Saxon who wore a short byrnie. The readjustment by Ulfcetel the Bold was working and we would not enjoy the success we once had.

Even as I resigned myself to a glorious death here on the banks of the Yare, I heard a distant horn and Griotard's voice as he roared, "Hold, Agerhøne! Karl Three Fingers and Cnut have fetched our men!"

The battle did not end then. I still had time to slay another two of the mailed enemy but the Saxons saw the approach of our men and I heard Ulfcetel, at least I think it was him, shout, "Fall back!"

Had we not been fighting for hours we might have followed them, but it would have meant many unnecessary deaths. We had done all that could be expected of us and saved the ships, but it had been the hardest battle I could remember since Svolder and the only one where the Saxons gave a good account of themselves.

Chapter 11

We lost many men that day. Even the clan of Agerhøne had lost fathers, sons, and brothers. The majority of those who had died were the men of Heiða-býr. Four drekar would need new crews such had been the slaughter. Cnut and Karl had fetched just five hundred men from the main warband and the reason for such a small number was clear. They rode and only that number of horses could be found. The king had retained twelve horses to pull the wagons with the vast treasure we had taken and the rest were ridden by our rescuers. Cnut was deemed, quite rightly, to be a hero. Had he not ridden so hard and been so accurate in his navigation then Karl Three Fingers might have arrived too late. The Saxons licked their wounds and watched us; they were not defeated but they had no fight left in them. We had a truce to recover our bodies and I retrieved Saxon Slayer. It was good that we would not be fighting again this season for I would have to make a new shaft. We burned our bodies. The truce meant we were not able to recover the mail and swords from their dead but that did not matter for we were just grateful to be alive.

We left the burnt-out city of Northwic five days later after we had fitted our masts and crewed the drekar of the warriors we had left, the dead. The famine in the land meant that there was no food, and we were reduced to eating the food we had brought for emergencies. The Saxons kept pace with us all the way to the mouth of the river. I saw Ulfcetel the Bold astride a horse, and he waved his sword at us as we left. I did not know if it was a salute or a sign that he thought they had won because he had made us leave. It mattered not, we had treasure and our crew were largely intact. Just one warrior, Ulf Black Tooth, had died and five were wounded. Many other ships sailed with half a crew. Our training had been vindicated and saved us.

The king was grateful, and we received a good share of the coins taken from the mint. He was not as generous as he made out as there were many of his men who now lay dead and unlike the widows of Ribe and Agerhøne the families of his dead would not receive one silver penny. With favourable winds, we did not have to row and we had neither slaves nor animals. The famine meant that we had been forced to eat the animals we had taken. It mattered not for we had enough silver to travel to the markets of Normandy and Frankia to buy them. In fact, we would not even have to do that for Aksel the Swede would be more than happy to use his increasingly large fleet of knarr to do so for us. It was as we sailed east that Cnut told us of his journey.

"There were bands of Saxons who were guarding the crossroads but my time with the clan has not been wasted. I became the bird which you heard but did not see. They were not mounted, and I was. I rode hard and I confess that I had to leave the horse when I found our men. Karl Three Fingers had also had a premonition of danger and he was already riding back having left Thetford at dawn. He had with him seven hundred men but only five hundred were mounted. He decided to take those and that was how we came to reach you before the flanks had collapsed. I rode with him and as we did so he said that so long as you and your crew survived there was a chance. He just feared that the Saxons would choose to attack you and eliminate the leader."

"We were lucky and I do not think that I will choose to raid next year. We have enough gold and silver. It is land we need and there is not enough in Denmark." Sweyn Skull Taker's words were like a cold shower for he was right. We had not been defeated and gained great glory. All the ones who had fought at Northwic spoke of the bravery of our clan but it felt like a defeat. He was right, men like Gandálfr, Snorri, Faramir and Dreng needed land and there was none to be had at Agerhøne. It came to me, as the coast of Jutland came into view, that we needed to share the land we had. A man was more likely to fight for his clan if he had land. I would speak to Mary about the idea which was fermenting in my mind.

My foster father came to speak to me when we neared Agerhøne. I had been aware that he had been looking for an opportunity but either Cnut or one of his sons was always close and he had bitten his tongue. Now the three were at the prow looking for the first sight of our home and he called me over to the larboard side of the stern. There was no one there. The crew lined the sides as the wind took us home.

"Sven, I would speak with you and I hoped to do so on the way home but…" I nodded, "Once we have unloaded the drekar then there will be too many people close by. On the morrow come early to the hall and we will walk."

I was intrigued, "Of course, jarl, but I know not why you wish to speak with me."

"And if I tell you now, hurriedly, then there will be no need to meet and I might choose the wrong words. I will speak with Agnetha for she helps to clear my mind and I know that you will do the same with Mary. Fear not it is nothing calamitous or should cause you to worry, but it has been on my mind since your father was killed."

A chill came over me. Had the Norns been spinning once more?

Egbert and the thralls were waiting for us but there was little for them to take. The coins we had taken were in my chest and they just carried the chest and my shield. "Was it not a successful raid, my lord? There are neither animals nor slaves."

"There is gold and silver. Your land is enduring a famine, Egbert, and there is little to take."

He nodded, "That explains the merchants who have been coming here to buy from us. The preserved herring and salted pig are in great demand. I did not know whence the merchants took it."

Aethelred's policies still had an influence on every person who lived in his land for he was spending his country's taxes on food rather than giving it to us. How much longer could he continue to do so?

We had not been away for long and yet I saw a change in my children. Gunhild could now run and she babbled. I caught a few of the words but Anna and Mary seemed to understand them all. I knew that my ear would become attuned to their sounds in time. That I was whole pleased my wife. I did not tell her all that we had done for I knew that it would upset her, but I told her of the famine that her land endured. She frowned and that was a sure sign that she sought a reason which would sit well with her beliefs. When she could not come up with an immediate explanation she said, "And now you must bathe, husband for you have the smell of war about you."

She was right of course, and I nodded.

"There are clothes I have had made for you. One of the thralls will show them to you when you have bathed. Seara, hot water and food for your lord."

Seara was another of the slaves taken when we had been in Wessex. They had all adjusted well to life in Denmark and it was proving not to be as terrible as they had imagined. That night we ate well. This raid had not enjoyed the range of food we normally consumed and the feast at my table tasted better than I remembered. When we had eaten and were seated before the fire, I brought up my idea.

"My love, you know that land is scarce here in Agerhøne?"

"Aye, I do, and it is becoming more crowded, too."

"We have plenty of land and it is producing a great deal. I thought to let those who live in my hall farm some of our land."

She smiled, "A Christian thing to do. I commend you, my husband, and while I think it is a good idea the men to whom you will be gifting this land are not poor. Charity is for those who cannot help themselves. I like the idea but I think that they should share our gift with us. That way it is in their interests to be productive farmers."

I could not think of an argument against her and, to be fair, it seemed a better idea than mine. The warriors who lived in the thrall hall, there were just three, Gandálfr, Faramir and Siggi, were all proud men and would not simply accept my gift. They were all grateful to have a roof over their heads and rooms where their families could live. I decided that I would tell them of my offer, but I would wait until I had spoken to the jarl. His request to speak to me still had me a little worried.

Sleeping in my own bed with my wife cradled in the crook of my arm was one of the pleasures I looked forward to the most and when my children burst in to join us in the bed, I felt slightly resentful but after a few moments of tickling them, I remembered that they would soon become a different kind of pleasure for me. The cooks had prepared all the food I enjoyed the most so that when I went to meet Jarl Sweyn, I felt replete.

He was speaking with Cnut when I arrived at his hall and I waited politely for them to finish. Cnut was growing and as he had shown in Northwic was becoming a warrior with a mind. I knew that the next raid would see him fighting in a shield wall. It was what his father wished and would show King Sweyn what kind of leader his son would be. His training would have to intensify and that meant I would have to devote more time to him.

He smiled and waved as he returned indoors, and my foster father strode over to me. He gestured towards the north. There was a good beach there and the wind was not too strong. It would be a pleasant place to stroll. "My other foster son did well, did he not, Sven?"

"He saved us, jarl, and the clan owes him much."

"Aye, you are right and he has a place in his heart for the clan. That is down in no small part to you."

"Me? But Hawk and Sweyn spend more time with him than I do."

"Perhaps but it is you he speaks of when he talks to me. I would have you spend more time training him. He needs to be a warrior who is as good as you."

I nodded with relief because now I knew what he had wished to say, "I had already planned on doing so. He is now old enough to stand in the shield wall."

"He is and that is not the matter I wished to discuss with you." I had been wrong! "Although we did not try the Boar's Snout formation at Northwic on the Yare, you showed me that day your skills as a leader. Once again it was you who managed to penetrate the enemy line and the clan was willing to follow you. Had our flanks not been so threatened we could have driven deep into the enemy lines and we might have won without the need for Karl Three Fingers."

I shook my head, "I am not so sure, for Ulfcetel the Bold was a cunning enemy. He chose to attack where we were weak. Had he fought against us from the start then I doubt I would have made any inroads."

"You are modest and that is good." There were some dunes covered in marram grass and he gestured for me to sit next to him. "Despite what you thought, your father and I were friends and between us, we led the clan. There were differences of opinion and you know that. We differed in that he sought glory and fame. You already have both but I know that you did not seek either. That speaks well of you. Just as your father and I led the clan and, his last raid apart, worked in harmony, I would have you and I do the same. I release you from duties as my hearth weru. Hawk is now in Ribe, and I have my eye on a couple who have been brought to my attention by Lodvir. Would you agree that Dreng and Snorri are the best young warriors?"

"Aye, and they showed great skill when first I trained them. Nothing I have seen since makes me doubt my first view of them."

"My sons agree with you and I will ask them to be my hearth weru with my eldest son. When you train new warriors, I would have the best two from each group identified. I want hearth weru who are young so that they can strengthen the clan and show every young warrior that there is the chance to be given a byrnie and serve the jarl." He smiled, "Thanks to our victories I have more mail shirts than I can ever wear. I shall give two to Dreng and Snorri if they agree."

"Believe me, they will agree!" I stared west, towards England. "But I still do not see what you mean about me leading with you."

"After your father died, then Lodvir took over and helped me to lead. It meant that when we went to battle, I could rely on him to organise our warriors. He now has a wife and lives in Ribe. He still fights with us but the men of Agerhøne no longer look to him. They already look to you and I would have you use it." He smiled, "They call you Oathsword and when you take out your weapon, they all call out its name. For them, you and the sword are the same. What say you? The ones in your wedge will be the core of your warriors and the ones who stood behind them will be given the chance to join you."

"Join me? It sounds like we are to be a different clan."

"No, not different but you will be the head of the spear that is the clan of Agerhøne. Twice it has been you and those who follow you who stepped forward and broke the enemy line. I am not a fool and the Norns have spun. I now see what they are trying to tell me. When they put that sword in your path it was to change not only your future but also the future of the clan. I would be a reckless fool if I ignored them." He stood and stretched, "If you wish a suggestion I would say that if you have them all paint a sword on their shields it will help for when an enemy sees it then they will know what they face. Cnut told me that his father desires the sword more than anything. There are many other warriors who agree with him. You have a name, foster son, and men will seek you in battle. You cannot change it for it was spun. You can, however, use it. What say you?"

I smiled, "You are right, foster father, and I cannot escape my fate. I might wish to be anonymous, but I know that I cannot. If I am to be the warrior that my father and you wished me to be then I must embrace this change. I will do as you ask, and I will help you to lead the clan."

"Then you are now hersir of Agerhøne. The king gave his permission when he gave me the silver. I had this in mind then." He took, from his pouch, the torc which was worn on ceremonial occasions by the hersir. I had not seen it for years. I nodded my thanks and took it. I confess that I was unable to speak for a while. I was so young and had achieved so much. Sweyn Skull Taker was right. When the sword had called to me then my life was changed.

"What of Sweyn One Eye? He is your eldest. Would he not expect to be hersir?"

"King Sweyn said that when I die my eldest shall inherit the title of jarl. Sweyn knows that and he is content."

That pleased me for I did not want to rob my cousin of his birthright.

I told Mary when we returned, and she was delighted for she understood the status it brought with it. I then sought out the warriors who were in my wedge. I did not want to order any man to follow me and so I asked each of them in turn. It took the rest of the day to speak with them all, for Lars and Lief lived some way from the sea. To my amazement, they all agreed with such alacrity that I was taken aback. It was almost as though they had conspired. My last visit was to Cnut and One Eye. I spoke to my cousin first for I wished no animosity that I was hersir. I told Sweyn that I would happily relinquish the title if he objected. He laughed.

"Cousin, you have been marked for greatness since the first time you went to war and you followed me. I knew then that Sweyn Sweynson would never be the warrior that you were and when my eye was taken it was confirmed. My greatness will come because a hundred years from now men will still sing my songs! Besides, I shall be jarl one day and that suits me."

I gestured for Cnut to join me outside, "Our foster father has asked me to spend more time training you to be a warrior. Are you happy for me to do so?"

"Of course, Sven, and I know that your training will make me a better warrior than my brother, Harald. Since I first watched you as a youth, I have wanted to be like you. I am not sure that I will be able to use the same skills as you for you seem to know when a blow is coming before the warrior who strikes it. That is a gift from God, but I hope that I can pick up enough to give me a better chance of surviving a battle. The four dead crews I saw when we rode to your side at Northwic were a warning of what can happen when leaders make mistakes."

It was as close to a criticism of his father as I had heard but it was just vague enough to be deniable. Perhaps it was a test. Cnut was his father's son and a more cunning man than his father I had yet to meet. His son must have inherited some of his traits.

That first day exhausted me and I was chastised by Mary when I entered my hall, "You have barely spent an hour with your children. They are upset that their father ignores them. Steana may not yet be able to form coherent words but I saw the hurt in his eyes. Today you gave your time to the jarl and the clan. Good. Tomorrow, you give it to your children!"

Most Danish warriors would have resented being spoken to like that by their wives, but I was not like most warriors and I agreed with her. "Of course, and you are right." I kissed her and she beamed. All was well.

Gunhild's babble soon sounded like words and I found, to my delight, that I could speak to her. Steana tried to talk and I am guessing that in his baby head he was speaking like we did but it just came out as grunts. At first, I forced myself to play with them and ignore the tasks which tapped inside my head. Then the tapping stopped and I found myself enjoying their company. When Mary fed Steana I had Gunhild to myself although Anna was always close by in case I needed her. I learned that Gunhild did not like the word, *'no'*. I had tears and that was when Anna came to my rescue.

"Lord, Mistress Mary is firm with her when she weeps. She must learn to accept discipline."

I nodded but found it hard to do so. In my heart, I wanted to stop her tears by acceding to her demands and to make her smile.

On the third day, it was such a pleasant morning that I thought to leave the hall and seek the ash haft. I asked Mary if Gunhild could accompany me as it was a walk. "Of course, but make sure she is wrapped well and," she nodded towards the hand axe in my belt, "be careful!"

I knew I could not manage two of them and Gunhild and I slipped out of the hall while Anna distracted my son. It was a long walk but Gunhild was a curious child and as I explained what we saw she replied to every piece of information with the same word, '*why*'. I found myself struggling to find some answers and that was good for it made me question what I knew. We found the stand of ash and I gave her a drink of the cow's milk Anna had given to me.

"Now let us find the piece of wood I need. We are looking for a piece which is straight and longer than I am, yet it should be no thicker than your leg or arm."

She nodded attentively and, taking my hand, we searched for the perfect piece of wood. Gunhild took the task seriously and even seemed to enjoy it. I had resigned myself to the single one we had found which was not quite as tall as I was when Gunhild, who had disappeared behind some ash shouted, "Here! Is this one right?"

I hurried around, grateful that my wife would never know that I took my eyes from her and saw that she had found a copsed ash tree. Six branches had sprung and grown upright. She had seen and found what I had not, there was the perfect spear shaft, but it was in the middle of the others. The other five would make serviceable spears but not for me. I would have to cut those away first before I could take the perfect one in the centre. I seated her on the lightning struck tree trunk and gave her some honey cakes while I toiled. I took my time for I saw that there would be six spears I could have. There were younger warriors who would need a spear and all the ones I cut were the perfect thickness. Gunhild squealed with delight as each branch fell. I stacked them close by to her. The last one would become the new Saxon Slayer and I took the greatest care in its cutting. It was after the sun had begun to dip that I finished, and I hefted the ash branch over my shoulder.

"What about the others? Are they just to stay here?"

"No, I shall send men for them. They will be useful. You did well to find what I did not."

That pleased her. "Father, are there any girls who become warriors?"

I had heard of some but not in our land and I did not think that her mother would approve, "No, it is just boys who train as warriors."

"Why?"

"That is the way it has always been."

"Why?"

I saw that I had entered the circle of whys and there was only one way out, break the circle. "Girls are different to boys, Gunhild. They can do things that boys cannot do. Your mother gave birth to you and your brother. I cannot give birth."

"Because you are a man."

"Aye." There had been no why but it soon followed!

"Why are there men and women? Why are they not the same?"

I almost used the word Allfather but I knew that Mary wished our children to be Christian and so I said, "God, in His wisdom made us either men or women. It helps to keep the world in harmony. Warriors protect the women from danger and women ensure that our people grow."

"I am tired, father."

I leaned the ash shaft against the sheep fence of Galmr Galmrsson and hoisted her upon my shoulders. Picking up the shaft in my right hand I continued home. "You would not like being a warrior, Gunhild."

"Why? Do you not like it?"

Her question, as simple as it was, made me almost stop as I struggled to find an answer. My thoughts were just a heartbeat ahead of my words as I answered her, "I am good at what I do, Gunhild, but I do not enjoy killing even though the men I kill are trying to kill me. If I did not have to kill again then I would be a happy man for it would mean that there was no need." Even as I said the words, I saw the lie. The need was not mine it was the king's and his ambition. When I had defended Agerhøne against the raiders then there was a need but all the men I had killed in England and at Svolder had been at the behest of the king, yet I could not refuse him for he was my king. I now understood those men who had decided that they did not want to obey a king and had sailed to the land of ice and fire. I could never do that but I understood why men did.

"Father?"

"Yes, Gunhild?"

"You are quiet; why?"

"Because, my love, you have put thoughts in my head and that is what men do, they wrestle with the demons inside them."

"Like the ones who come at night."

"Come at night?"

"Yes, when you were away at sea, and I sleep, creatures, horrible ones, come into my head and I wake up crying. Anna sings me to sleep but it is hard for I fear that the demons will come back."

I squeezed her hand with my left one. "No demons will come into our hall. You have my word."

She was silent for a while and then said, somewhat sadly, "That is good for you are home. When you sail away again then will the demons come again?"

I had no answer for that and the joy of finding the ash evaporated as I thought about her words. One day the king would call, and I would have to go to war again. I had not thought about this before but now, when I was at sea, I would know the effect it had on my children.

We had a workshop close to the hall. Egbert had made it when I had been on one of my raids. There was an anvil and a furnace. Anna brought Steana and Gunhild to watch when I attached the spearhead to the haft. I had smoothed and polished the haft and I was pleased with it. I had prepared the socket end but this time Saxon Slayer would be different. I still had some byrnie metal and I had made a metal collar. Before I sank the spearhead into the socket I prepared the collar around the top of the spear. An enemy would not be able to hack it off so easily and it would blunt the sword which struck it. I poured molten metal in the socket to bed in the spearhead then I used the fire and my hammer to beat the collar and make the head secure. That done I left it to cool. I was sweating heavily when I had finished.

"Come, let us leave Thor's workshop and go where it is cooler." The words were barely out of my mouth before I regretted them.

"Who is Thor? Is he one of your men?"

I saw Anna grasp her cross and I shook my head, "You know the stories from the Bible, the ones Anna and your mother tell?" She nodded. "Well, Thor is like that. He is from a story we have here in Denmark. He makes weapons and armour."

She seemed satisfied with my answer. She liked stories. I would have to watch my words from now on.

I had done as I had promised and I had spent three weeks giving every moment to my children, but I was now a leader of men and Cnut came one morning to ask when I would do as I had promised and begin to train him. Mary was there and she gave a nod. I had done what she had asked and she understood that I was a warrior.

"Now! We can do some spear work. I will call Gandálfr and the others."

Cnut smiled, "They are already waiting, Sven Saxon Sword."

I had also finished the other five spear hafts and, without their metalheads, were perfect for training. With my young warriors who had fought in many battles, we were able to teach Cnut what he ought to do. He had seen us do this but watching and doing were two entirely different things. He tripped and fell three times. Faramir had also had the same problem and he gave Cnut the solution. "We always move with our sword leg first. Think sword and move that leg."

It solved the problem and Cnut began to improve. He also found it hard to hold the long ash haft for long periods and there was no simple answer to that. I told him how Lodvir had made me hew down trees and carry them back to strengthen my arms. "You will need to be stronger for some battles, like the one on the Yare, may last hours. A battle is not only a test of skills but strength and endurance. When you are not training with us then you should be training alone and making your arms stronger."

I was aware, while we trained Cnut, that I was also training what were, in effect, my men and so we began to modify the way we fought in a wedge. Lars and Leif were not close by and so I alternated other warriors to stand behind me when we were in a wedge. Who knew what might happen in the maelstrom of a battle? We worked on my commands to change formation. Speed could win a battle and after many days of training, we were able to move seamlessly from one formation to another. As winter began to bite and the days became shorter, so our training intensified.

Hawk and his wife, Frida, now lived in Ribe. They had a fine hall but that of Aksel the Swede was almost palatial. Hawk and his wife often stayed in Aksel's hall. Aksel seemed to really like Hawk and the two got on. It was from Aksel that we learned more of Aethelred and England. The famine had caused many deaths. Aethelred had also become something of a tyrant. The massacre on St Brice's Day was just one of a series of savage and ruthless acts which eliminated any opposition to him. A new name was mentioned and, when we feasted in the jarl's hall to celebrate the birth of the White Christ and the winter solstice, Hawk still visited regularly and it was on one such visit that he told us of the new eoreledman of Mercia, Eadric Streona. The man had come from nowhere and now appeared to rule Mercia for the king. He appeared to be the antithesis of Ulfcetel Snilling in that he was not a warrior but a plotter. It said much about King Aethelred that he advanced men like Eadric Streona whilst, seemingly, ignoring warriors like Ulfcetel.

"There will be no raid this year for the king." Hawk had looked at his father who knew what the look meant.

"And there will be no raid from Ribe and Agerhøne. Our young men who are yet to be trained have time to develop and to grow while those who have married can father new warriors."

I nodded, "And land? Where will these fathers and warriors get land, foster father?" I saw Cnut look up at my question.

Sweyn Skull Taker shook his head, "That I cannot answer. Perhaps we should farm the sea. We can use more men to fish and gather the sea's harvest."

I nodded, "If they choose to do so."

"Men always have choices, Sven. You chose to give land to your men. That has proved successful. Other men must make their own decisions. We cannot make them for them."

The jarl was clever. By planting the idea at the feast, by the time the days lengthened then many of the warriors who had no land built fishing boats and began to do as he had suggested. In a year without war, we became richer through our hard work. They became better seamen and learned about weather, waves and the wind. When war came we would be better prepared. The jarl was also correct about the growth of the clan. Mary as well as many other of the women in the clan were with child. Steana and Gunhild would have a brother or sister soon. Hawk and One Eye would also be fathers. That year was the most peaceful any could remember yet for Hawk there would be a worry.

Chapter 12

1006 Cent

It was Thorkell the Tall who was the reason we went raiding again. While the king and the rest of us had enjoyed a peaceful time, he had sailed with the Jomsvikings and enjoyed great success. He urged King Sweyn to come and join him for he said King Aethelred had given himself up to wine and women and appointed men to lead who were not warriors. The jarl was summoned to Heiða-býr and, when he returned, we were told of our target as well as news of the troubled kingdom.

Cnut sat with the jarl and his hearth weru. He listened intently for he was almost ready to take a greater interest in his father's kingdom. "We are to raid Cent. There are ports there that are rich and are not protected by a burh. Karl Three Fingers is a clever man and he wishes to keep the Saxons guessing where we will strike."

"And the famine?" My question was born because I did not know why we needed to raid.

"It is over. The last harvest was a good one and they have begun to sell their goods abroad once more. There will be coins, animals and slaves."

I shook my head, "I need no more slaves. Since I gave land to my men I need fewer workers in my fields. I have good slaves now and it would be foolish to risk bringing bad ones into my fold."

Their silence told me that the others wanted slaves. Cnut said, "You know that there is an old English song which says that if the Danes were to get to Cwichelmeshlaew or, as they call it now, Cwichelm's Barrow, then all their land will become Danish. Do we know if this barrow is close to Cent?"

None knew but I knew someone who would, "I will ask my wife, Cnut. She has a great knowledge of the land for we read through many parchments when we were seeking information about the dragon sword."

Cnut came with me and he asked Mary the question. She had heard the rhyme and she knew where the place was. "Oxnaford where I believe many of your people were killed on St Brice's Day is close to the barrow. It lies just a hundred miles or so from Wiht."

That seemed to please Cnut, "Then when we meet him, I will speak to my father for it seems to me that if we had a foray to the north then we might find this barrow. It could not hurt."

After he had gone Mary said, "The princeling is ambitious. He would have the crown which Aethelred wears." My wife was a clever woman who could read people as well as she read parchments.

"He is the son of a king, what else can you expect? I would not take a crown if it was thrust upon me!" Mary smiled for she knew that I meant every word.

Before we left Aksel the Swede delivered some news to Hawk which, at the time, seemed unimportant but later was of great moment. The king had appointed a man called Eadric Streona as the ruler of Mercia. Hawk had told us this the previous year but now we saw the manner of the man. Eadric had invited a great noble from southern Northumbria, eorledman Ælfhelm, to hunt with him and had him murdered by one of his men, Godwin Porthund. That it was done at the behest of the king was clear when Ælfhelm's sons, Wulfheah and Ufegeat were taken by the king and blinded. It made Aethelred the effective ruler of half of Northumbria. What it showed us was how ruthless this apparently Christian king was. The only one of Ælfhelm's family to escape was his young daughter, Ælfgifu and her whereabouts were unknown. Once more Cnut showed how sharp was his mind for he saw immediately the importance of such an action.

"This Ælfhelm of Jorvik was well thought of and there will be people in Northumbria who are now resentful of the king. Many Danes and Norse live in Jorvik. My father could seize the opportunity. Jarl Svein Hákonarson raided the north of Northumbria and knows the land well."

The boy who had come to us to be trained was now almost a man and I marvelled at the change. The warrior in him was down to the training we had given him but the mind of the leader was from within himself. Just as the sword had chosen me it seemed that Cnut had been chosen to lead. I wondered if this would lead to conflict between him and his brother. Since the raid on Exeter, he had seen nothing of him. Although King Sweyn appeared hale and hearty no man lives forever. Who would be the next King of Denmark?

Our fleet left Danish waters just as the English were beginning their harvest. After the long famine, it was eagerly anticipated and every man who was available was working in the fields to gather as much food as they could. We used the same course as when we had raided Northwic, the difference was that when we saw the smudge of a coastline, we headed due south knowing that the next place we saw, after the estuary of the Tamese, would be the granary of England, Cent!

Aboard our ship, there was an air of confidence. The jarl's idea of a crew within a crew had worked. The men who followed me now felt special and others, who were neither in the jarl's hearth weru or my warriors were desperate to impress us for they wished to be chosen. There was no moaning and when we had to row then the crew put their backs into every stroke. When we hove to, just off the coast of Cent there was such a positive mood as we donned our mail and stepped our mast, that I felt there was nothing beyond us. Whatever the men of Cent threw our way we would overcome. We waited until dark before rowing silently towards the coast. We knew, again from Aksel, that there was a river with a prosperous town, Sandwic, at its mouth. We liked to use rivers for we could moor our ships where they would be safe from the vagaries of the weather and the tide. We rowed in and this time it was the king who led the way. We sailed half a mile up the river so that we could moor safely without being rammed by one of the other drekar. We passed the town and, of course, we were seen. We heard the cries of alarm. We had to row beyond the king's ship. The result was that we did not have the benefit of a wooden quay and so while the ship's boys tied us up, we leapt ashore. This would be the first time that I led my wedge and it felt good as I ran, ahead of the jarl, back towards the town.

King Sweyn had caught the men of Sandwic unawares and, despite the alarm being given, he had breached their poor defences almost instantly. The result was that as we ran back down the river to the port, we met refugees fleeing from danger. Some of the women were so terrified that they hurled themselves in the river only to find more of our ships looming up to land their men. Lodvir's drekar struck three of them. The men who faced us had weapons, but they were no match for my men who were mailed. The men died and the women who did not hurl themselves in the river prostrated themselves before us. Lodvir took them aboard his ship. By the time dawn broke, we had the port and all the ships which were tied up there. The men had either fled or been put to the sword and any women and children who remained were taken and secured.

There was no time for complacency and the king sent us out in three columns to take as much plunder and grain as we could from Cent. The men of Ribe and Agerhøne were one of the columns. I like to think that we were one of the best. The reason was not arrogance it was based on the fact that we had lost the fewest men in the raids thus far and yet we had taken, the mint apart, the greatest treasure. We were sent north and we ran, even while Sandwic was still being looted. We had to outrun any news of our arrival and when we came upon half a dozen Saxon men also running north then we knew that we would have surprise and that there would be a settlement for us to raid. The men tried to defend themselves, but they were not warriors.

We found the small port of Hremmesgeat just five miles from Sandwic. It was nowhere near as big but there were three large trading vessels in the harbour as well as a dozen fishing boats that had just returned from a night of fishing. We had been lucky that they had not seen the approach of our fleet. The three trading ships were laden with goods for trade and were awaiting the tide. We took their crews and placed our own men aboard the ships. The small town had fine houses and we had ample time to search them for treasure. While the three trading ships were sent back to Sandwic and while the men of Ribe completed the emptying of the town the men of Agerhøne continued to head north. We left Hremmesgeat in the early afternoon and our noses took us along the coast to cross low-lying ground and marshes towards the smoke we could see rising from another fishing port. We discovered an even smaller one than the one with the three traders. Meregate was a huddle of houses and fishing boats with a jetty. It did not yield much in the way of treasure but once again we had the catch from the fishing boats.

After burning the houses we boarded the fishing boats and, even though they were overcrowded, sailed back around the coast to Hremmesgeat. We ate well that night and the next morning, after burning the town and sending the fishing boats back to Sandwic, we headed inland. We had taken fish, cargo and a little treasure but we knew that there had to be great quantities of grain. Even as we headed north we could see it ripening in some fields while others had already been harvested. For the next two months, we rampaged through Cent without ever having to fight a battle. We saw warriors who, when they spied our numbers, melted back towards the Tamese. They were not ready to face us. We had taken some thegns as prisoners and before we executed them, they were questioned and we learned that Aethelred was in Mercia with his new favourite Eadric Streona. England was leaderless!

Cantwareburh, despite its name and its mighty church, did not hold us up and it yielded even more riches than the mint at Thetford. I thought then that we might return to Denmark but as Gormánuður came to a close we boarded our already laden ships and sailed not east but west. The traders we had taken in our raids, all eight of them, were sent home. Half went to Ribe and Agerhøne and the other half to the king's home. We landed at our second home in England, Wiht! The people who had lived there when we had first used it as a camp had long since departed. We had returned too many times for them to stay. I thought we might overwinter there. I did not want to. If we were not going to fight warriors then I wanted to go home. The reason we did not was

Cnut. The princeling had raided with us but once we had taken all there was to be had he had visited his father in Sandwic. He planted the seed of the idea of taking the army to Cwichelm's Barrow. It appealed to the king and as we would have to march close to Wintan-ceastre, he saw it as a way of further humiliating King Aethelred. Leaving our ships well-guarded, two thousand warriors marched north towards Oxnaford and Readingas which was where the Saxon king's father was buried.

The jarl was given the honour of leading the march. It was a double-edged honour. While it showed great faith in us, we would also be the first to face an enemy. If they chose to ambush us, then it was we who would suffer. My wedge was given the task of scouting. We marched a quarter of a mile ahead of the rest of our warband and they were two hundred paces ahead of the main body. When we marched on the Roman sections of the road there was little to be feared for the roads were straight but, in some places, the roads had not been well maintained and trees had been allowed to grow alongside the road providing places of ambush. We had less than ninety miles to go and it took us just three days. Readingas proved to be the hardest part of our journey for the Saxons defended it. They did not ambush us and when Jarl Sweyn Skull Taker arrived he quickly ordered an assault on its wooden walls. With no spike lined ditch, we took it within half an hour and before King Sweyn could even order his own attack.

The next day, with information taken from prisoners we headed for the barrow. It was a mighty monument and stood out along the skyline. This time the king and his son led the procession to the top. We were relegated to watching from the base. We did not mind. At the top King Sweyn raised his standard and shouted, "I claim the land of Cwichelm for Denmark and my sons!"

It was, in many ways, meaningless for we had not fought a battle and had no intention of staying there but it seemed to inspire our army. We camped on the barrow, eating all that Readingas had to offer and then we headed south. The king's words must have had an effect for the Saxons waited for us at the River Kennet just five miles from Readingas. They lined the river and held the bridge.

King Sweyn quickly convened a council of war. I was not included this time but it mattered not. When Jarl Sweyn returned it was with the news that our crew would be the ones who would force the bridge while those warriors who had no mail would make crude rafts and cross the river. The thought of attacking the men guarding the bridge seemed daunting for they were all mailed but we had the chance to take that mail and their weapons. We did not shirk from the honour. Cnut would also fight with us. He would be behind the jarl and his men. It was my wedge that would lead the attack!

The bridge was a wooden one and only wide enough for four or five men. As the men who waited for us in the centre were mailed then it would be four of us who faced them. While our archers showered the Saxons with arrows I spoke with my men. "We will use the wedge and drive between the two men in the centre. Our three spears should be able to strike the two of them and we will split them asunder. The wooden sides of the bridge look weak and we may be able to make them fall into the river. They have only managed to block the bridge with sixteen men. The rest await us on the other side, and they are not mailed. We just keep going for we know that behind us are the men of Ribe and Agerhøne." The bridge was just eighteen paces across, and I knew that speed would help us. The men grinned their agreement.

The jarl had waited patiently while I had spoken to my men, "Are you ready, Sven?"

I nodded, "Aye, foster father! We will run at them."

"Then begin your attack!"

I began banging my shield with Saxon Slayer and started to stamp my feet in time. The others formed up behind me and did the same. When Lars tapped me on the shoulder then I knew that they were ready and pointing Saxon Slayer towards the south, I shouted, "Oathsword!" and began to run to the bridge.

The men who awaited us had their shields raised to save them from the fall of arrows and the slam of stones. It was our feet stamping on the ancient bridge which told them that we were coming, and it was only then that they attempted to lock their shields. I was right and speed was our best weapon for we struck the middle of their line before they had locked shields and before the second and third ranks had pushed their shields into the rear of the front rank. Saxon Slayer grated off mail and then found flesh as it hit the Saxon in the second rank. I heard a crack and a cry as one was knocked over the side into the river taking part of the wooden parapet with him. The boss on my shield saved me from the spears of the mailed men on the bridge and the spears of Lars and Leif enjoyed great success. My boots ceased to pound and echo when we burst through the last of the bridge defenders and faced those on the riverbank.

It was as I stabbed a surprised warrior in the face with Saxon Slayer that I heard first, a mighty crack like thunder and then screams. Faramir shouted, "The bridge has collapsed! We are alone!"

It would do little good to bemoan our position. The Norns had spun and the bridge had been old. My leadership was being tested. The

Saxons saw that they had the wolves surrounded and they began to close with us. Without turning I shouted, "We are the men of Agerhøne and we do not fear these Saxons. Hold the formation and trust in each other." I might have had more words to say but the Saxons rushed us in an attempt to drive us into a river which, although I could not see it must have been filled with the drowning bodies of men who were mailed. Were my foster father and cousins dead? Had the princeling, Cnut survived? The thoughts flashed through my mind for a heartbeat and then my battle instincts took over.

I thrust Saxon Slayer at the eager warrior whose own spear was shorter than mine. Gunhild had found a good stand of ash that day and the spear head drove into the man's chest and I turned the head and dragged his dying body to the side. The ones following fell over his corpse and as they did so I withdrew my spear and stabbed down again on the unprotected back of one of the fallen. A Saxon spear struck my shield, a second my helmet but the straps on both held and I punched with the shield as I stabbed another of the writhing bodies on the ground. I now had a wall of four bodies before me as Leif had managed to spear one too. It made the enemy move to my right. They were surrounding us but on our right they faced spears and they would die. The ones on our left had shields before them and spears which jabbed over the top.

I heard Lodvir's voice behind me. I had no idea where he was but hearing it told me that he was alive, "Use the dead as a bridge! That is Sven Saxon Slayer and our best warriors fighting for their lives!"

It heartened me that help was coming and I gripped my shield a little tighter. If we were to die, then we would die hard! We would enable our men to win the battle. I heard a thegn exhorting his men to push us back into the river and saw five mailed men, two of them wielding axes lead a small mob of farmers to run directly at me. They could not have seen the bodies or else they would have angled their attack to my left. The swinging axes looked dangerous, but I had faced one before at Dean. With my left foot planted before me, I slightly raised my shield as I tried to work out where the axe would strike and then Saxon Slayer darted out as I saw that his byrnie's fastenings had not been tied tightly and I spied cloth. The tip drove into his breastbone and then the spearhead cracked it open and entered his body. His axe fell and he lurched to the side dragging his body from Saxon Slayer. The second axe man had been swinging his own axe at me and the falling warrior deflected his axe so that it struck my shield a glancing blow. His momentum and the weight of those behind made him an easy target for Lars whose spear skewered him.

The thegn and his other two mailed housecarls had swords and they closed with us. The men behind the thegn told me that Saxon Slayer was no longer the weapon I needed. As the thegn and one of the housecarls closed with me I punched with my shield and then stabbed Saxon Slayer to pin the housecarl's foot to the ground. He screamed in pain and that allowed me to draw Oathsword.

Behind me, I heard Gandálfr shout, "Oathsword!" I knew it would give heart to my men.

I smashed the hilt into the face of the thegn as my shield took the strike from his sword. I then used the pommel to strike into the side of the head of the pinioned housecarl. He tried to raise his sword but Oathsword's freshly sharpened edge slid down and across his neck. The spurting blood showered the thegn and me as Lars used his own sword to kill the last housecarl. I lifted my shield sharply and the metal rim smashed up and under the chin of the thegn.

"Agerhøne!" Lodvir's voice and the sudden pressure in my back of Leif's shield told me that men had made the south bank of the river. We were no longer just hanging on. Now we needed to move!

The thegn's head jerked back, and I knew that I had hurt him. He had a mail byrnie but I had Oathsword and I drove the tip towards him as I stepped onto my right foot. It was not just the strength of my right arm that helped Oathsword slide through mail and into flesh. It was also the weight of the men behind me as not only the thegn was driven back but also the mob of men who were behind him. We were mailed and they were not.

The falling thegn was like the bursting of a dam. We moved forward with such speed that it felt like we were back at Agerhøne on the training ground and charging invisible enemies. The farmers we faced were not prepared to face the metal demons who had just slaughtered their lord and his oathsworn. They broke and when they did, so I saw that we had broken through their whole army. As they fled south, I raised Oathsword and shouted, "Turn!" I whirled left and saw the Saxons hurriedly trying to turn and face the sudden threat we posed. I knew that there would be others behind me doing the same, but I had heard Lodvir's voice. He would deal with those. Karl Three Fingers' warriors who wore no mail had already crossed the river and were engaging the Saxons on the riverbank. I knew what we had to do.

I risked looking behind me and I saw that I had a wedge of twenty men. More were joining me, and I saw the backs of others that told me Lodvir was doing as I had done and clearing the other side of the riverbank. When I spied my foster father, cousins and Cnut clambering up from the remains of the bridge then I knew that the Allfather wished us to win.

I raised Oathsword and pointed it at the Saxons who were trying to form a shield wall but one without mailed warriors. "One more charge and we will end this. Let us tell them who we are!" I began to sing and not only my wedge but the rest of the clan sang too. It gave us the rhythm and the beat. We marched quickly towards the shield wall.

We are the bird you cannot find
With feathers grey and black behind
Seek us if you can my friend
Our clan will beat you in the end.
Where is the bird? In the snake.
The serpent comes your gold to take.
We are the bird you cannot find
With feathers grey and black behind
Seek us if you can my friend
Our clan will beat you in the end.
Where is the bird? In the snake.
The serpent comes your gold to take.

We charged into spears but some spears were just fire-hardened points and even the ones which had metal heads were not particularly sharp. My shield shattered the first two and even the metal one which scratched across my shoulder did no harm. Oathsword, in contrast, smashed into the helmet and then the skull of the first Saxon and my shield brushed aside the man to his right. I pulled back my arm and drove Oathsword towards the terrified face of the next Saxon who brought his shield up in an attempt to save himself. His spear was thrust blindly at my head and I easily avoided the clumsy strike. The shield stopped my sword from finding flesh but it found the crack in the boards and split the shield in two. The boss of my shield struck him in the face and with a shattered nose his body fell to the ground and I trampled across it as we moved deep into the hastily formed Saxon defences.

There was an eorledman and he was mounted on a horse, no doubt to give him a better view of the battle. He must have not liked what he saw for I saw him point to the south and then give a command. The words were lost for he was four hundred paces from me, but the meaning became clear as those closest to him joined him as they fled south and east. I stabbed another Saxon as the ones behind him turned and saw that they were fleeing. They joined the rout and within four swings of Oathsword, the Saxons were gone!

We could not have chased them even had we wanted to for we were all weary beyond words and besides we had done all that was asked of us. King Sweyn and the bulk of the mailed portion of our army still stood on the north bank of the river. They had not yet crossed. The only mailed men who had managed to cross were those of Ribe and Agerhøne.

I turned to my wedge. I saw that young Thorkell was no longer there. I had lost one of my men. That made me sad, but I realised that it could have been worse. Thorkell was one who had not fought in the wedge but the shield wall behind it. He had been unlucky for the rest, Faramir, Gandálfr and the rest were still whole. Their mail was bloodied and some had cuts but they stood.

"It was an honour to lead you this day!"

I raised my sword in salute, and they all shouted, "Oathsword!"

"Now let us reap our reward before the men of Heiða-býr find the courage to cross the river and take the mail from the warriors we slew!" They cheered again. "And before someone takes Saxon Slayer."

I had just retrieved my spear from the foot of the dead housecarl when my foster father, limping and supported by my cousins found me. "What happened?"

"The bridge collapsed, and we found ourselves in the river. It was not as deep as we had thought but I managed to turn my ankle as we fell. We climbed out of the river using the Saxon dead and the wooden piles. We followed Lodvir. You have the honour of the victory, foster son."

Sweyn One Eye nodded, "Aye, that was worthy of a saga. Twenty of you faced a Saxon army and you won!"

I looked around, "And where is Cnut?"

Hawk laughed, "He went to chastise his father for being so tardy! He urged us to get to your side and when the Saxons fled his face was filled with anger that his father's men had not done what we did."

"We did what we were asked. A man cannot be responsible for the actions of others. The Norns spun and we have another victory. My men have mail and the battle made us closer. Thank you, foster father, for giving me the chance to lead."

"It is in your blood and you did not disappoint. Now you will have every young warrior clamouring to join you!"

We reached our ships a week later having left a trail of destruction as we headed south. We had destroyed the only army the Saxons had and their churches, monasteries and nunneries were emptied of all that they contained. We even halted at Wintan-ceastre to taunt the Saxons who were waiting, terrified behind the walls of the mightiest burh in England. When we reached Wiht the king sent for me and presented me with a beautifully made jewelled encrusted dagger. Too pretty to use it was a symbol and showed that my star had risen. The king planned on wintering on the island but at the end of Mörsugur, King Aethelred sent an envoy. He had endured enough, and we were paid thirty thousand pounds in weight of gold to leave his land. We reached Agerhøne by the end of Þorri. We were all richer!

Chapter 13

1007 Agerhøne

The ships we had sent home had kept our people well fed over the winter and now they provided another source of income as the jarl sold most of them to Aksel the Swede. They were sound ships and added to the growing fleet the Swede owned. We kept one for we saw the opportunity to trade too. We benefitted from the profits. The Swede also asked if he could hire some of the younger warriors to act as guards for his ships. Sweyn saw no problem with that as it would keep them occupied when they were not needed by the clan and give them experience. There were pirates but a handful of armed Danes were often enough discouragement to make them choose easier prey.

I came home, as did many other men, to a son. This time Mary had named him Bersi, after my father. He had already been christened by the time I saw him. Gunhild and Steana had also grown and were now, clearly children. I even understood much of what Steana had to say. I looked forward to some weeks of their company before the demands of the clan and my lands took over. Mary was delighted that we would not be raiding, and another year of peace loomed up.

Cnut spent more time with me. He accepted that I needed to be with my children and I could not resume his training yet but he was full of questions both about Oathsword and, surprisingly, Mary. I knew that he admired her for she was both clever and well-read. He had always spoken to her when they had met and he had, especially when he had been younger, rained questions on her. Now he asked me about her and her background. I had no idea why he wished the information, but I found it easy to talk to him about the woman I loved and the mother of my children. She had been my mother's crutch through her last years and, I believe, kept her alive long after she should have died. He also asked Mary, directly, about some of the names of the people we had heard while raiding. Some were totally unknown to her: Eadric Streona for example but others, like Ælfhelm and Uhtred the Bold, both lords of Northumbria were the names of men she knew.

It was while we were talking that I asked him about his relationship with his younger brother. It had become clear while we had been raiding that King Sweyn saw Harald as his heir and I wondered if Cnut resented that. It might explain his questions.

"I know that my stepmother has bewitched my father and no matter what I do in battle, my younger brother will still be King of Denmark. I am resigned to that but England? That is a different matter. Your wife is from that land and she does not see Aethelred as a worthy king. From the way the Saxons failed to fight with any determination, I am inclined to agree."

"Do not forget Ulfcetel."

"I do not, and I see him as a serious threat but he is out of favour with their king and that is surprising for he almost defeated us. I see these raids to England as a way to take their land. I would have my father stay there longer to raid. When I am old enough, I will ask if I can lead an army there."

"You are a warrior now."

He laughed, "A warrior who has yet to kill. That will come and I will gain the skills I need but I do not plan for this year or even the next. I see far into the future and you, Sven Saxon Sword, will be the key to my success."

His laughter was infectious as were his fanciful ideas which had as much chance of coming to fruition as I had of becoming an Archbishop, "I am just a hersir from Agerhøne. I am content."

He nodded, "But I am not!"

I put his words from my mind for they seemed like one of Sweyn's sagas, not based on the real world but a warped vision, a stylised telling of a tale with a few pieces of reality thrown in. I threw myself into the task of training men, playing with my children and watching my land prosper. When, in the summer, Cnut left us to return to his father, I thought we had seen the last of the engaging princeling. I saw that he was as ambitious as his father.

Sweyn One Eye's son, Sweyn, had been training with us for some time. A little older than Cnut he was now ready to join the shield wall and when we began to train the new warriors, I saw the nervousness from my cousin. He knew the pressure to be a successful warrior and as the grandson of the jarl, he had much to live up to. Griotard no longer helped us to train the young warriors. He had become a captain and enjoyed that. It meant we were the ones moulding the young men and my cousin normally deferred to me. The two new hearth weru just kept quiet. They had been trained by me not so long ago! Some of those who farmed my land like Gandálfr and Faramir often joined us. The work on their land was not arduous and both had thralls. It was useful to have them for it meant we could demonstrate our formations easier. A wedge with three men rarely worked.

Sweyn Sweynson proved to be one of the most gifted warriors I had yet seen. He was at least the equal of Dreng and Snorri. Perhaps he had inherited the skill from his grandfather for his father had never been the greatest swordsman. When we used the wooden swords, he could soon best all the other new warriors and gave Dreng and Snorri a hard time. As we watched them, I said to my cousin, "Your son has skills which will soon put him in the forefront of a shield wall. Are you happy about that?"

He smiled, "We both know that is out of our hands. He has been given skills and it would be wrong to deny him the chance to use those skills. Of course, his mother will not wish it but that is in the nature of mothers."

Hawk occasionally visited and when he did he helped us. He had become wiser since he had married, "The odds on his death are less than they would be in another crew." We both looked at him. "I know not if it is your skill, cousin, or the magic of Oathsword but we lose few men do we not? Even when the bridge collapsed, we did not lose many warriors."

We were silent as we took that in and then a thought struck me, "You will need to curb, cousin, any tendency to seek glory. Remember the jarl who died in Hamtunscīr?" They both nodded, "They were a good war band but one man's desire for glory and recklessness caused a whole crew to perish."

Sweyn One Eye changed that day. He became his son's guide and mentor. I still showed him how to use his weapons, but his father taught him how to use his greatest weapon, his mind!

It was after the harvest and the blót feast that Cnut returned. He rode a fine horse and was now dressed as a prince of Denmark. He had his hair trimmed and his beard and moustache had been shaved. He looked even younger than I remembered but he did look more like a prince. He had with him six warriors and I saw their herkumbl, they were his hearth weru. His father had accepted him as a leader. The training in Agerhøne had been worthwhile and we had made a man of the boy. I did not know if we would reap any benefit from the work we had done, but I had a deep sense of satisfaction for I would happily fight alongside the princeling and that said much.

He and his men dismounted, "Welcome, Cnut, you are now a warrior with hearth weru?"

"My father said I needed hearth weru and he chose these six from his own oathsworn. They will do for now." Cnut was unafraid of upsetting people and he spoke loudly enough for the six to hear him; I had seen that when he had spoken to his father and refused the chance to go to Thetford. He knew his own mind.

"And now you are returned." I wanted to know why they had come back for I did not think it was in the nature of Cnut to come and show off his fine clothes, horse, weapons and hearth weru.

"I have come because my father wishes to speak to you, and I must ask a favour of Jarl Sweyn Skull Taker."

My heart sank for I did not wish to travel back to Heiða-býr and yet as the king had requested it, I could not refuse. "Of course. I take it that we would be leaving soon?"

"On the morrow."

"Then while you have a conference with our foster father I will speak to Mary."

Mary was more intrigued than upset. "And he wants just you? Perhaps it is the sword he wants."

"Perhaps but he said he had to speak to the jarl." I shrugged, "We will find out, soon enough, I daresay."

When no one came to speak to me before I retired for the night I was a little concerned. Was there a problem? I had expected the jarl, at least to tell me what this was about. I rose early and prepared my horse. Magnus was an indulgence for I did not need a horse but when I had seen him for sale in the market at Ribe, I had to have him for he was pure black except for a white blaze in the centre of his head. This would be my first long ride with him, and I looked at the horn of ale as half full. Whatever the outcome of the meeting I would enjoy the ride.

Jarl Sweyn and Sweyn One Eye came with Cnut and his oathsworn. The jarl said, almost apologetically, "I would have come to speak last night but we feasted and talked until late."

"It is of no matter, jarl." There was a question in my eyes if not my words.

"King Sweyn has need of Agerhøne's greatest warrior and Cnut asked my permission." He smiled, "I believe that the task which you will undertake must be worthwhile." He turned and looked pointedly at Cnut.

"Jarl, the task was requested by me, but my father insists that he speaks with Sven Saxon Sword first. He will return, I promise, and it will be soon."

I was even more intrigued for Cnut would not be profligate with my life. The king might but not, I believed, his son.

As we rode, with the six men twenty paces behind us, Cnut said, "I will let my father tell you the task for he ordered me to remain silent. I need this to succeed and so I agreed. I am sorry that it is such a mystery. It need not be, but it is my father's way. I would be more open but..."

I nodded, "The six men who protect you, you trust them?"

He frowned, "My father chose them."

"That is not what I asked. If you had the choice would you have chosen them?"

The question sank in and he shook his head, and said, quietly, "I do not think so."

"Then appoint your own as soon as you can. You know that the men in my wedge all chose to follow me. They are not hearth weru, but I trust them like my family. When we fought on the Kennet, I knew that I could rely on them and they helped us to win. That is what you need, my young friend."

"Then I will begin to seek out those that I think would be trustworthy."

Over the next miles, I told him how to choose men he could trust. The six behind us were undoubtedly good warriors. They had battle bands and scars; their mail and weapons were the best but those who protected needed good hearts and a desire to protect their charge. I knew that when they discovered what I had said the six men might become my enemies. I did not mind for I owed Cnut and I knew not them! On the other hand, they might resent having to serve the princeling when they were the king's hearth weru.

King Sweyn had used the coins we had been paid well and his hall was the most palatial I had ever seen. It was some years since I had been here, but I could see that he had paid workmen to gild some of the wood with gold and silver. The cross which adorned the top was also well carved and inlaid with silver. To the world, he seemed like a Christian king, but I knew the reality, and this was just for show. He had shown when we had raided crueller traits than any barbarian.

As we entered the huge gates, manned by warriors in gleaming mail, Cnut said, "You will be staying for at least one night, Sven."

He said it almost apologetically, but I had known that I would have to. I determined that I would drink as little as possible, I dared not give offence, but I would not succumb to the drunkenness which had once left me so ill.

There were stables with grooms for our horses and I watched the one who attended to Magnus. He seemed to know what he was doing and after patting his neck I followed Cnut into the hall. It was filled with warriors and they were drinking ale and mead. It was a loud and raucous gathering and that surprised me for I thought King Sweyn would try to appear more regal. His wife was well named, Sigfrid the

Haughty. She seemed to permanently look down her nose which was already raised so high as to make me wonder what she could actually see.

"My lady, this is Sven Saxon Sword."

She barely glanced at me and sniffed, "He does not smell as bad as some of the other warriors here." That was the sum of her words to me and she never spoke to me again.

King Sweyn smiled, "You are a warrior, Sven Saxon Sword, and I would not have you smell any other way. First, we eat and drink. Tomorrow, when time allows, and we have clear heads then I will speak with you." I saw that Karl Three Fingers and Thorkell the Tall were seated close to the king. Karl waved at me and then resumed his conversation with Thorkell.

The food was good, for living on the eastern side of Denmark the king had a greater choice of animals and fish. We were served beaver tail and I found it delicious. We had no beaver near to us and this must have come from the Frankish Empire. The ale and mead were good too, but any warrior will tell you that the best ale and mead come from his own hall. Cnut kept me apprised of who the warriors were that we saw. That he knew them and their skills impressed me. When he was a leader such observations could make all the difference. When men began to fall over drunk and after Sigfrid the Haughty had retired, men began to fight. Cnut and I slipped away to the hall where we would sleep. As most of the men were still in the mead hall we were amongst the first in and we chose two fur lined beds in the corner, away from the doors. When the latecomers staggered in then anyone close to the door risked being stepped upon.

It was not the best night's sleep I had ever had for there were too many men in the hall. I was used to my quiet hall. Even when we raided, we did not have to endure such a cacophony of noise. I could understand why so many drank themselves to oblivion. I was amongst the first to rise and I went into the fresh air just so that I could breathe! I was reluctant to enter a mead hall I knew would stink of urine and vomit. The doors were open, and the thralls were busy cleaning it. Instead, I walked the walls of the town for this was a fortress. Had it been in England then it would have been called a burh, but it was far stronger than even Wintan-ceastre.

I knew that I was recognised for some of the sentries must have been at Svolder or raided with us and they spoke to me. Of course, while their words were addressed to me their eyes stared at Oathsword. It was pleasant speaking to them for these were real warriors and they were keen to speak of Dean, Exeter, Svolder and Northwic. Cnut ended my walk for he waved to me and I descended.

"My father wishes to speak, Sven!"

"Good for I am intrigued."

"All you need to know is that this idea came from me and it was I asked for you."

"Then you stir more intrigue and mystery to this interesting pot!"

We did not enter the mead hall. Obviously, King Sweyn had the same aversion to the smell as I did. Instead, Cnut led me to a small, more intimate hall closer to where he and his family lived. Karl Three Fingers was there with the king but that was all. Food and ale were on a side table. The king waved a hand, "Take what you will and then sit. The servants will be leaving us."

This was private, that much was clear. There were no guards and no hearth weru. I picked some fried salted pig meat, pickled cabbage and rye bread which I placed on a wooden platter. I poured myself some ale and sat. The others had already taken their food.

The king began without preamble. "The time you have spent with my son appears to have made his mind sharper. For that I thank you. He is now a man and a warrior. He has come up with an idea in which I find merit." He suddenly stopped eating and jabbed his eating knife towards me, "What is said here remains a secret! You will not reveal a single word! Do you understand?" His voice was harsh and commanding. I did not like his tone.

I put down my own knife and said, "King Sweyn, I did not choose to come here. I was summoned. I do not appreciate being spoken to as though I am a thrall and threatened with a knife. I am happy to go back to Agerhøne and continue my life there!"

I saw Karl cover his smile with a hand. The king looked shocked and Cnut said, "Father, I trust Sven Saxon Sword. He has shown that he is a true warrior and has fought for you too many times to be disparaged so."

The king shook his head, "This is your plan, Cnut and I hope you have chosen your man well! To me, he still seems a little young. You can speak and I will eat and watch." His eyes glared at me.

Cnut smiled and nodded, "You remember that Ælfhelm of Jorvik was murdered?" I nodded, "He was not only an eorledman of Northumbria but through his mother was related to Elfweard who was the brother of Aethelstan."

I was intrigued, "Related? How?"

Cnut became irritated and waved an airy hand, "Ælfhelm of Jorvik's grandmother claimed to have slept with Elfweard before he was murdered."

That sounded so vague that it was unlikely that Ælfhelm would have believed he had any claim at all to the crown. For all Aethelred's faults, and there were many, he was the rightful king of England. I just said, "Ah."

"King Aethelred must believe the story for he has had the daughter of the murdered man, Ælfgifu, imprisoned in a hall along a tributary of the Humber. Thurbrand the Hold is the lord of that part of the land and he has many men guarding her." He paused, "I propose to rescue her and bring her here to Heiða-býr. She will be kept safe and when we deem the time to be right, I shall marry her."

I was shocked by the audacity of the plan but I saw it all clearly now. He wanted a crown, and this was a way for him to give himself some legitimacy. Harald might have Denmark, but Cnut saw a richer prize, England.

"I have spoken with Jarl Sweyn and he has agreed to let us use one of the trading ships we took at Sandwic. He only knows that I wish you to sail with me to England and take your band of warriors. The clan will be recompensed for your time away. We do not need a large crew. It will be your wedge who will crew and we have the man whom Aksel loaned us when we raided, Edgar. He has agreed to steer."

I felt myself becoming angry. I had thought better of Cnut and that I had raised a good man. He was happy to use my warriors and me to get his own ends. "And none of us have any say in the matter?"

King Sweyn's eyes narrowed, "Did my son not make it clear? Agerhøne and Ribe will be paid for this raid. You will be doing it not as a Danish warrior, but as a pirate. We have taken Aethelred's coin and I will not break the agreement."

"King Sweyn, they will know we are Danish."

Karl Three Fingers spoke for the first time, "Perhaps not, for even now the ship is being disguised with a new sail bearing a Norse design. They will think that you are disgruntled Norsemen."

The planning was incredible. My foster father must have known more than he let on, why was he going along with this?

"And if my men say no?"

Cnut gave me a sad smile, "We both know that they will not. It was another reason for choosing you. Your men are loyal to you."

"And I bear Oathsword! I am Sven Saxon Sword, and every Viking knows that!"

"But not the men of Northumbria and Holderness. They have never even heard of you. We slip up the River Humber for eight miles and sail a little way up the River Hull. We cross just a mile to the hall and the tower. The Lady Ælfgifu has just two serving women, all the rest are men from the retinue of Thurbrand the Hold, the lord of Holderness. He does not live there but he has his warriors guarding her."

I pushed away the platter for I had lost my appetite. I drank the beer, but it tasted sour. I had thought to have a year free from war and instead I would be risking not only my own life but the young warriors who followed me not to mention Lodvir's ship. All for a wild plan which would not, so far as I could see, get Cnut anything. The abduction of a Saxon lady by Vikings would add fuel to the argument that we were all barbarians. They would not see fine motives.

"I have no choice in the matter?"

King Sweyn said, flatly, "Your jarl has agreed." He smiled, "It is not just the money we have paid; Aksel the Swede has been granted trading rights here in Heiða-býr. Your foster father understands the way the world works. Your clan will all reap the benefits."

This was not the place to argue. I would save those for Agerhøne. I rose, "Then if you have done with me, I had better head back to my home. I have much to do."

The king's hand dismissed me, and I left. Cnut scurried after me, "Sven, do not be angry. I thought you would have been pleased for me. I plan for the future!"

"And if things go awry then there will be no future for the young warriors I trained." I strode to the stables and he had to run to keep up with me.

As I saddled Magnus he said, "I will be at Ribe in five days. I will meet you at the ship."

That gave me five days to persuade Jarl Sweyn to cease giving his support to this ridiculous notion. If we needed more coins then we could raid Frankia!

When I reached my home, I went directly to the hall of Sweyn Skull Taker. Far from dissipating my anger, it had grown all the way back to Agerhøne and when I strode into the hall I was seething. My foster father must have been warned of my approach for the hall was empty and my feet echoed on the wooden floor.

Sweyn approached me and said, "You are angry!" His voice was calm, and I nodded but before I could speak, the words were a torrent in my head and ready to pour out and drown him, he said, "And you are right to be angry. Let me speak and then, if your anger has not left your face, your heart and your mind then we can send a message to Cnut and tell him that we will not do as he asks." He gestured to the table, "Come let us sit. Is your horse outside?"

"Aye."

"Folki, take Sven Saxon Sword's horse to his stable!"

A disembodied voice from outside the hall said, "Aye, jarl."

"There is no need for your horse to suffer for your anger." We sat. "What you are asked to do is a good thing. You and I are not Christians, but your wife would applaud what you do. Ælfgifu is young and not yet a woman. Aethelred has shown that he is a cruel man. The warrior who holds her, Thurbrand the Hold, is a dangerous and ambitious man. He is the Eadric of the north."

"How do you know all this?"

"I checked Cnut's words. Now that more ships visit us, I was able to go to the port yesterday and ask the captains. I did so discreetly implying that we sought to trade. It was the Saxon traders who confirmed that Ælfgifu is being held against her will. Her father was popular and there is sympathy for the maid. It is another reason for Cnut's decision. He seeks to use that support when the time is right. He will be the man who saved the maiden. That still does not give a reason why it should be you who goes. The reason is you. Cnut admires you. He watched you closely when you trained him, and he followed you to war. While the rest of us were fighting alongside you he was watching. He wants this to succeed and he believes that you are the only man who gives his plan a chance."

"But the other warriors...why should they take a risk?"

He laughed, "For the same reason. They chose to follow you. When I made you and my sons hearth weru, I did not give you a choice. I like to think that you did not mind but there was no choice for you. Gandálfr, Lars, all of them chose to fight alongside you. I offered some the chance to be my hearth weru with Dreng and Snorri. They chose you."

I was silent and somewhat humbled.

Sweyn said, in a quiet voice, "Now that you are calm and no longer thinking that you have been used as a piece in a chess game, ask yourself, do you think that you can succeed? Be honest with yourself. Do you have the skills to lead men through hostile land and effect the rescue of one who is little more than a girl? Can you do that and return here to Agerhøne?"

I sighed and closed my eyes.

My foster father said, "You are not like your father in this respect, Sven. He would not have hesitated, but he would have taken his drekar and a full crew and he would have charged in without any thought to survival. That was his way. You are more like your mother. You are thoughtful. You have your father's courage, but you have much of your mother's mind and heart in you."

I opened my eyes and knew that he was right. I did think, perhaps too much. "Sailing a trading ship will mean that we should escape notice. We will have to disguise the large crew in some way. Perhaps we could board the ship at night." I realised that I had accepted the idea and was already planning it. My foster father was a clever man. "If we land at dusk it will give us the chance to scout out the hall and then attack when all save the sentries who watch her are asleep. The hard part, if we succeed in persuading her to come with us, will be timing the tide and dawn so that we evade notice. I do not know this River Hull nor the Humber and there may be ships belonging to this Thurbrand the Hold. We cannot outrun a Saxon warship."

He nodded, "Then it could be done. Remember Sven that Cnut will be with you. He is risking his own life and that says much about the young man. He wants to make sure that he has power when he gets older and he is planning now. He is not sitting idly by and hoping that the Norns spin him a good future. Personally, I do not think that marrying this girl, at some point in the future, will help him to gain the crown. The story he has heard is too thin but that matters not to Cnut. He is taking the future into his hands. It is a gamble but one I can understand."

"I liked Cnut before this but now I am not so sure."

"You remember your first raid when you rowed with Snorri?" I nodded, "You liked him."

"I still do."

"Yet he chose not to become a warrior and now raises pigs."

"That was his choice. He is different from me. If we were all the same, it would be a dull world."

"Cnut is different from you. Look into your heart and ask yourself, has he changed, or did you have an idea of a perfect prince who might become a perfect king?"

Even as he said the words I knew that he had read my mind, "You are right. I suppose now I will have to tell Mary what it is I do. She will not be happy."

He nodded, "One more thing I need to tell you. I know you were angry with me because I agreed. You thought I was bought off or bullied by threats. Neither is true. I only took the coins after I had agreed. I think Cnut will be a good king for Harald has been influenced too much by his mother and is like his father, ruthless. Cnut has a ruthless streak too, but he is also honest, and his motives are good. My grandson, Sweyn, will be on the ship with you. He overheard the conversation and said he wished to sail with his uncle. If I thought that you would fail, would I let my eldest grandchild go with you?"

I left the hall with a mind filled with so much that I thought it would burst. I needed to speak to Mary.

The Hall · River Hull

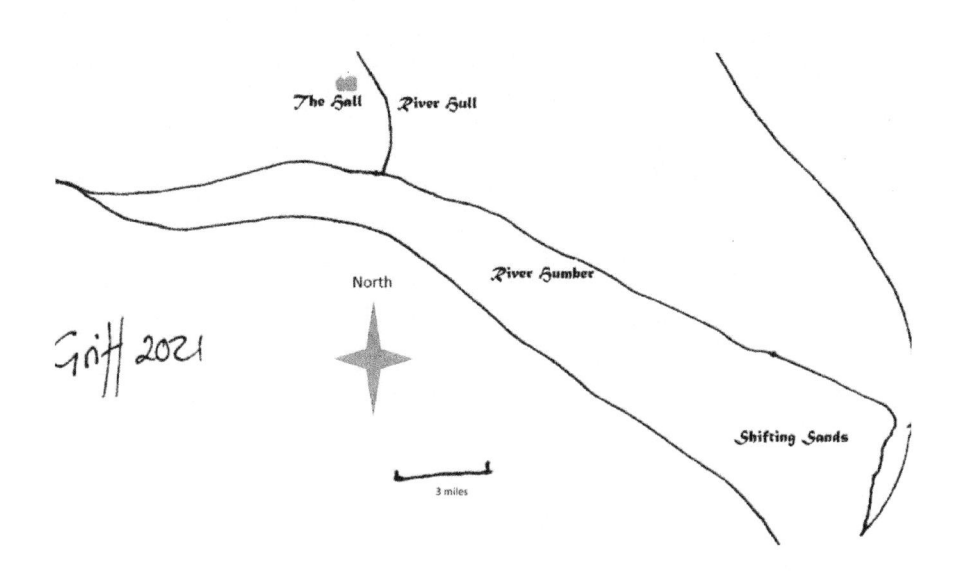

River Humber

North

Griff 2021

3 miles

Shifting Sands

Chapter 14

The return of my horse had alerted Mary. She is a Christian and can have not a drop of volva blood in her but sometimes she knows things that she cannot know! As I approached my two eldest ran to me and I swept them up in my arms. They both babbled about presents and I felt guilty that I had not brought any. Then they asked to play with me, and it confirmed in my head that I did not need this risk for a future king's desire.

"Children, go and prepare for food. Anna, take them to wash. Your father will put you to bed tonight and tell you stories but first I need to speak to him, alone!"

My wife had a firm voice which brooked no argument and the four of them left without complaint. "Sit and tell me all." Mary poured me some ale. "I know that there is something going on. Agnetha came yesterday to speak to me and she rarely visits. Others have been arriving to speak to me. I thought that you had been summoned to the king for punishment and I was relieved when you returned whole but tell me so that my mind can become at peace once more."

I swallowed some of the beer and then began. I told her of the task and then of my misgivings and how I had thought to confront my foster father. Finally, I told her that I believed I would have to do this.

When I had finished, and it took less time than I had thought she smiled and took my hand in hers. "That you worry about the lives of others rather than your own is one reason I love you so much. In all your words you never said that you were afraid or that you might die. It was a concern for the men you lead. This is a dangerous thing you do. I have heard of this Thurbrand. His family are ruthless. When I read the parchments to your mother his family name was mentioned, and it made me afraid. Now I know that you risk meeting him I am even more fearful. Sweyn Skull Taker is right. The only chance for Ælfgifu is you. One young girl may seem unimportant and if she died then the world might not even miss her, but I am a Christian and know that every life is important. What happened to her family was inexcusable. If this was Gunhild would you want her held against her will expecting death, or worse, when she went to bed each night?"

Mary's words were like a dagger to my heart. I would fight all the demons of her God's hell to save my daughter. I kissed my wife's hand, "You are right. Thank you."

"God sent a good man to take me from my home. When I think of the warriors who could have taken me, I wake shivering and shaking. You are still, despite my efforts, a pagan but one day you will see the Christian who lies within your heart."

The next morning I began to assemble my crew. I approached each one individually so that I could explain the dangers and that there was no expectation from me that they would go with me. To my amazement, all wished to sail with me. I had sixteen men and I stopped at that number. More would have been useful if we found ourselves facing many enemies but sixteen would be a reasonable number for the crew of a large trader. Sweyn Sweynson would be the ship's boy and that left the helmsman, Edgar. He still worked for Aksel, but he had taken a Danish wife and lived in Ribe. He was keen to sail with us despite the danger. I discovered the reason within the first moments of speaking to him. He had been promised that he could captain the trader we used. It belonged to Cnut for his father had given it to him and Edgar knew the profits he could make. He also knew the two rivers and that convinced me. We had a crew but the motives of all of us were different. I think that I was the only one sailing to rescue a young girl. Cnut hoped to win a crown, Edgar a boat and the rest did it out of duty to me!

When Cnut arrived in Ribe, we sailed the trader, **'Raven's Wing'**, down to Agerhøne. Our original plan to load the ship at night had long been abandoned for the whole village knew that we would sail west. They did not know where we sailed but as it was filled with warriors, they all assumed that we were raiding. However, to maintain the illusion that we were traders we would not be taking either shields or spears. Our mail would be kept below the deck in the capacious hold. We would wear beaver skin and seal skin hats and simple kyrtles. Half of the crew would stay hidden beneath the gunwale if we closed with any other ship and we had some almost empty barrels of pickled herring and salted meat on the deck to add to the deception. We left at the start of Ýlir. The days were getting shorter and that would help but, at the same time, it added to the danger as we would be sailing at night. There would be fewer ships on the sea and that too would help. When we landed, we would have more darkness to help us. The last night was spent in my thrall hall when we went over everything we planned. Sweyn Skull Taker had mounted a guard on our ship so that Edgar and Sweyn could attend.

I spoke and made certain that I could see the eyes of all, "The voyage will take four or five days and nights. We will have three watches and that means two thirds will be sleeping or be hidden. That is intentional. I lead." I looked at Cnut who nodded. "That means that if I think we cannot succeed then I will abort the mission, and no one shall argue." They all nodded. "Edgar, the river and the hall?"

Edgar answered confidently, "The River Humber is as wide as a sea but the entrance has a shifting sandbank called Spurn Head but once we have navigated that the Humber is easy. The Hull can be tricky but as we have no cargo then *'Raven's Wing'* will ride higher in the water and the shallow waters will not hurt us. Indeed, if we are pursued, when we escape then the enemy will be more likely to fall foul of them."

"Pursued?"

"Yes, Sven Saxon Sword. Thurbrand has his own warships. They are on the Humber but if word gets out he can send them after us." He shrugged, "It is a risk and there is no getting around that." I nodded. "The hall has a stone tower attached. I think that one of Thurbrand's ancestors built it from the stone of a Roman signal tower. It is not high, but it gives a good view, during the day, over the flat lands that surround the hall. There is no ditch, and the hall is similar to this one. The warriors and the captives will all live in the hall."

"Thralls?"

"Aye, there are thralls and, at night they are locked in a thrall hall." Locking thralls at night was a normal procedure.

Gandálfr asked, "How do you know so much about this place, Edgar?"

"When I was young, I sailed on a ship from Jorvik to Lundenwic. I travelled the river each month and the hall can be clearly seen. It is the last home you see before you reach the open sea, and I was young and curious. I last saw it five years ago, but I cannot see that they will have changed it much." He paused, "They might have, I do not know."

"And that is why we land when the sun has set, and we have darkness to scout out the land. Before you ask, we do not know how many men guard the captives. It is a maid and two servants. It could be just six men but, equally, it is a large hall, and it could be the crew of a ship. We might have twenty or thirty men to face." I wanted none to be complacent. "We will take bows with us for some of you are good archers and an arrow is silent. It will not be honourable work. My seax and Norse Gutter are more likely to be used than Oathsword. We cannot spare any of the guards. If the alarm is given, we cannot fight off a warship."

There were an hour or so of questions and then they all retired. Edgar and Sweyn went to the drekar and my men returned to their families. I went to watch my children sleeping. Mary came to slip her arm through mine, "All will be well, and this is more honourable than raiding nunneries, is it not?"

"Perhaps." I was still unconvinced.

The next morning I was at the ship early. It was moored at the furthest end of the quay and the least popular berth. We had decided to have the men join us in pairs. There were other ships in the port and we could not control them. I was trying to make my men almost disappear while walking to the ship. We had decided to sail without fuss and so none came to see us off. We had said our farewells in our halls. We all looked like sailors rather than warriors. We had brought our weapons the previous night and our mail had been stored for a couple of days in the hold. We loaded the barrels and, as the last of the crew boarded, we set sail. We were advised by Edgar who told us what to do. The ships we passed saw just five of us for the rest were hidden from view by the barrels which would be our disguise. We headed north for the simple reason that we spied no ships and any of the ones in Agerhøne that had seen us leave would assume we headed to Norway or Østersøen. It was also the natural way to go around the offshore islands. Once we had an empty horizon we turned to head west and with Sweyn as the lookout, the crew were able to stand. The time of year ensured that the sea was empty. Winter was not the time to sail. The wind was fresh and helped us but also brought squally rain. That too helped as it made the visibility poor.

After the speed of a drekar, the tubby cargo ship seemed to barely move. It would take a long time to reach Holderness. I mentioned this to Cnut and Edgar. Edgar smiled, "We do not reef the sail at night for there are few ships and we do not travel fast enough. With a good watch then any danger can be spotted. We keep the same speed no matter what the time of day. Slow and steady that is the way of the trader."

He was proved right. I took one of the watches while Edgar slept. It was unnerving to sail into the dark. Until dawn, we would not know if we were on course or not but Edgar had given me some tips on how to steer without the stars. By keeping the forestays and the mast in line with the short prow it was possible to sail in a relatively straight line. It meant we lost a little speed when the wind changed but that was acceptable. I woke Edgar who took the rest of the night watch. When we woke to a cold but bright day then he had another sleep once he had checked the compass and put us on the right course. We had not deviated by much. We saw not a single ship that day. Lars and Leif were happy to steer and with four of us sharing the steering board none were overtired.

Cnut was quieter than I had expected. With little experience of sailing a ship he was not given the steering board, but he stood his watches with the rest of us. Here he had no opportunity to be pampered.

His hearth weru had been left with his father. That had been my decision. This would be hard enough without having men I did not know with me. I had trained all the men with me with the exception of the brothers Lars and Leif, I had fought alongside them since before I found Oathsword.

As Cnut and I watched the smudge that was England approach, and we took in the sail a little so that Edgar could find the estuary, I asked him about our quest. "And what if the girl does not wish to come?" I waved an arm at my men, "To a maid, these will look worse than Thurbrand's guards."

Cnut smiled, and gestured to his face, "Before I returned to my father, with the idea still growing in my head, I asked Mary what she found so attractive in you when you took her by force. She told me you looked less threatening because you were clean-shaven."

I laughed, "I barely had a whisker in those days."

"The times I have spent with your wife and your children's nurse has improved my words and enabled me to use gentler ones than I might otherwise have. When we find her, Sven, I will see her alone and speak to her."

"Do not worry, Cnut, we will have plenty to occupy us. So, your plan is to make her like you?" He nodded. "Good luck with that. We may have to carry her and that can hardly be done in silence. I hope you succeed in convincing her for the alternative may well bring down the wrath of the men of Holderness. It might be sparsely populated but they have horses and fast ships. We are a barrel with a sail."

Edgar knew the waters. He found the estuary and I still know not how for I did not see it. The shifting spur of sand was, to me, invisible, but Edgar turned us around it and then headed into the widest estuary I had seen since the Tamese. We reefed the sail just to keep way and then followed the setting sun towards the River Hull. We took out the twelve oars and the men began to row. I was taking a chance and we would not don mail until we were closer to the hall. Sweyn hung over the prow and I stood with Edgar watching my cousin's son as he directed us away from shoals, sandbanks, and the shore! I was relieved that the river did not twist and turn as much as many other rivers I had used. I was also grateful for the lack of dwellings on the marshy shore for when we surprised a flock of sea birds and they took off, the noise was enough to wake the dead! I regretted not making a blót. If I could I would take one of the birds and make a sacrifice with it! The seven or eight miles we rowed seemed to take an age. Had we been in Wessex or Cent we might have heard the tolling of a bell but there was nothing to mark the passage of time. I could see why Aethelred had chosen such a remote place to keep his hostage to fortune. Cnut had told me that the young girl might be used to make an alliance with some important warrior. The King of England was grooming the child to become marriage material. What Cnut was doing was similar but, knowing Cnut as I did, I hoped that he would give her a choice.

When we turned to sail up the Hull then all of us were needed for it was narrow. In places, it was just twice as wide as the ship but Edgar was confident we would find somewhere we could turn. The wind had shifted a little, in any case, and there was no room to tack. When it widened a little and we saw, to the north-west, what looked like smoke we stopped and prepared to land. The smell from the building reached us a mile before we knew where it was. A mixture of animal and human waste combined with woodsmoke and cooking food told us that we had reached our destination. We turned the ship around and Sweyn and Folki tied us to the shore. Edgar said, quietly, the tide is almost completely out and explains why it took so long. If you can be back within two hours, then we have a chance of using the tide to reach the sea before dawn. The wind has already changed."

I knew that because we had smelled the hall and seen the smoke before the sun set completely. I nodded, "You and Sweyn take care. If you are disturbed and have to leave then we will head downstream to find you."

"I hope that it will not come to that!"

"As do I."

I was the leader and I led. I placed Cnut six men down the line of warriors and it was Leif, Lars, Gandálfr, Faramir, Ulf and Harold who followed me. They were dependable. I had my swords and neither shield nor spear. I carried my helmet for I needed my ears and my eyes. We saw the hall and the tower within half a mile of leaving the river. They stood against a western sky. I saw a glow from a door as someone came out. We were too far away to see but it showed me how close we were. I held my hand up and we stopped. We moved again once I saw the door open and close. When we were within a quarter of a mile we stopped, and I waved my arm for my warriors to form a half-circle and squat. My arm arrested Cnut and I put him behind me. We waited and we watched. I studied the top of the tower and I saw no movement. More importantly, I saw no glow. It was cold and the wind from the northwest brought a chill to the land. Nor could I see any sentries patrolling outside. That made sense as the girl had been here for some time. Boredom would bring complacency. None of us had moved and we were invisible. There was a building attached to the tower but it was relatively small and I guessed it might be a sort of armoury or workshop. A door to the hall opened, I saw the glow and when a door to a second building opened to the east of the main hall I froze. I saw movement from the main hall and people heading into the second building. When the light disappeared, and I heard a bar being dropped into place then I knew that it was the thrall hall and the slaves had been locked away for the night. As soon as the light went from the main hall, I circled my arm and spoke quietly. The wind would take my words away from the hall but I was succinct in any case.

"Ulf and Harold, head around to the back of the hall and see if there is a second door. If not, then guard the door to the thrall hall. The rest follow me. Cnut, stay at the rear. This is warrior work!" This was not the time for any heroics from the prince.

I donned my helmet and drew Oathsword and Norse Gutter. This would be close and bloody work. We had not been able to ascertain numbers and, as we neared the hall, I heard the sound of laughter. The Saxons were awake. We would not be able to slit throats and kill silently. We would have to rely upon surprise. As I neared the door, I realised that I did not know if it was barred. If it was then all surprise would be gone. The noise from inside was louder. It was the sound of men talking and some were laughing. I was fifteen paces away when I heard the neigh of a horse. It came from close to the single tower and I saw what had been hidden when we had spied the buildings, a small stable. Of course, there would be a horse, perhaps more than one for we were many miles from anywhere. The neighing horse must have alerted one of the guards or it may have been that he needed to make water. As I almost reached the door it opened and, thankfully, it opened outwards which meant I was shielded by it. The light from within would have blinded the man in any case. I waited until I saw his back and then drove my sword up, through his ribs to rip through his heart. He died without a sound. I swung his body around so that Lars could lower it to the ground. Leif stepped over the body and into the hall. I quickly followed.

I saw that the men were seated around a table and drinking. Of the girl and her attendants, there was no sign. That would be the task of Cnut. Leif leapt towards the nearest man and the eighteen or so warriors, I did not have the time to count, all looked up in surprise. Perhaps they thought that it was the man who had just left, returning. Whatever the reason the first man died at Lars' hand and I was on the second, swinging Oathsword across his neck. The warriors reacted quickly. I realised if I had waited longer, they might have been abed. I had not done what I had planned! The rest of my men were in the hall and we held the advantage for we had swords drawn already and they did not. Even so, they were tough men and one lunged at me so quickly that even as I used Oathsword to block the blow and turn, his sword slid along my mail byrnie, damaging some of the links. I backhanded Norse Gutter across his throat, and he fell. Faramir was struggling to defeat a large warrior who, unlike the rest, still wore a byrnie. When Faramir slipped on a pool of blood, the mailed warrior raised his sword to end my young warrior's life. I brought Oathsword across his back with such force that it sliced through mail links and into his flesh. He was a hard man and he started to turn. I used Norse Gutter to end his life, "Go to your God!"

I saw that my men were whole, and the guards lay dead or dying, "Cnut! Find the girl." Just then I heard the sound of hooves and while my men looked at each other I ran from the hall and was just in time to see two men on horses galloping west. The door to the tower lay open.

Ulf and Harold ran towards me. "We were about to come around to the thrall, for we found no rear door when we saw the two men come from the tower and mount the horses. They saw us and fled. They did not even bother to saddle the horses."

I cursed myself. Even if men could not see far from the tower, they would keep it manned. We had just been lucky that the two men had slept. Awoken by the fighting and seeing Vikings they had fled. The Norns had been spinning and time was now against us.

"Get to the ship and have Edgar prepare for sea. We will be right behind you."

When I entered the hall, I saw that Cnut had found the captives. He was speaking to them and they cowered in the corner.

"Is anyone hurt?" They shook their heads, "Two men have gone for help. I know not how far away it is but Thurbrand has ships of his own and they are warships. We must run, Cnut! Now!"

"I have explained to them what we must do and they are content. Afraid but content. I will come now."

Turning to Lars and Leif I said, "Open the door to the thrall hall. Perhaps when they run it will confuse our pursuit. Make them run north and west!"

"Aye, Sven."

"Gandálfr and Faramir, help Cnut. The rest of you fire the hall. I want the Saxons confused!"

Setting fire to the wooden building was easy. The chairs were hurled upon the fire and the rest laid close by. Even as Gandálfr and Faramir urged Cnut and the three Saxons towards the door the fire bit and the wooden chairs began to burn. As the table was thrown on top of the fire the flames leapt higher and soon the roof would be alight. It was

Cnut with Ælfgifu who led us back to our drekar. Gandálfr and Faramir had slung the two women over their shoulders but it was Ælfgifu who determined our pace and she was not quick. I saw as we neared, **'Raven's Wing'**, that Edgar had the sail raised and the ship was tugging at its moorings. It was maddening to have to follow Cnut and Ælfgifu who were moving too slowly. Gandálfr and Faramir reached the ship first and dumped the women in the ship. They then stood at the two lines securing the ship to the land and waited. Leif and Lars almost hurled Ælfgifu over the side as my men scrambled aboard.

I shouted, "Gandálfr and Faramir, get aboard, we will cut the ropes!"

The seamen in them had thought to save the ropes but I knew that the two men risked being stranded ashore. Their lives were worth more than two ropes. As soon as they were aboard, I sliced through one rope and Ulf the other. Our ship belied her tubbiness. A combination of the tide and the wind made her leap downriver. There was a chance!

"Cnut, secure your," I hesitated for the word, "ladies at the prow."

"Aye, the lady is grateful, Sven, for lately the guards had begun to cast covetous and lewd glances at them. They feared for their virtue. They were afraid of us until I took out my cross and swore that no harm would come to them. They believed me."

I said, in Saxon, for the benefit of the three, "And it is true for I, Sven Saxon Sword, do not make war on women!"

I saw a smile and a nod from the youngest, Ælfgifu.

Turning to my men I said, "We are not out of this yet. Prepare bows and then eat and drink. If those riders reach the Northumbrian ships, they will follow us and if they are warships then they will be rowed and faster. They will catch us! Eat while you can and let us hope that we can lose them in the vastness of the sea."

I went to stand with Edgar and took out the stopper of the ale skin. I drank deeply. Edgar's eyes never left Sweyn astride the prow as he spoke to me, "If we can make the sea before they appear then we can try to hide. It is like the game, fox and geese. The foxes will not know where we have gone. If it is just one ship that follows then we might well disappear but two or more make it less likely. They can spread out and all they need to do is to seek a sail. If we were one of your drekar we could take down the mast and simply row. We cannot do that and even though we are unladen we are still far from fast."

"Do the best you can."

He smiled, "Of course, and should we survive then when I have children this will be a tale to tell to make their eyes widen!"

The men had opened the barrels of salted herring. They had been put aboard for show and none were anywhere near full. They ate and an idea grew in my mind. I let it spin there while I went to partake in the feast.

Faramir said, "I owe you a life, Oathsword!"

I shook my head, "We fight for each other. The Norns spun and you slipped. I was handily placed, and it was nothing. If we get out of this then we will all be better warriors."

Ulf asked, "Do you think we will escape?"

I pointed to the northwest. The fired hall could be seen as a glow in the distance. All else was blackness, "The Northumbrians may well seek us close to their hall, but we have to assume that they will not and that they will sail their warships down the River Humber to retrieve their property. The people of this land have Danish blood and may well have drekar or their own version of a drekar. Whatever they have will be faster than this ship but we can hope that we make the sea before dawn and disappear."

We reached the Humber far quicker than on our journey upriver and when we left the narrow waters of the Hull, I was relieved. However, it soon became clear that no matter how fast we were moving we would not reach the sea in darkness. The black sky behind was contrasted with the slight glow ahead as the new day began to dawn. By the time Sweyn was no longer needed for the estuary was wide, it was daylight and the empty sea beyond the shifting sands beckoned us. I joined Edgar.

"The wind is from the north and west. If we sail south and east then we will travel faster but it means that, at some point, unless the wind changes, we will be forced to tack and sail more slowly to reach our home."

"And if we sail due east?"

"Then we keep a steadier speed to Agerhøne." I heard the caution in his voice.

"The Northumbrians do not know we came from there. They may think we are Norse. Aye, you may be right. When Jarl Svein Hákonarson raided last year he did us a favour. The Norns have already spun. Let us sail due east and hope that they either think we were Norse or that we are tricky Danes who try to throw them off the scent."

The sun was rising in a chilly blue sky and we thought we had escaped when Harold, who along with Faramir was watching astern spotted the sail. We turned to look. The exception was Edgar who stared ahead. "Sweyn, up to the top of the mast and see if you can identify it. It may be another trader."

The son of Sweyn One Eye clambered to the top and sat astride the mast, his legs dangling over the yard. He stared and when his words drifted down it was like a crack of doom, "It is a drekar with shields along the side and they have oars out."

We could all see the sail which lay to the southwest of us. We had taken off our mail for if it came to a fight with such overwhelming odds as we seemed likely to face then it would only slow an inevitable end. "Take your bows. Cnut, you guard your ladies."

"It may not be them." He was still seeing everything as half full and it was not.

Shaking my head I said, "It is them and the Norns have spun."

As if to confirm it, as the pursuing ship drew a little closer Sweyn shouted, "There is a second one. It is further away and to the northwest."

Edgar said, "Aye, they have kept each other in sight and with lookouts on their masts would have a better view of the sea. I can go no faster and they will catch us. It is just a matter of time."

I nodded, "Unfasten the barrels of herrings. When they get close, I want the barrels hurled overboard. Who knows, they may be careless and hit one?"

That made the crew smile and Gandálfr said, "And that would be a great jest!"

In truth, it just gave them something to do and stopped them worrying about how they would die. Lars and Leif had been at Svolder and they knew what happened in a sea battle. They would have told the younger warriors.

The two ships began to converge, and we could see that they were smaller than a threttanessa but of a similar design. The nearer one, the ship we had first spotted had a red sail while the other had one which might have had a colour at one time, but it had faded to a dirty white. Neither had a dragon prow, but they had shields hanging along the side. I estimated there were thirty on each one. That mattered little for the two of them had enough men aboard to easily outnumber us. One advantage we had was that we all had bows. We could shower them with arrows, and it was unlikely that they would be able to respond in kind. We might take some of them and a fouled oar from a dying man might well slow them down. Such are the thoughts of a drowning man who clings to any hope. I wanted to live and see my family and I hoped that the Norns had not spun my death!

"When they are close enough send arrows at them. We will wait until they are much closer before we use the barrels. Sweyn, come down and help us to move them."

The ship was wider than a drekar and that would help us. The six barrels were all almost empty. They had just been to disguise our intent. They would float and bob about. They could be avoided but in such a manoeuvre then the warship would lose way and any carelessness might be rewarded with a sprung strake. When the barrels were ready, I saw that the two ships were almost within range of our bows and that there was no one at the prow. The oars were biting, and the ships were drawing closer, but their speed did not suggest that they were double crewed.

Lars had a good arm, and he drew back his bow first to send an arrow soaring towards the nearest warship, the one we had seen first. It plunged into the wooden prow. It was the signal for the rest of my men to loose their arrows. Half of them managed to drop their missiles into the rowers. I knew that for I saw one oar foul another. The ship slowed and that allowed the other to close with us. After another shower at the first ship, Lars and my men switched to the other. The two ships were now closing rapidly and our arrows were too few to hurt two warships.

"Sweyn, help me with the barrels."

My plan was simple. We just used the weight of the almost empty barrel to tip it over the side. We had to use the larboard side for fear of fouling the steering board. The first barrel splashed and then bobbed towards the second warship. It was seen at the last moment and the ship veered to larboard as Sweyn and I dropped over the second barrel. The ship which had veered gave my archers a view of the steering board and they sent arrows towards it. The steersman steered a little further away as the arrows struck the boy next to him. The barrels now lay astern of us in a line and the two ships tried to avoid them. We heard the crack as the first ship, the one with the red sail, hit one a glancing blow. The effect was to drive it further from us. The barrels had done their job and the two warships now had to use a different approach. They would try to come alongside us but that meant that one would reach us before the other for the dirty sail would have the wind and the red sail would be fighting it. We had bought time but not much of it.

"Concentrate your arrows on the one which has the wind gauge."

Leif said, "That means we will be loosing into the wind."

"It cannot be helped."

Cnut was peering over the prow and he shouted, "I see a sail ahead. Could this be another of them?"

The trading ship was much shorter than a warship and his words were easily heard. Edgar shook his head, "Unlikely. It will probably be another trader. They will be wary until they recognise that we are a trader too."

"Might they intervene?"

He laughed, "When they see the two warships they will head away as fast as the wind will carry them."

The dirty sail was now closing with us. Some of the rowers had been taken from the oars and they held their shields over the steerboard so that we could not hurt the men there.

Gandálfr said, "The other ship, the one with the red sail, is not closing as fast as the other."

Edgar risked a glance, "The barrel must have hurt her. With a sprung strake, she will take on water. There is hope!"

Dirty sail suddenly put their steerboard over to come directly for us. They were trying to drive us in to the path of her consort. Edgar edged our steerboard over and our speed increased but it meant we risked being rammed by the ship which had been damaged by the barrel.

The white-sailed ship was going to hit us, that was clear but if they wanted the girl back then they would not try to sink us, "Prepare your weapons. We need to stop them boarding!" I turned to Edgar, "Keep moving away from them and tempt them to hit the stern. At the last moment put over the steering board and try to take out their oars!"

I thought I might have intimidated him, but he looked delighted, "This is indeed a joke. The sheep becomes the wolf!"

I drew my two swords, "Cnut, can you make out the ship yet?"

"Not yet but it looks a large one."

Cnut was not one of the clan. We would have all known the type of ship and how many oars it had. I feared that this was a Norse pirate and we could end up being picked over by two enemies. My first priority was the white-sailed ship which was now barrelling towards our larboard side. Edgar cleverly kept us parallel to them. The red sailed ship was barely keeping pace with us but once the other hit us we would have to stop and then we would be lost for we would be fighting two crews. Only Sweyn was still loosing arrows and he gave a victory cry as his arrow slammed in to the chest of the Saxon whirling the grappling hook. Another took his place and I saw that we were just a ship's width away. The Saxon was going to lay alongside us.

"Now Edgar!"

As he put it over Cnut shouted, "I recognised the sail, it is *'Sea Serpent'*!" The women of Agerhøne had made the sea serpent on the sail and Cnut had recognised it.

The clan was coming to our aid and even as I began to believe we might live I wondered how. There were cries as the oars on the side of the white-sailed ship were shattered and some of the crew were impaled or stabbed with sharp shards and splinters of broken oars. I leapt up onto the gunwale and held on to the backstay with my left hand. Edgar's move had made some of the Saxons lose their footing while I had jumped on the side of the more stable trader. I swung Oathsword at the head of the nearest Saxon who lunged at me with a boarding pike. Leaving go of the stay, I used my other sword to deflect the head and Oathsword bit into the skull of the man. I saw that there were twenty or so men aboard and many were still struggling to their feet or trying to stem the bleeding from wounds. I did something foolish but, at the time, I thought it was necessary. I did a Hawk and jumped down to the Northumbrian's deck. It took both crews by surprise and enabled me to swing both of my swords at head height. I hit men straight away and then I ducked, dived, blocked, and stabbed. I knew that whatever flesh I hit would be an enemy's.

My men shouted, "Oathsword!" and jumped down to join me. It was a mad thing to do and left '***Raven's Wing***' with just Cnut, Edgar and Sweyn to guard the women against the red sailed ship which was looming up from steerboard. Then I heard a roar and as I whirled to block an axe coming at my head while stabbing up into the throat of a Saxon, I saw the prow of '*Sea Serpent*' as our drekar smashed into the prow of the already damaged red sailed Northumbrian ship. My men had the joy of battle in them and even though when we had boarded, we had been outnumbered, my berserk attack and their anger had slain every warrior who was still alive. I saw the helmsman and three of his crew hurl themselves from the stern. It reminded me of King Olaf Tryggvasson, but the motives of the Northumbrians were less noble, they were trying to save their lives.

I heard Lars shout, "Oathsword, the ship is sinking. We have yet to lose a man! Back!"

I nodded, "Aye, the red mist has left me!" I was the last to be pulled up by Cnut and the water was already lapping around my sealskin boots as I did so. Even as I stepped aboard there was a gurgle of air and the ship slipped beneath the waves.

'*Sea Serpent*' loomed over us and Thorstein the Lucky leaned over, laughing, "I think, Sven Saxon Sword that you must be the luckiest warrior I have ever met!" I saw that the other ship was wreckage and men were clinging to it and kicking as far away from us as they could get.

Cnut came and put his arm around my shoulder, "No, Thorstein, the bravest and, maybe, the greatest warrior! Sven Saxon Sword, Oathsword!"

The cry was taken up by both crews and nodding, I kissed the hilt of Oathsword.

Epilogue

We did not discover the whole story until we landed at Agerhøne. The decision to bring the drekar to see if we needed help had not been the jarl's. He was certain that we would survive. I was not sure about that! It was the clan who did not like the idea of Oathsword, the weapon and me, being lost. After he had left us Sweyn One Eye said that no one gave a second thought to Cnut. It was me and my warriors who were their concern. I was touched. They had been sailing towards the mouth of the estuary when they had seen our sail and Thorstein told me that the ship had never travelled as fast. If we had wanted a sea trial to see her potential, we had it.

Cnut and the three Saxons stayed but three days. By that time, his father had sent a wagon and an escort to take the maiden to a sanctuary. We learned that she would be housed in a nunnery close to Heiða-býr and for that I was glad. There she would be looked after, protected, and safe. Cnut's plans could wait. I had felt sorry for Ælfgifu. She was no more than eleven or twelve summers and yet she had been used and abused by those who did not care for her. I hoped that Cnut would not be the same, but I did not know him as well as I thought I did. When he said farewell and clasped my arm like a warrior, I thought I had seen the last of him. We had raised him to be a warrior and while he would never stand in our shield wall, he could lead armies from the rear and defend himself. The Norns were, however, still spinning, they had not done with me and my threads were irrevocably bound up with Cnut's! And although I did not know it then I had made an enemy of Thurbrand the Hold!

The End

Norse Calendar

Gormánuður October 14th - November 13th
Ýlir November 14th - December 13th
Mörsugur December 14th - January 12th
Þorri - January 13th - February 11th
Gói - February 12th - March 13th
Einmánuður - March 14th - April 13th
Harpa April 14th - May 13th
Skerpla - May 14th - June 12th
Sólmánuður - June 13th - July 12th
Heyannir - July 13th - August 14th
Tvímánuður - August 15th - September 14th
Haustmánuður September 15th-October 13th

Glossary

Beardestapol – Barnstaple
Beck- a stream
Blót – a blood sacrifice made by a jarl
Bondi- Viking farmers who fight
Bjorr – Beaver
Burgh/Burh-King Alfred's defences. The largest was Winchester
Byrnie- a mail or leather shirt reaching down to the knees
Cantwareburh- Canterbury
Chape- the tip of a scabbard
Denshire- Devon
Drekar- a Dragon ship (a Viking warship) pl. drekar
Dun Holm Durham
Dyflin- Old Norse for Dublin
Eoforwic- Saxon for York
Føroyar- Faroe Islands
Fey- having second sight
Firkin- a barrel containing eight gallons (usually beer)
Fret-a sea mist
Fyrd-the Saxon levy
Galdramenn- wizard
Gighesbore – Guisborough
Gippeswic- Ipswich
Hamtunscīr -Hampshire
Hamwic- Southampton
Heiða-býr – Hedeby in Schleswig- destroyed in 1066
Herepath- the military roads connecting the burghs of King Alfred
Herkumbl- a badge on a helmet denoting the clan
Hersir- a Viking landowner and minor noble. It ranks below a jarl
Herterpol – Hartlepool
Hoggs or Hogging- when the pressure of the wind causes the stern or the bow to droop
Hremmesgeat – Ramsgate
Hrofescester- Rochester, Kent
Hundred- Saxon military organization. (One hundred men from an area-led by a thegn or gesith)
Isle of Greon- Isle of Grain (Thames Estuary)
Jarl- Norse earl or lord
Joro-goddess of the earth

kjerringa - Old Woman- the solid block in which the mast rested
Knarr- a merchant ship or a coastal vessel
Kyrtle-woven top
Lydwicnaesse- Breton Point, Exmouth
Mast fish- two large racks on a ship designed to store the mast when not required.
Meðune –River Medina in the Isle of Wight
Midden- a place where they dumped human waste
Miklagård - Constantinople
Northwic-Norwich
Njörðr- God of the sea
Nithing- A man without honour (Saxon)
Ocmundtune- Oakhampton
Odin- The 'All Father' God of war, also associated with wisdom, poetry, and magic (The Ruler of the gods).
Østersøen – The Baltic Sea
Oxnaford - Oxford
Ran- Goddess of the sea
Roof rock- slate
Saami - the people who live in what is now Northern Norway/Sweden
Sabrina - The River Severn
Sandwic – Sandwich (Kent)
Scree - loose rocks in a glacial valley
Seax – short sword
Sennight - seven nights- a week
Shamblord - Cowes, Isle of Wight
Sheerstrake - the uppermost strake in the hull
Sheet - a rope fastened to the lower corner of a sail
Shroud - a rope from the masthead to the hull amidships
Skald - a Viking poet and singer of songs
Skeggox – an axe with a shorter beard on one side of the blade
Skreið- stockfish (any fish which is preserved)
Skjalborg- shield wall
Snekke- a small warship
Stad- Norse settlement
Stays- ropes running from the masthead to the bow
Strake- the wood on the side of a drekar
Tarn- small lake (Norse)
Teignton- Kingsteignton
The Norns- The three sisters who weave webs of intrigue for men

Thing-Norse for a parliament or a debate (Tynwald in the Isle of Man)
Thor's day- Thursday
Threttanessa- a drekar with 13 oars on each side.
Thrall- slave
Trenail- a round wooden peg used to secure strakes
Úlfarrberg- Helvellyn
Ullr-Norse God of Hunting
Ulfheonar-an elite Norse warrior who wore a wolf skin over his armour
Verðandi -the Norn who sees the future
Volva- a witch or healing woman in Norse culture
Walhaz -Norse for the Welsh (foreigners)
Waite- a Viking word for farm
Wiht -The Isle of Wight
Withy- the mechanism connecting the steering board to the ship
Wintan-ceastre -Winchester
Woden's day- Wednesday
Wyrd- Fate
Wyrme- Norse for Dragon
Yard- a timber from which the sail is suspended

Historical Notes

The dragon sword is a blade of my own imagination although King Alfred did give a sword to the illegitimate son of Prince Edward, the king's son. Aethelstan became the first king accorded the title King of England. As readers of my books will know swords are always important. This series will reflect that.

A word about Denmark, the maps and the place names. If you look at a map of modern Denmark, you will see that Ribe is not where I place it. Names change over the years and you will see, as the series progresses, the reason for some of the changes. The Heiða-býr of King Sweyn is also no longer there. It was destroyed sometime after King Sweyn died. There are some ruins where it once was but as the Danes built using wood they are not as substantial as Roman ones would have been. The Battle of Svolder did take place but the island from which the allied fleet sailed is not marked on any map as Svolder. My research indicates that it was north of Øresund which is close to Copenhagen. There are two islands that fit the detail and I have used the one called Anholt which is a triangular island and would have fitted the events of the battle. If any of my Danish or Norse readers have better information then please let me know.

The raids on Hampshire, Devon, East Anglia and Cent are all documented by the monks who chronicled the Danish raids. The events happened almost exactly as I wrote them. History has helped me. The fiction is the clan of Agerhøne. Thorkell the Tall is reputed to have been Cnut's foster father but as Cnut is not mentioned until 1014 I have used that lack of information to make up a story. The rescue of Ælfgifu is pure fiction and there is not a shred of evidence that she was held captive. However, she does eventually marry Cnut and as her family were killed on King Æthelred's orders I thought it was a reasonable storyline.

Some of the events I write about are incredible such as King Æthelred paying gold to the Danes and, in the same year, butchering every Dane in his kingdom including the sister of the Danish king. It beggars belief but, apparently, happened. The bodies of the dead were discovered some years ago. Ulfcetel Snilling was also a real character and he almost managed to destroy the Danish fleet. Oathsword's part in saving the fleet is also fiction. As I keep saying I am a storyteller! The saga will continue until Cnut becomes King of England.

- King Cnut- W B Bartlett
- Vikings- Life and Legends -British Museum
- Saxon, Norman and Viking by Terence Wise (Osprey)
- The Vikings (Osprey) -Ian Heath
- Byzantine Armies 668-1118 (Osprey)-Ian Heath
- Romano-Byzantine Armies 4th- 9th Century (Osprey) -David Nicholle
- The Walls of Constantinople AD 324-1453 (Osprey) -Stephen Turnbull
- Viking Longship (Osprey) - Keith Durham
- The Vikings- David Wernick (Time-Life)
- The Vikings in England Anglo-Danish Project
- Anglo Saxon Thegn AD 449-1066- Mark Harrison (Osprey)
- Viking Hersir- 793-1066 AD - Mark Harrison (Osprey)
- National Geographic- March 2017
- British Kings and Queens- Mike Ashley

Other books by Griff Hosker

If you enjoyed reading this book, then why not read another one by the author?

Ancient History

The Sword of Cartimandua Series
(Germania and Britannia 50 A.D. – 128 A.D.)
Ulpius Felix- Roman Warrior (prequel)
The Sword of Cartimandua
The Horse Warriors
Invasion Caledonia
Roman Retreat
Revolt of the Red Witch
Druid's Gold
Trajan's Hunters
The Last Frontier
Hero of Rome
Roman Hawk
Roman Treachery
Roman Wall
Roman Courage

The Wolf Warrior series
(Britain in the late 6th Century)
Saxon Dawn
Saxon Revenge
Saxon England
Saxon Blood
Saxon Slayer
Saxon Slaughter
Saxon Bane
Saxon Fall: Rise of the Warlord
Saxon Throne
Saxon Sword

Medieval History

The Dragon Heart Series
Viking Slave
Viking Warrior
Viking Jarl
Viking Kingdom
Viking Wolf
Viking War
Viking Sword
Viking Wrath
Viking Raid
Viking Legend
Viking Vengeance
Viking Dragon
Viking Treasure
Viking Enemy
Viking Witch
Viking Blood
Viking Weregeld
Viking Storm
Viking Warband
Viking Shadow
Viking Legacy
Viking Clan
Viking Bravery

The Norman Genesis Series
Hrolf the Viking
Horseman
The Battle for a Home
Revenge of the Franks
The Land of the Northmen
Ragnvald Hrolfsson
Brothers in Blood
Lord of Rouen
Drekar in the Seine
Duke of Normandy
The Duke and the King

Danelaw

(England and Denmark in the 11th Century)
Dragon Sword
Oathsword

New World Series
Blood on the Blade
Across the Seas
The Savage Wilderness
The Bear and the Wolf
Erik The Navigator

The Vengeance Trail

The Reconquista Chronicles
Castilian Knight
El Campeador
The Lord of Valencia

The Aelfraed Series
(Britain and Byzantium 1050 A.D. - 1085 A.D.)
Housecarl
Outlaw
Varangian

The Anarchy Series England 1120-1180
English Knight
Knight of the Empress
Northern Knight
Baron of the North
Earl
King Henry's Champion
The King is Dead
Warlord of the North
Enemy at the Gate
The Fallen Crown
Warlord's War
Kingmaker
Henry II
Crusader
The Welsh Marches
Irish War

Poisonous Plots
The Princes' Revolt
Earl Marshal
The Perfect Knight

Border Knight
1182-1300
Sword for Hire
Return of the Knight
Baron's War
Magna Carta
Welsh Wars
Henry III
The Bloody Border
Baron's Crusade
Sentinel of the North
War in the West
Debt of Honour
The Blood of the Warlord

Sir John Hawkwood Series
France and Italy 1339- 1387
Crécy: The Age of the Archer
Man At Arms
The White Company
Leader of Men

Lord Edward's Archer
Lord Edward's Archer
King in Waiting
An Archer's Crusade
Targets of Treachery
The Great Cause

Struggle for a Crown
1360- 1485
Blood on the Crown
To Murder a King
The Throne
King Henry IV
The Road to Agincourt
St Crispin's Day

The Battle for France
The Last Knight
Queen's Knight

Tales from the Sword I
(Short stories from the Medieval period)

Tudor Warrior series
England and Scotland in the late 14th and early 15th century
Tudor Warrior

Conquistador
England and America in the 16th Century
Conquistador

Modern History

The Napoleonic Horseman Series
Chasseur à Cheval
Napoleon's Guard
British Light Dragoon
Soldier Spy
1808: The Road to Coruña
Talavera
The Lines of Torres Vedras
Bloody Badajoz
The Road to France
Waterloo

The Lucky Jack American Civil War series
Rebel Raiders
Confederate Rangers
The Road to Gettysburg

The British Ace Series
1914
1915 Fokker Scourge
1916 Angels over the Somme
1917 Eagles Fall
1918 We will remember them
From Arctic Snow to Desert Sand

Wings over Persia

Combined Operations series
1940-1945
Commando
Raider
Behind Enemy Lines
Dieppe
Toehold in Europe
Sword Beach
Breakout
The Battle for Antwerp
King Tiger
Beyond the Rhine
Korea
Korean Winter

Tales from the Sword II
(Short stories from the Modern period)

Other Books
Great Granny's Ghost (Aimed at 9-14-year-old young people)

For more information on all of the books then please visit the author's website at www.griffhosker.com where there is a link to contact him or visit his Facebook page: GriffHosker at Sword Books

Printed in Great Britain
by Amazon